Walk a Mile

Copyright ©2024 by Eliza Lane

Cover Design by Lorissa Padilla

All rights reserved.

No portion of this book may be reproduced in any form without written permission from the publisher or author, except as permitted by U.S. copyright law.

Also by Eliza Lane

Somebody to Love You

Chapter One

Now

"It's a month out." I fight to keep my voice calm and controlled, even as my stress hormones kick into overdrive. I stand tall on the raised patio, hands on hips, looking out over the formerly green and gorgeous rolling hills where I envisioned my wedding taking place. Now the area is half-submerged in floodwater after the torrential rains that pounded the East Coast last week. "Surely it will retreat by then."

Matilda, the country club's event coordinator, clears her throat uncomfortably and pats the coil of deep brunette hair that rests at the base of her neck. "Yes, but it will be extremely muddy. Even now, you can see the leaves and debris floating in the water. The grass will have to be—"

"So you're telling me I can't have my wedding here," I interrupt.

"Of course not," she says quickly. "You'll remember that we have a beautiful indoor space. We can easily relocate—"

My mother chooses that moment to cut in. "How do you justify charging fifteen thousand dollars just to use a space," she says, arms crossed, manicured nails tapping against her linen blouse sleeves, "that's not properly protected against flooding? This is Coastal Carolina, for god's sake."

I watch as the first tinges of red color Matilda's cheeks. "We've done everything we can, but unfortunately, there are many properties in the area that are being affected by the storm. I apologize for the inconvenience, truly."

"My daughter and her fiancé planned for an outdoor wedding and reception," Mom says. I'm beginning to feel like a kid at the pediatrician's office, listening to others talk about me and my life while I'm right here. Still, I don't jump in—that would only turn my mother's ire onto myself, which wouldn't be helping anybody. "All the decisions—even her dress—were made with that in mind. Nothing will match if we move the wedding inside."

"We can certainly reschedule for a later date. Actually, I just had a spot open up for the outside area on a Saturday in August." Matilda turns to me with a tight smile and tries to draw me back into the conversation. "Would that work for you, Nina?"

"Can I trust that the lawn will be back to its previous condition by then?" Mom fires off, not giving me a chance to respond. I note her use of 'I' instead of 'we', and not for the first time, I wonder who this wedding is really for.

Matilda lets her professional mask slip, and I see a glimpse of annoyance cross her face before she covers it. "Yes, ma'am, assuming we don't get rain like that again."

Mom looks at me, one eyebrow arched with interest. "Nina, maybe we should—"

"No," I burst out, breaking my silence. "No. It's fine. Let's go look at the ballroom and figure it out."

"But the flowers will clash—"

"Let's go look," I repeat, an edge coming into my voice, "and see what we need to change."

Mom purses her lips. Her narrowed eyes hone in on me, and I stare right back at her. "I'm not asking Travis to pay for this wedding to be completely redone from top to bottom, Nina Lynn."

I turn on my heel, wincing at the cramp in my foot. Even after years of wearing heels almost every day, my legs still regularly beg me to make a different choice. "Then I'll pay for it."

What I really mean is that my fiancé, Daniel, will pay for it. I wonder if, once we're married, it will stop feeling so strange to claim his money as my own.

The three of us form a chorus of clicking heels as we go back through the ornate French doors that bring us back to the club's offices. Mom is breathing loudly, not because she's actually out of breath—she's in a committed relationship with her Peloton, after all—but because she wants me to hear her seethe.

Matilda walks ahead of Mom and I and leads us down the hall. She glances back at me, fake customer service smile firmly in place. "You must be eager to start your life together."

I blink. "What?"

"With your fiancé."

We move forward a few more steps. Matilda is looking at me expectantly, and after my silence goes on a bit too long, so is Mom. "Oh," I get out eventually, hoping my voice doesn't sound as flat to her ears as it does to mine. "Of course. Absolutely."

"Do you want to video call him so he can see the ballroom?"

I just barely stop myself from laughing. It's two in the afternoon. I can't even imagine how Daniel would react if I called and interrupted his workday with wedding details. "No. He's an investment banker. He has more important things to worry about than this."

"Ah," says Matilda. She treats me to the same expression she had when my mom was being a bitch, and I belatedly realize that I've come off as a snob.

We arrive at the entrance to the ballroom. Matilda stands to the side, extending her arm to signal us ahead of her. Mom walks in like she owns the place, hiking her Coach bag up her shoulder as she goes. I step in behind her and immediately inhale.

It's true that we were shown this space before, but I barely took any time to notice the details, since I had already decided that I wanted to have the wedding on the lawn. Now I turn in a slow circle, taking in the large round room with purposefully weathered stone walls, a high domed ceiling, and large stained glass windows.

It's beautiful, like a church. Many people would love to be married here. But it doesn't look anything like the open, emerald-colored field where I wanted my wedding to take place.

Mom begins interrogating Matilda, and I wander off under the pretense of getting a closer look at the guest chairs pushed against the wall. I run my hand mindlessly over the upholstery and think about what I'll say to Daniel when we speak tonight. He doesn't understand why we can't just get married in New York City, where we've lived together for the past three years. It's been a point of contention with us throughout our entire engagement—which is strange, because we didn't used to be a couple who argued often. In our relationship, his preferences have tended to be the default, and I've generally been happy to go along with them.

But on this, I have fought, and on this, we've disagreed. I already dread telling him that we're going to get married in an elegant but generic ballroom that has a thousand equivalents back in the city. I know exactly how the conversation will go—he'll start by expounding on how it's ridiculous to have the wedding in North Carolina in the first place, how it's my choice that has put us in this position of having to make last minute changes. The complaints about the travel and the days he'll need to take off work will ratchet up. Just anticipating it makes me tired.

My mind flickers back to what Matilda said earlier, about the possibility of pushing the wedding back. I had been quick to dismiss the notion, but—

No. My first instinct was right, I decide: better to go ahead with the original date, even if the wedding turns out to be wildly different than the one I had envisioned. There are so many of Daniel's business contacts on the guest list; changing the date would be way worse than moving everything inside.

Matilda and Mom walk over to me. There is tension in Mom's shoulders and a frown playing on her lips, and I wonder what they've been talking about.

Matilda gestures to the chairs I've been pretending to look at. "We have slipcovers for these, if you don't like the cream color."

I try to refocus on the present. The plans. The details. The things I flew all the way here to take care of. "What options—"

"Excuse me?"

Startled, the three of us turn to see a man standing in the doorway. He's wearing clean but faded jeans and a polo with some kind of logo on it. A baseball cap is pulled low over his brow, casting a shadow over his face. Something about his posture—feet planted apart, hands in his back pockets—strikes me as familiar.

Matilda steps forward. "Can I help you?"

"I'm looking for Wendy," the man says, and now his voice sounds like one I should know. "She called me about the flooding on the lawn."

"Oh, yes. Great." Matilda pulls a radio from her pocket and speaks into it. "Wendy? Hoyt Landscaping is here for you."

There's a reply, but it's background noise to me as my mind processes the name she's just uttered.

With a flash of panic and a mind to flee, I straighten quickly. At that exact moment, he notices my mother.

"Kelly?"

He pushes his hat up, and... yes. There he is. Now that I can see his face, it's undoubtedly him—of *course* it's him.

He has the same hazel eyes, the same square jaw, the same slightly overlarge nose. I'm completely unprepared to see him here, and I find myself clasping my hands behind my back, letting my nails dig into my palms.

Matilda is still speaking into her radio, seemingly oblivious to the reunion unfolding in front of her. Her voice is the only sound in the room as the man and my mom stare at each other.

I watch as he flicks his gaze from my mom to me, just briefly, and then snaps his entire head in my direction. It's taken him this long to notice me, I realize, because I don't look at all like the girl he used to know. A lump rises in my throat, and I force myself to swallow it down.

He takes a few steps further into the ballroom but leaves a healthy distance between us. I don't know how I didn't recognize his voice earlier, because I remember exactly what it used to sound like as the soundtrack of my life when he breathes, "Nina."

There's no hiding now.

I see the moment he notices the three-carat diamond on my left hand, and I raise my chin defiantly, letting the boy who was once my entire world know—and reminding myself—that he has no place in it now. "Hi, Theo."

Chapter Two

Then

Even today, old memories from a lifetime ago sometimes come out of nowhere. I'll remember drawing with chalk in the one-car driveway of the aging bungalow where I grew up, or swimming in the local pond with my older brother, or the bumpy ride down gravel roads that I took each day in the back of a school bus.

And in nearly every memory I have, there is Theo: showing me up by drawing a bigger, better castle. Laughing maniacally as he cannonballs into the pond. Sitting next to me on the bus with his homework in his lap, urgently trying to finish it before we get to school.

We were born and raised in Amity, North Carolina, about an hour southeast of Raleigh, just as our parents and grandparents were. Our families were always acquaintances in the way that most families in small towns are, but when Theo's father and mine began working together at the local manufacturing plant, they became good friends. Their wives didn't quite share the same camaraderie—Theo's mother was the warm and gooey to my mother's cold and stingy—but a few years later, when the men fell victim to a wave of layoffs, the four of them decided to go into business together.

Theo was three and I was two when our families opened Walk a Mile, the only shoe store—the only place that sold shoes at all—in Amity. Up to that point, people in town would have to go over to Goldsboro for anything beyond basic pantry staples that could be found at the Wilsons' general store. We stocked shoes and socks and random other things that Randi and my mom thought the women of the town would enjoy, like hair clips and scented lotions. Despite Amity being very blue-collar, very working-class, the store performed better in its first years than anybody had ever hoped.

I don't remember the very beginning of the store, but it is the setting of the earliest memory I do have. It was shortly after Theo's fifth birthday, which I remember because he was still wearing his cardboard party hat, or trying to. It really should have been trash at that point, but he kept wearing it despite the grease stains and the shapeless elastic that hung loose around his rounded chin. Even then, he was stubborn. Determined. Always so sure of what he wanted, regardless of what anybody else had to say about it.

The hat was perched precariously atop his dark hair as he ran around the stock room, bent at the waist, arms extended like a superhero, making *pew-pew* noises. His mom was in the office just around the corner, and I heard her sigh shortly after Theo darted inside. "Go sit with Nina."

I was cross-legged on the foam mat our parents kept at the store, playing with some plastic building blocks. At my name, I glanced up and saw his face bunched up in distaste before he turned away from me. "You always say to sit with Nina," he whined, stamping his foot. "I'm *bored* of sitting with Nina."

"She's being such a good girl." I smiled, pleased at the praise. It was much more than I received from my own mother, who tended to refer to me with words like *loud* and *ornery* and *wild*. I hoped she would come back to the office and see how well I was behaving. "She has the blocks out. You like the blocks, buddy."

"But I built somethin' already. I want to go outside. Daddy said we could go out later and—"

"Daddy's busy with customers," Randi interrupted. "And I'm busy, too. You don't want Nina to be lonely, do you?"

"No," he said, defeated, and then he reappeared, shoulders slumped low. Slowly, he trudged back toward me, collapsing dramatically onto the mat when he got close enough. "Okay," he sighed, rolling onto his stomach and propping himself up on his elbows, "whatcha makin'?"

"A castle."

And just like that, he seemed to forget how much he didn't want to be down here playing with me. "With a moat?"

"Maybe," I said, not really knowing what that was.

"Here." He grabbed a couple of long rectangular blocks and started arranging them in front of my tall tower. "You do the castle, I'll do the moat."

And we did. Randi finished her work and went out to the floor, and we stayed bent over our project, diligently building our castle and our moat and eventually turning the green blocks into a forest surrounding it. Then, wanting to protect our creation, we slid the entire mat up against the wall and lay down on the edge of it, the tops of our heads touching as our feet stretched in opposite directions. We stayed there, creating a human barrier between our castle and whichever of our parents would walk around the corner next.

He was talking, and I was listening—or trying to—but my eyelids became heavy and I drifted off. Sometime later, I opened them again and he was still there beside me and, somehow, *still* talking.

"Nina," he said after a while. "Are you lonely still?"

I looked over at the castle we'd made together. My mom hadn't come by, but that was okay. I'd had fun with Theo anyway. "No."

"Okay. 'Cause Mama said you were, and that's sad. Did you know I love you so much?"

I grinned. "Did you know I love *you* so much?"

"Yeah," he said somberly. "You smile at me a lot."

From then on, "love you so much" became our refrain. It was something that Theo's parents said to him, and since verbal professions of love weren't the norm in my house, I latched on to the opportunity to exchange those words with him. As we grew older and started school, we naturally said it less often and with less sentiment.

"Love you so much," I said with a saccharine smile after beating him in checkers.

"Love you so much," he hollered as he barreled past me in a game of Red Rover.

"Say 'love you so much,'" Randi prompted us once when she was refereeing some argument we'd gotten into. We said it, voices hollow as we glared at each other. Five minutes later, we were over it and back to normal.

I might have thought that the words had lost all meaning, but one day when I was in kindergarten and he was in first grade, Theo found me crying on the bus after school.

"What's wrong?" he asked, seeming a little alarmed at the sight of my tears.

I wiped my eyes with one hand and used the other to gesture vaguely at the oblong birthmark beneath my left eye. Haltingly, since I had been crying for ten minutes and had to catch my breath after every other word, I said, "Misty said—there's mud—on my—face."

Theo sat down next to me, looking confused. "There's no mud on your face."

"No," I wailed, pointing directly to the birthmark. "She meant this!"

He squinted as if he'd never noticed it before. "Well, she's stupid. That doesn't look like mud at all."

The bus engine started rumbling as we pulled out of the parking lot, and I used the neckline of my shirt to wipe my face. I felt marginally calmer now that he was here, speaking with sense and logic as always.

"She meant because it's brown," I said miserably, "and ugly."

"It's brown, but it's not ugly," he said. "It's just your skin."

I stared into my lap, wishing that everybody would treat me the way Theo did. It *was* just skin, wasn't it? But it didn't feel that way when Misty was making fun of me, and it didn't feel that way when my mom sighed about how pretty my face could have been.

"Nina?"

I looked up at Theo. Back then, when his hair got a little long, he had a cowlick that his mom couldn't smooth down for the life of her. It was pointing straight up toward the roof of the bus. "What?"

"I think you look pretty."

I sniffed. "Really?"

"Yeah." With one hand, he played with the end of my ponytail. "Your hair looks pretty today, too."

I could feel the clouds around me lifting, giving way to the sun. The corners of my lips crept up, up, until I was beaming at him. Suddenly, I didn't care what Misty thought. Theo thought I looked pretty today, and that was enough to make me happy.

We started talking about other things—the broken swing on the playground, what our moms had packed us for lunch, the book Theo checked out from the library—and before I knew it, the bus had reached our stop.

I flounced down the stairs, letting my ponytail bounce behind me so that Theo could appreciate it some more. On the sidewalk, I started walking backward in the direction of my house. "Bye, Theo!"

He raised his hand as if to wave, but abruptly dropped it back to his side. "Wait," he said, hurrying after me.

"What are you doing? Your house is that wa—oof!"

I got my answer when Theo grabbed me in a tight hug. Despite being nearly a year older than me, he was only a little bit taller, and I found that I could comfortably rest my chin on his shoulder. There were a couple of older kids who had gotten off the bus with us standing nearby. They were laughing—probably at us—but I didn't care. I just hugged Theo back.

When we pulled apart, Theo looked me in the eye and said, as seriously as a seven-year-old could, "Love you so much."

And that was the very first time Theo Hoyt gave me butterflies.

Chapter Three

Now

"Theo." My mother pastes on a stiff smile. "How nice to see you."

Theo takes his hat off and holds it in front of him with both hands, ducking his chin toward her. Randi was always very cognizant of his manners. "Nice to see you too."

Matilda puts her radio back in her pocket and turns back to us, seeming oblivious to the tension in the air. "Wendy will meet you back at the lawn," she says to Theo.

Theo nods. "Alright." He looks over at me, his gaze lingering. I avert my eyes and stare hard at the floor. Silence reigns for a few long seconds before he clears his throat. "Have a good day, ladies."

"You too!" my mother calls, her voice lukewarm on the surface, downright chilly underneath. "Give my regards to your folks."

"Of course, ma'am," Theo says, and I chance a second glance at him. Damn it—his eyes are *still* on me. My protective instinct says to glare at him, so I do. The corner of his mouth lifts in a smirk, and in that instant, I feel like the world has been ripped out from beneath me. Memories come in a flood, sending me adrift.

I'm ten and Theo has won four straight games of Battleship.

I'm thirteen and Theo has just figured out how to overwrite the store's playlist with his own.

I'm seventeen and lying in the back of his truck, counting the stars above me.

As if he knows exactly where my mind is at, Theo's hazel eyes flash mischievously. With his left hand—there's no ring, I notice—he puts his cap back on his head, taking longer than necessary to position it, and then gives me a knowing nod before striding out of the ballroom.

I find myself staring at the place where he just stood. Mom clears her throat. "Well," she huffs. "I see he hasn't done anything with himself."

I blink, remembering the way Matilda had announced his arrival on the radio. "He owns the company," I say. "Or his family does."

She casts me an annoyed glance. "You should know better than anyone that being a business owner and being successful are not the same thing." With a scoff, she adds, "There is no way Cecil Hoyt or anyone related to him is running a successful company. Not an honest one, anyway."

I choose to ignore that last dig, because it's a can of worms we don't need to reopen today. I do open my mouth to point out that the company is being used by this very expensive, very exclusive country club and, therefore, is most likely doing pretty well, but Matilda clears her throat. "Sorry about the interruption, ladies. As I was saying, the slipcovers..."

She continues, my mom interrupting her every so often, while I try to calm myself down. There's no universe in which I could run into Theo again and *not* be impacted, but of course, Mom isn't concerned about that. The next time Matilda turns her back, she elbows me in the side, just hard enough to be uncomfortable, and I force myself to check back into the conversation.

After we come up with a rough idea of what the wedding will look like now that it's going to be inside, the decision is made to reconvene in a week. In the meantime, I will make adjustments to the decorations, seating, and other aspects that will need to change now. Then Matilda bids us goodbye and disappears back toward the offices. I watch her go, and I notice that the further she gets from us, the more her shoulders relax.

"Well," Mom sighs, "that was eventful."

"I need the restroom," I tell her. "I'll meet you at the car."

She walks off, heels clicking on the ground. I duck into the hall where the restrooms are and push through the frosted door that says *ladies* in fancy script. Instead of heading for a stall, I go to the sink and grip the edge.

It's true that I still think about Theo more than I would like, but I've become very practiced at not dwelling. It's like a mental game of Whack-a-Mole: something reminds me of Theo, a thought pops up, and I promptly tamp it down. My emotional survival over the past ten years has depended on my ability to separate the past from the present, to remember that Theo left *me*, that whatever we had as kids was over and done with.

Now, with a single short conversation laden with fake pleasantries, he's somehow managed to knock my entire world off its axis.

Again.

My full-coverage makeup does a good job of hiding the flush on my cheeks, but I can see a hint of red peeking through. I can't splash cold water on my face without ruining my makeup, so I wet my hands and hold them to the back of my neck, eyes closed, trying to ground myself that way. Breathing deeply, filling my lungs with as much oxygen as possible, I put my purse on the counter and pull out my setting powder. I reapply a thin layer across my cheeks and forehead, trying to get my mask back in place to hide behind.

The door opens. I continue what I'm doing, focusing intently on my own reflection in the mirror, not interested in making small talk with whoever has just walked in.

Then the person steps up behind me, and I nearly drop my compact in the sink.

"Theo," I hiss, whipping around, "what the hell are you doing? This is the women's room."

Ignoring me, he squats down to peer under the stalls. "You alone?"

"Yes!" I shriek, losing all sense of decorum. This is Theo, and even though I haven't seen him in ten years, he was always the one person I could be genuine with.

So I don't bother trying to keep up appearances. I just throw my make up back in my purse and fling my arm toward the door. "Get out!"

Theo crosses his arms over his chest. There are some smudges of dirt on his jeans that weren't there before, and I wonder what he was doing outside. "I just want to talk to you."

My name sounds the same coming off his tongue as the last time I heard it, and I feel it all the way to my toes. "About what?" I demand, angry at the effect he still has on me. "What could you and I *possibly* have to talk about? I don't even know you anymore."

"Funny," he shoots back. "I was going to say the same thing. What the hell is all this?" He gestures broadly, and it takes a minute for me to realize that by 'all this', he's referring to my face. "You don't even look like yourself."

"I don't look like myself ten years ago, no," I snap, although I can't help but notice that he looks *overwhelmingly* like he did the last time I saw him. So much so that it makes my heart pound. "People grow up, Theo. People change."

Theo shakes his head. His expression is some combination of disappointed and sad and puzzled. The last time we saw each other, he was certainly all of those things, but I try not to think about that. His eyes skate over me, assessing. The combined cost of my outfit is about twelve hundred dollars, and I think he can tell. "So who's the guy?" he asks.

I move my left hand, just to make sure he has a good view of the three-carat diamond on my fourth finger. "His name is Daniel."

"And is he the reason you got a nose job?" There's an edge to Theo's voice. "Is he the reason you had your birthmark removed? Bleached your hair?"

Anger surges through me, and I know my nostrils are flaring. "Fuck you, Theo."

I turn my back on him and shake my purse, checking that all my things are inside before hiking it up my shoulder. The thing is, Theo is a lot closer to the truth than I'd like to admit. It's unnerving how much he can still read me. I feel like I'm under attack right now, like all the parts of me I keep locked down are about to be extracted by the only person in the world who could do it.

With my head held high and my shoulders back, I begin to walk purposefully toward the door. There isn't room to completely avoid Theo's muscular frame. I try to brush past him, but he steps in front of me, looking troubled.

"You are insane," I snap, starting to lose my patience. "We are *strangers* and you are in the women's restroom, blocking me from leaving. I should call the police."

"Really?" he asks wryly as his eyebrows hike up his forehead. "You want the police involved?"

The breath leaves my lungs. I'm amazed that he's able to bring up our last day together so cavalierly—I never allow myself to think about it.

"No," I admit.

Theo's voice softens. He leans in, fixing me with that penetrating gaze that I've never been able to escape. "You know you're safe with me."

He's right, but he doesn't need the satisfaction of knowing that. At no point in this interaction have I felt unsafe. Even after all this time, I still know with absolute certainty that Theo wouldn't hurt me.

Not physically, anyway.

"I'm going to count to five, Theo, and—"

"Fine." He steps aside, sweeping his arm toward the door. "Go."

"Thank you."

I stomp to the door and yank on the handle. It opens so hard that it bangs against the wall, but I can't bring myself to care. I'm halfway into the hall when I hear, "See you around."

I stop and look around. Nobody else is in the hall. Just to be safe, I lean back into the bathroom and lower my voice. "Like hell you will."

Theo is still standing in the middle of the women's restroom, hands in his pockets, looking completely unbothered. He puts two fingers to his forehead and gives me a sarcastic salute. "Better go find Kelly," he quips. "You guys probably have a Botox treatment to get to."

"You're looking a little wrinkly yourself. I'll get you a referral."

The beginning of that trademark smirk appears on his face. It does something to me, seeing it again, and although I was prepared to stalk away, I find that my feet are firmly planted on the floor.

Theo sees his opportunity. He takes a step toward me, his face full of intent. "I told you I'd find you."

"Yeah," I say, sarcasm dripping from my voice. "And it only took you ten years. Great job."

Pain flickers over his face. "Sass—"

"Don't call me that," I snap, and then I take my hand off the bathroom door, allowing it to swing shut between us.

Chapter Four

Then

Because Theo and I were close in age and my brother Brock was five years older than me, Theo was the one I usually spent my time with. As we grew older and started school, we began to receive the message that Brock had gotten from the very beginning of the store: that our contribution was vital to keeping roofs over our heads and food on our tables. When Brock got old enough to start running the cash register—according to our parents, not child labor laws—Theo and I were pulled out of the stockroom and given menial tasks like straightening shelves and sweeping floors and standing next to Brock while he rang people up, finagling shoe boxes into thin plastic bags that ripped about half the time.

The adults generally seemed to regard Theo and I as one entity. We were nearly always given the exact same tasks and then left to our own devices to complete them. Over the years, we created our own world within the shoe shop, one that only the two of us knew existed. We had routines for our chores and would perform them seamlessly, side-by-side. Sometimes we made games out of it. Some of the games, like the one where we competed to end up with the dirtiest cloth after dusting, went over well with our parents. Others—namely what we called "bin throw", where one of us would sit in a giant plastic bin while the other slung it across the floor as hard as they could—did not.

It was usually on the heels of one of these incidents where I had been acting "unladylike" that my mother would step in and separate us. If she deemed that I was being too loud or too noisy or too active, she'd make me sit in the time-out chair behind the counter. Very rarely was it used by either of the boys.

"Theo was doing it too," I complained one day. He had been shushed and reminded to walk when we were caught having a race through the sandal aisle; I, on the other hand, was currently swinging my feet so wildly that the front legs of the time-out chair kept rising a few millimeters off the ground.

My mother didn't even look up from the price gun she was using to tag a shipment of socks. "Boys can't always control themselves, but you can."

I didn't think that was true. Theo was in second grade and I was in first, but since our school was so small, first and second graders were combined into one class that year. Under the watchful eye of our strict gray-haired teacher, Mrs. Everett, Theo seemed perfectly capable of sitting quietly at his desk and walking calmly down the hallway, only to let his energy explode once he stepped foot outside for recess. But I knew from experience that arguing would get me nowhere with my mother, so I slouched low in the chair and spent the next ten minutes glaring at her back.

When I turned nine, my parents decided that I was old enough to walk two blocks to the bus stop by myself, and those unsupervised few minutes before my bus rolled up was the most freedom I ever experienced in my childhood. Every day, when I turned the corner at the end of our street and knew that my mother couldn't see me, I did all the unladylike things I could think of. I sprinted. I did cartwheels. After it rained, I jumped in puddles and plucked earthworms off the sidewalk to deposit back in the grass.

Theo lived in the same neighborhood as us but came to the bus stop from the opposite direction. I almost always beat him there. Sometimes, I'd be about to climb on when a shout would come from behind me, and there would be Theo, running down the hill with his backpack banging against his back and one of his shoes untied. The bus driver, Ms. Pam, always sighed in irritation, but she never left Theo behind.

Toward the end of that school year, when we were starting to get a bit too comfortable, there was one day where Ms. Pam had had enough of the chaos happening on her bus. She pulled over onto the side of the road, got up, and did the clapping thing teachers did when they wanted everyone's attention—*clap-clap-clap-clapclap*. Only about half of the bus clapped back. I did, but Theo was shuffling through his backpack for a multiplication table and ignored her.

Ms. Pam clapped again. Again, she was ignored by Theo and the rambunctious kindergarteners across the aisle from us and the fifth graders two rows back who were busy testing out new curse words.

Losing patience, she gave up on the clapping and simply roared, "Be quiet *right now!*"

Everybody turned silent. Theo's hand stilled in his backpack, and he grimaced at me.

"I am not going to listen to another second of this," Ms. Pam carried on, voice still raised louder than we'd ever heard it. She moved down the aisle to make sure everyone could hear her. "Starting right now until we get to school, I don't want to hear a sound. No talking. None. Understood?"

"You're talking." I meant to mutter it, but it rang out clearly in the dead silence surrounding us. Ms. Pam was standing about three rows up, and I felt my eyes widen in realization at the exact moment hers widened in disbelief.

Ms. Pam wasn't a large woman, but she did have the air of somebody who should not be messed with. When she beckoned me toward her with a crook of her finger, it was like all the air got sucked from the bus. I stood up, taking my backpack with me, feeling everybody's eyes on my back as I moved behind Ms. Pam down the aisle. She motioned for me to sit in the empty seat right behind hers, which was where she made kids sit when they got in trouble. It was my very first time sitting there, and it felt a lot like being in the time-out chair at the store, with one key difference: this time, I felt bad about what I had done.

We got to school and I stayed put. Everybody knew that if you were in the seat behind Ms. Pam, you would be the last one to get off. The other kids shuffled down the aisle, still silent. When Theo walked by, he slipped out of line and sat down beside me.

"What are you doing?" I whispered.

"Waiting for you."

"You're gonna get in trouble."

"No, I won't."

Ms. Pam suddenly appeared, twisting around the barrier behind the driver's seat so she could see us. "Quiet. Theo, I don't know what you're doing there."

"Just waiting for Nina."

"Well, hush while you do it."

Once everybody else was off the bus, Ms. Pam came and stood over us. "I was going to go buy some new sneakers today." Her tone was conversational, but her gaze was sharp on me. I slunk down in the seat. "Do I need to tell your mama you were being sassy on my bus, Nina Sullivan?"

"No ma'am," I said quickly.

She turned to Theo, propping a fist on her hip. "What about you?"

"I didn't do anything."

I thought *that* was kind of sassy, even though it was true, but Ms. Pam just looked at him. "Go to class," she told us after a long moment. "I don't want either of you sitting up here again, hear me?"

"Yes ma'am," we chorused in the most deferential tone we could manage. Ms. Pam stepped to the side and held out her arm, motioning for us to get up and go.

I followed Theo off the bus. By then, the other students had gone inside; the only people on the sidewalk were our principal and the art teacher. They were talking to each other and didn't seem to notice us.

The bus doors *whooshed* shut, and I heard the rumble of the engine as Ms. Pam drove away. I felt laughter bubbling up my throat and glanced over at Theo. He was already grinning at me.

"I didn't mean to!" I shrieked. "It just came out!"

Theo started cackling, and so did I. We doubled over, arms banded over our midsections, gasping for air. It wasn't even that funny. It was the high, I think, of getting off easy and having Theo, ever-present, ever-dependable Theo, there beside me.

"Hey," called a male voice. Still giggling, I looked up to find the principal glaring in our direction. "You're late! Go to class!"

That sent us into a fresh burst of laughter, and we hurried inside, trying not to get yelled at again. We reached the cafeteria, where Theo would eat breakfast—I wasn't allowed to eat school food—and I waved goodbye to him.

"Wait," he said, one foot in the cafeteria and one in the hall. "Sassy."

I stopped. "What?"

"That's your new nickname." Theo beamed, proud of himself. "I'm gonna call you Sassy."

"No you aren't," I argued, putting my hands on my hips.

"Don't be sassy, Sassy."

Behind Theo, through the doors that were still propped open, I could see the principal walking toward the building and knew that I needed to go. Still, I stuttered out, "Well, I'm gonna call you—I'm gonna call you—"

But Theo had caught sight of the principal, too, and he was hurrying into the cafeteria, leaving me alone in the hall. "Love you so much, Sassy!" he called, disappearing before I could respond.

All the way to my classroom, I tried in vain to come up with a nickname for him.

I never did come up with one. Theo, as promised, called me Sassy for about a week before dropping the second syllable. I lost interest in fighting it pretty quickly, especially after I realized how good it felt to have a nickname that only one person used. It was just a silly nickname with a silly backstory, but unlike the store and our time and our space and our families, it was something that existed between Theo and I alone. Something just for us.

I really liked that.

Chapter Five

Now

"You know we passed a black cat on the way there."

I sit on a pristine white ottoman in my mother's living room, holding a glass of the sugar-free lemonade that she insists tastes just like the real thing. "Did we?"

Mom is sitting on the futon across from me, a marble coffee table filling the space between us. When I was growing up, Mom always kept our house neat, but she didn't attempt to erase all evidence of a family living there. Sitting in the five-bedroom house she lives in now feels like taking a break in a furniture store. "Mm-hmm. Explains our bad luck, doesn't it?"

"I guess."

She takes a dainty sip of her own lemonade, studying me over the rim of the glass. I try not to squirm. For the majority of my adult life, I have twisted myself into knots to become the daughter she always wanted. Most days I'm confident in who I've become, but every time I come back to visit, I constantly second-guess myself, wondering if I'm being too loud, too opinionated. Too much.

"You have a good life ahead of you, Nina," she says. "Marrying a man like Daniel means the only thing you'll ever have to worry about is what to wear in the morning."

There are multiple implicit meanings in her words, and I hear them all: *Don't ruin this. Make sure not to upset Daniel with the changes to the wedding. Get Theo out of your head right now.*

"I know," I tell her, because I do. "Everything will be fine."

Footsteps approach, and I turn to see my stepfather in the doorway. He's dressed in his usual outfit of slacks, a crisp blue button-up, and brown loafers. My mother does not believe that shoes belong in the house—neither of us are wearing them now—but she rarely pushes back against anything he does. I guess spotless floors are one of the things she gave up in exchange for marrying real estate mogul Travis Weldon and becoming a multimillionaire overnight.

"How did it go?" he asks, sinking onto the couch beside my mom. He puts his arm around her, squeezing her shoulder with his large hand. I look away. I did not grow up seeing my parents share physical affection, and even though Mom has been married to Travis for several years now, it's still strange to see him touch her. "Everything still on track?"

I expect Mom to answer, but she flicks her eyes at me.

"Their lawn is a mess from the storm," I say. "But we're going to keep the date the same and move it indoors."

"What about the flowers?" she asks. "Your dress?"

"I already sent the florist an email," I tell her. "She said it's not too late to make changes. The dress I have will just have to do."

"It's an outside summer dress," Mom says, a *tsk* in her tone. "There's no fullness to it at all. You're going to be drowned out by that big room."

Travis laughs. It's a big, booming sound that echoes off the high vaulted ceilings. "There's not a set of walls in the world that can overshadow a bride on her wedding day."

"He would know," I point out.

She purses her lips, the telltale sign that she is putting her desire to be an agreeable wife over her natural inclination to tell me I'm wrong. "Well," she concedes, "I suppose if Daniel sees it that way, there's no problem."

"I'm sure he does," says Travis, placating.

I sip on my lemonade and say nothing. I could mention the fact that how I feel about my own wedding dress has not been mentioned once, but there's no point. I save my breath.

Mom clears her throat. "Things are working out for you, Nina Lynn. I used to worry that they never would."

I glance at Travis. In the years they've been together, I haven't been able to figure out how much he knows about our lives before him. He's obviously aware that Mom is divorced, that she used to be a small business owner, and that she no longer speaks to her ex-husband or son. Surely she had to give him some reason for the estrangement, but my gut feeling is that she has never been completely forthcoming about what happened the summer before my senior year.

Travis gives me an oblivious smile. "We all have to sow our oats when we're young, huh?"

I glance at my mother. "Right."

Even though Travis was the one who said it, her perturbed exhale and disapproving look are directed at me. "You better call Daniel and run all of this by him," she says pointedly. "We don't want to do anything concrete without his permission."

I bristle at the use of the word *permission*, but tamp it down and take the dismissal as the reprieve it is. "I'll go out to the patio and call. He said he might leave work early today."

I drain the rest of my flavorless lemonade and drop it off in the kitchen. Mom and Travis begin talking about a client of his. Their voices follow me out to the back patio until I shut the door behind me, enclosing myself in blissful quiet.

I highly doubt Daniel actually left work early, so I tap out a text about moving the wedding inside and send it. I watch the screen until the word *delivered* turns to *read*, then wait a couple more minutes to see if he'll respond. No bubbles pop up. No reply comes.

Accepting that my fiancé has chosen to ignore me, I scroll through my texts until I find my last conversation with Dad. I blanch when I see that we haven't spoken since he wished me a happy birthday last October. It's been even longer for me and Brock—nearly a year has passed since he sent a picture of his kids watching fireworks on the Fourth of July.

Most of the information I have about Brock's life comes from social media, so it was strange to receive a picture from him out of the blue. I wonder if he realizes how much weight the Fourth of July still holds for me. How hard I try not to think about it, and how much I still dread it every single year. It's part of why I scheduled my wedding the eighth—the hope being that with so much to do, I wouldn't have time to dwell.

Of course, that plan would have gone a lot better had Theo not reappeared in my life.

Chapter Six

Then

When we were growing up, other kids often thought that Theo and I were brother and sister. By the time we were in fourth and fifth grade, it was well-known that we weren't. Instead, kids started asking if we were dating.

"No!" I would protest, my disgust completely sincere. "He's just Theo."

We grew older, though, and as we did, things did start to change. At first, the changes were so incremental that I hardly noticed them. One summer day right before I started middle school, I was stacking paper bags under the register when a realization popped into my mind. I gasped out loud. Theo looked up from the book he was reading at the counter. "What?"

"We haven't played one of our games in here in *forever*," I said, already amping up, ready to go. "We should do something."

Theo looked at me for a moment. He was nearly thirteen, and his face wasn't as round as it used to be. I also thought that his eyebrows were getting longer. They looked dangerously close to connecting in the middle. "We're too old for that," he said stiffly, and my excitement evaporated.

"Said who?" I demanded, because that didn't sound like Theo at all. I knew for a fact that he still had a fuzzy cartoon blanket that he slept with in the winter.

He put a sticky note in his book to mark his place and set it aside, his movements measured, like he was buying time. "My mom told me that I needed to set a better example," he said, "so that you would stop getting in trouble with your mom."

My face heated up at his implication: that I needed someone to set an *example* for me. That Theo was my superior somehow, when all my life, I'd thought of us as being equals. "That's stupid."

"It doesn't always feel like it," he said, "but I'm older than you, Sass."

After shoving the last stack of bags into place, I sat back on my heels. I looked up at him, but decided that I didn't like him towering over me and jumped to my feet. "That doesn't make you better," I snipped. In my eleven-year-old brain, it seemed like a real zinger, and I punctuated it by turning on my heel and walking away.

A while later, I was still pouting when Theo found me. He approached with both hands behind his back, and when I looked at him, he smiled sheepishly. "Wanna play a game?"

"No," I sniffed.

"Come on," he said, and showed me the dust cloths in his hands. He shook one in my face, tempting me. "I call the top of the water fountain."

I stayed stubborn for just as long as it took him to turn on his heel, as if he was about to leave me behind. Lunging forward, I snatched one of the cloths from his hand and then took off at a sprint toward the back of the store. Theo's footsteps were loud behind me as he followed.

"Theo," called Theo's dad from somewhere. "Nina. Stop running."

"Sorry!" we yelled, but we didn't stop.

Theo edged in front of me. I grabbed his elbow, trying to hold him back, but all I accomplished was causing a crash. We went tumbling to the ground in a tangle of limbs, me shrieking, him laughing. I tried to get to my feet, but Theo's body was draped perpendicular to mine, weighing me down. I lay back on the floor and burst into giggles, our spat from earlier forgotten.

We were still laying there when Cecil, came around the corner. He sighed when he saw us, but I knew he was concealing his amusement. "Guys, come on. Get up."

Theo pushed himself up on his hands. I caught his eye and returned his grin, feeling like my face was about to split in two.

That was the second time I felt butterflies around Theo. It was just the tiniest flutter in my belly, almost undetectable. But it was there, and I spared only a quick thought to wonder about it before stumbling to my feet.

I don't remember another moment like that until I was thirteen, Theo was fourteen, and we were doing our after-school chore of restocking the shelves. We had perfected our routine at that point: I would start at one end of the aisle and stock the shoes on the bottom half, and he would start at the other end and stock the top half.

When we met in the middle, Theo stepped around me as he usually did. I wasn't really paying attention to him, but then he lost his balance and his hand landed on my back. I startled, my stomach turning over at the warmth of his palm, the press of his fingertips through my shirt.

"Sorry," he said, using me to push himself back up to standing. He grabbed two shoeboxes from the cart behind him and shoved them into the gaps while I blinked at him, confused by my body's reaction to a touch that was as familiar to me as my own.

As his body grew and changed, I carefully cataloged the broadening of his shoulders, the sharpening of his jaw, the deepening of his voice. I was later to start puberty than most of the other girls, but this didn't really bother me much until Theo got a girlfriend who had at least one full cup size on me. Suddenly, I found myself overcome with insecurity, and that led to one of the lowest points of my adolescence: my mother walking in on me shoving socks in my bra.

"You'll fill out," she said once I'd yanked the nearest shirt over my head. "But make sure you're trying to impress the right kind of boy."

My face was already flaming hot, but when Theo popped into my head, I felt my blush deepen. "What do you mean?"

I was expecting her to talk about a churchgoing boy—we did go to church back then, although it was mostly for the sake of appearances—who would treat me well. Instead, she said, "There's a lot more to think about than how cute a boy is. You need to think about his family, where he comes from. *What* he comes from." At this, she rubbed her thumb and first two fingers together, as if stroking money. "Whether being with him is going to take you someplace new, or leave you stuck right here."

I truly didn't know what she was talking about, but I mumbled something in agreement so she'd go away. Once she was gone, I grumpily removed the socks from my bra and resigned myself to the fate of my flat chest.

Over time, I began to understand what Mom meant that day. I understood what it meant for me—I was not to become romantic with Theo or anyone else who was in the same economic boat as us—and I understood the implications for her: she wasn't happy, stuck there in Amity running a failing shoe shop. It was disconcerting. I didn't know what to do with that knowledge except try to pretend I didn't have it.

When I started to get involved with boys, I was indiscriminate. I didn't worry about who or what they came from. I generally didn't think of Theo as someone to pursue; most of the time, Theo was still just Theo to me. But there were moments, few and far between, when I felt something else. There were even times when I wondered if he did, too: moments when I caught him staring at my lips or my butt, light touches on my back that seemed to move lower each time it happened. It would be disconcerting for a moment, and then I would shake it off, and life would go on.

Until the summer after my junior year.

That was when everything—*everything*—changed.

Chapter Seven

Now

"This is gorgeous," Matilda says, looking at me with what may be the first genuine smile she's shown in our presence. "You have an eye for color."

Beside me, my mother huffs. "That green will look so out of place."

"It's only an accent color," I tell her. I take the paint swatches back from Matilda and hold the green one up to the closest window. "These big windows make it so that the land outside is part of the room. If we have a bit of sage green in here, too, it'll tie it together."

"Hopefully it's land we'll be seeing," Mom snarks, "and not water."

Matilda's short-lived smile falls. "Don't worry about that. Everything should be drained well before the wedding."

"But will it be picturesque? You know, that landscaping company you hired isn't all that."

"Is that so?" Matilda asks, eyebrows knitted together. She almost looks interested in hearing more.

I'm not, so I cut in.

"The blush and champagne are the main colors I want to use," I say, fanning the paint swatches in front of me like a deck of cards. "The bridesmaid dresses are close to this mauve color, so we'll tie that in as an accent, too."

"Absolutely," says Matilda. She moves over toward the edge of the ballroom, where several tables are covered in fabric, ribbon, and centerpieces. "This is what we already have in stock, but keep in mind that we can always order more from the supplier or use anything you bring in. These are the fabric swatches for the table linens. I think this off-white might look nice."

Mom shakes her head vehemently. "Oh, no. We don't want any messes to show. We'll need something darker."

"Like the green?" I quip.

She sends me an annoyed look, and I glance away, biting my lip to keep in a laugh. It's been a long time since I smarted off at my mother. I forgot how much I enjoy it.

We work through the tables, making decisions on the linens, the drapes, the vases, the ribbon for the flowers. Mom has an opinion on everything, of course, and both of them keep asking what Daniel would think. I'm exhausted and relieved when we're done, because I'm running out of polite ways to say that he doesn't give a shit about any of this.

Matilda tucks her clipboard under her arm. "I'll come back and clean up," she says, gesturing to the tables. "Before you go, I did want to go over your account, just to make sure all the services you want are booked and the charges are paid for."

"I believe we paid in full upfront." Mom's eyebrows knit together. "Surely there aren't additional charges because of your inability to properly protect your property from rain."

An icy smile turns Matilda's lips. "No, there wouldn't be anything extra related to that. It's just something we need to check off the list. Let's head to my office and take a look."

With a haughty tilt of her chin, Mom starts for the door, not even pausing to let Matilda lead the way. I hike my purse up my shoulder and start to follow when something on the lawn outside catches my eye.

It's a white work van with a blue logo on the side. I saw Theo in a polo with that logo on it when we were here last week, but I hadn't paid much attention to it. Now, with the words *Hoyt Landscaping* stretching across the side of the van in blue, I can see that the dot on the *i* is actually a tiny star.

In the split second that my breath is caught in my throat, I made a decision.

"Mom," I say, and wait for her to turn back toward me. "I'm going to go outside and call Daniel, just to make sure he's okay with everything before we settle the account."

"You could have called him earlier, when we were actually making the decisions."

I move toward her, heels clicking on the floor. "I know, but he doesn't like to be interrupted at work. He's probably on lunch now."

Mom looks skeptically at her watch, apparently doubtful that someone would be taking their lunch at half past noon. Of course, Daniel generally has food delivered to the office so he doesn't have to take a break, but she doesn't need to know that. "Let's go then," she says. "Text me if we need to make any last-minute changes."

"Sure," I say, and wait for her and Matilda to turn the corner before I slip outside.

I stand on the patio and gaze out over the lawn, which looks significantly better than the last time we were here. Most of the water has been drained; only a few sparse puddles remain. I spot three men standing in a circle near the van, sipping from water bottles. The one with his back to me is shorter than the rest, and my heart leaps into my throat until he turns to spit into the grass. It's not Theo.

"Looking for me?"

The voice comes out of nowhere, inches from my ear, and I jump back with my hand pressed to my chest. "Holy crap," I gasp.

Theo smirks at me. "How ladylike of you, Nina Lynn."

There's an uncomfortable jolt inside of me, and I purse my lips, embarrassed and annoyed. All I wanted was to see if he was here and *maybe* talk to him—on my own terms. Being ambushed again almost makes me wish I'd just gone to Matilda's office with my mom.

"I was just about to call my *fiancé*," I say, stressing the last word.

"Sure." His tone is conversational, and he rocks back on his heels, thumbs hooked in the front pockets of his jeans. When he stood that way in school, Mrs. Everett always told him that he looked like a ruffian. "After you were done staring at my guys, right?"

"Yes, Theo," I say sarcastically. "I just needed a moment to reign in my unbridled lust for a bunch of guys in dirty jeans and shirts with your name on them."

I'm about to turn on my heel and march back inside, but then Theo bursts out laughing, and I freeze. His head is thrown back, sharp nose outlined against the sky, and the guffaw rumbling from his chest as familiar to me as the sound of my own name.

It's been ten years since I last heard Theo Hoyt laugh, and until right this moment, I forgot—or maybe just chose not to remember—that it used to be my favorite sound in the world.

His laughter fades into a low chuckle, and then he's just standing there grinning at me. Several seconds go by before I realize that I'm smiling back. Quickly, I try to school my expression, but Theo's grin only widens at my attempt to glare at him.

"Damn it," he says softly. "I missed you, Sass."

"Don't call me that." I repeat what I said last week, but it's pointless. My voice comes out soft, with not a trace of venom. I use my left hand to brush my hair over my shoulder, making sure to point my engagement ring at Theo.

It doesn't hurt to remind myself it's there, either.

"So," Theo says. "I didn't get a chance to ask last week, with you yelling at me and all. What's he like?"

I blink. "Who?"

He raises his eyebrows. "The fiancé whose ring you just flashed at me. The one you were about to call?"

"Oh, right." I clear my throat and fixate on the sky above Theo. I count six clouds before returning my attention to him, feeling marginally more grounded. "His name is Daniel. He's an investment banker on Wall Street."

"Wall Street?" Theo sounds surprised. "Where do you live?"

"New York. On the Upper East Side."

"Fancy." Theo adjusts the baseball cap on his head. His hair is long enough to curl around the brim—longer than I would expect this time of year. "What else?"

I blink at him. "What do you mean?"

"I mean, you didn't answer my question. I didn't ask what his job is. I asked what he's *like*."

My tongue is heavy in my mouth as I search for something to say. The adjectives that come immediately to mind—uptight, serious, conventional—aren't what he is looking for, and I know they won't come off as flattering to Theo. I try to think of the last time Daniel and I went on a date that wasn't also a work event for him. When did we last eat a meal or watch a show or even laugh together?

When I don't answer, a shadow crosses over Theo's face. He takes a step closer to me. There's less than a foot of space between us now. Against my own will, I remember our last night together, how we lay in bed talking with our faces close like this—closer, even—until sleep took us.

My heart begins to pound. Theo's gaze flicks to the base of my throat, and when understanding crosses his face, I know that he can see my pulse fluttering.

"See, Sass," he begins quietly. I don't bother correcting him. "I was hoping you'd say that he's kind and takes you on adventures and makes you laugh. I told myself that if he was a good guy who makes you happy, I'd say congratulations and leave you alone."

"He *is* a good guy," I argue belatedly.

"If he was, you wouldn't have frozen up when I asked about him. And you sure as hell wouldn't have led with the fact that he's an investment banker." Theo's gaze locks onto mine. "And you know what? You wouldn't be looking at me like that, either."

My phone buzzes in my pocket, and I suddenly remember that I'm supposed to be texting Mom so she can finalize the bill. "I need to go."

"Wait," Theo says, touching my wrist. It's just a graze of fingers against my skin, but it feels like a live wire is zipping up my arm. I yank my hand away, and he gives me an apologetic look.

"What is it?" I snap.

From his pocket, Theo produces a business card and a pen. He scribbles something on it, then holds it out to me. I see the logo, the star, his name. And, in the messy chicken scratch I remember, the same phone number he had as a teenager. "My personal cell is the same as it always was," he tells me. "I kept it in case you ever wanted to reach me."

I swallow around the lump in my throat. "Mine is different," I murmur.

"I know. Some guy who works in a butcher shop has your old number now." He pauses, letting the words land.

I wonder when he last tried to call. How long it took him to give up on me. "Call me, text me, whatever. Anytime. Day or night."

"No," I say, but he refuses to lower his hand. My phone buzzes again, and, growing flustered, I reach out and snatch the card. "Fine. Don't hold your breath."

"Oh, don't worry. I learned my lesson about that."

I'm in the process of turning my back on him when the sharp words land, striking a dormant nerve. A beat of silence stretches into more as I try to convince myself that I'm going to walk away.

My indignation wins out, and I round on Theo slowly, waiting to see if he's going to take back his own indignant response. But Theo always was stubborn, and he's just standing there with his eyebrows raised, daring me to challenge him.

"I called you," I tell him, my voice carefully measured. "I called you a *lot*."

"You called me for three days and stopped."

"Because you never answered. And you turned your phone off."

"Nina." He tips his head back momentarily, shoulders heaving with a sigh. "My parents were beside themselves, and I was scared shitless, okay? I thought I was going to jail."

Nausea churns in my gut at the unwelcome memory of a teenaged Theo standing on the side of the highway in handcuffs, chin tucked into his chest. I was trying so hard to get one more glimpse of his face, but he refused to look up. From the time we were little kids, Theo was always so capable, so confident. Not that day. I remember thinking that I'd never seen him look so small.

My hands drop uselessly at my sides. "So, what? I was supposed to keep calling, even though you were ignoring me?"

Theo crosses his arms. He's all lean muscle now—the result of manual labor, I suppose. "You were *supposed* to know what you mean to me. I was going to come for you, just like I said."

I spare a thought for his word choice—*what you* mean *to me*, present tense—but frustration wells up and takes over. I remember the pain of being ripped away from Theo so vividly. I must have called him forty times in those first days after we were separated. When the calls started going straight to voicemail, of course I got the message that he wanted nothing to do with me anymore—what else was I supposed to think?

As far as I was concerned, Theo had abandoned me, and it left me absolutely bereft. It was weeks before I got out of bed, months before I began to emerge from the fog in my head. *Years* before I accepted that he was gone from my life.

And now here he is, standing in the place where I'll soon marry someone else, acting like it's my fault.

I lower my voice, even though we're alone on the patio. It's the only way I can maintain my composure. "Nothing happened to you. I've looked it up. There were no charges. You could have picked up the phone."

"The second I knew I was in the clear," he says, matching my volume, "I tried. My parents hired this dumbass lawyer who took a week to figure out that North Carolina is a Romeo and Juliet state. There was absolutely nothing to pin on me. I was trying to call you back literally mid-conversation as he was telling us that, but your phone was disconnected by then."

I fixate on the tiny star on his chest. "My mom took it."

"I called your parents and your brother, and of course they ignored me. I went to your family's house, and nobody was there. I looked everywhere for you, Nina." His voice cracks on my name, and I glance up to find pain etched into his features. "I looked fucking everywhere."

Not everywhere. I may have had enough pride not to keep calling after he ignored me, but I wasn't hiding from him. In the Raleigh house an hour away that my parents hurriedly moved us to, I was spending my days staring out the window, very much waiting to be found.

"Theo—"

"Nina Lynn!"

We both jump as my mother sticks her head out onto the patio. Her eyes widen slightly when she notices Theo there, but she quickly schools her expression. "Oh, so this is why you aren't answering your phone," she says with fake cheer. "Theo. It's nice to see you again."

He ducks his chin. "Nice to see you, ma'am."

Mom turns her sharp gaze on me. "Nina, did Daniel want any changes? Or did you get a chance to speak to him yet?"

I clear my throat. "Yes, I talked to him. You can go ahead and sign off."

"Great."

The three of us stand in awkward silence for a long moment, and I have the feeling that I'm in a standoff of some kind.

"You should probably come in with me," she says finally, her tone making it clear that this is not a suggestion. "Just to make sure everything is as you want it, and then I need to get home and pack. Travis is taking me to the Catskills for the weekend."

I nod slowly. "Right. I'm coming."

"Great," Mom says again, and steps back so she can hold the door open for me.

I feel like I'm seventeen again, not daring to look at Theo for fear of what my mother will see. I slip back inside, subtly dropping his card in my purse even though I still know that number by heart.

Chapter Eight

Now

For the rest of the evening, thoughts of Theo dance in the corner of my mind, refusing to be ignored. I know that I have no business contacting him, and I don't plan to—but I can't seem to stop thinking about what I might say if I did.

It took me so long to pick up the pieces of my life, but eventually, I accepted things as they were. I even began to think that everything worked out for the best, once I met Daniel and moved to New York and realized that I was on the brink of seizing a life of security and ease. Armed with Daniel's credit card and endless time to do whatever I wanted, the version of me that once thought about sticking around Amity to run the store with Theo seemed impossibly naïve.

I'm better off now.

So why do I keep thinking, *What if I had called just one more time?*

***

It's half past nine and I'm in the middle of my nightly skincare routine when my phone buzzes with a call from

Daniel. Huffing in annoyance, I quickly dry my hands and barely manage to answer before it goes to voicemail. "Hello?"

"Hey, babe."

"Hey." I put the phone on speaker, freeing my hands to pick up my retinol. "Did you just get home? I called after we ate dinner."

I hear the *beep* of the microwave in the background. "Yeah, I saw. That merger has all of us working late. I thought it would be finalized before the wedding, but—"

"You're going to *make* the wedding, right?"

Daniel lets out an irritable sigh. "Yes, Nina. I'm going to make our wedding."

I bite back the urge to point out that on my last birthday, he was so late getting home from work that we missed the restaurant reservation I'd made months prior. I suppose missing his own wedding might be a step too far, though.

"Sorry," I say in my best placating tone. "We had to go to the venue and sort out all the new details today. It was a bit stressful."

He snorts. "I wish picking out ribbon was the most stressful part of my day."

Since he can't see me, I direct my glare at the mirror as I squeeze retinol onto my face. As always, two drops go along the thin line of scar tissue where my birthmark used to be. "I'm sorry you're under stress at work," I say evenly.

"It's just the same bullshit. This guy who transferred from Boston is the dumbest fuck I've ever met."

I smooth my hands over my face, rubbing in the product. "Hmm."

Daniel goes off on a tangent, and I attempt to listen as I switch out my retinol for eye cream. I know a lot about small business operations, given the way I grew up, but the finer points of Daniel's job evade me. I have a hard time conceptualizing his mid six-figure salary, much less the enormous sums he deals with on a daily basis, and when he complains, my sympathy is often lost under memories of my parents fighting tooth and nail to keep the lights on.

He works hard so you don't have to, I remind myself. *You have three hundred dollars' worth of skincare right here because of him.*

"Anyway," he says eventually as silverware clanks on his end. "I need to eat something and hit the sack. I have to be back early in the morning to get this sorted out."

"Hold on. Did you see the text I sent you earlier? I wanted to make sure you're okay with—"

Daniel cuts me off. "Nina, look, I don't have the time or energy to read a paragraph about wedding shit. I'm taking time off so we can get married in North Carolina like you wanted. I need you to let me focus on work until then."

I pause in applying my eye cream, fingers frozen on my cheekbones. In the mirror, I watch my face fall. It's not that I thought this conversation was going great, but his complete refusal to engage has taken me aback. "Alright."

Daniel sighs again. "My food's getting cold."

"That's fine. Go eat. I love you."

There's a beat before he responds. "Love you too."

"I hope tomorrow is bet—"

The line goes dead.

I finish up in the bathroom and head back into the guest room. Mom has it decorated like a high-end hotel room, but I've been here for over a week now, and I'm not a particularly tidy person. There's a pile of worn-but-not-yet-dirty clothes tossed over the armchair in the corner, my suitcase lays open on the floor, and various forms of entertainment—magazines, tablet, vibrator—cover the bed.

I turn off the overhead lights, leaving only the lamp on the nightstand to see by. I shove my stuff to the side and crawl under the covers. On the off chance that Daniel has sent a follow-up text, I pick up my phone and click over to my messages. Nothing.

At this point, Daniel's grumpy moods generally roll off my back; however, something about our conversation tonight has lodged a piece of discontent in my chest. I replay our exchange a few times, trying to pinpoint what's bothering me. It could be the fact that he acted like our wedding was an inconvenience to him. Or the fact that he didn't bother to ask about me or my day—except to mention how much more stressful his was.

I let out a sigh, equal parts frustrated with Daniel and myself. Work has always come first for him, and it's never been a secret. Three weeks before our wedding is not the time to start challenging that.

I roll onto my side, reaching to turn off the lamp, but pause when I catch sight of my purse a few feet away. It's on the floor, slouched against the wall, and I can see the corner of Theo's business card peeking out of the side pocket.

And then, before I have the chance to think too hard about it, I pull out my phone, open a new text, and type in the number I never forgot.

There are a million questions I need to ask him, a million things I want to know, but all I write is, *Hi*.

I hold my breath after sending the message, but he doesn't make me wait long for a reply.

Hey there, Sass.

Chapter Nine

Then

"Theo!" I sang out. "I have more for you!"

Theo looked up from the shelf he was arranging as I barreled toward him, pushing the old brown utility cart that we used to run stock. It was piled so high with shoes that I had to lean to the side to see where I was going. There were shoeboxes scattered all over the floor, waiting to be added to the clearance rack.

"All that?" he asked me. "Seriously?"

"That's what Randi said." I parked the cart in front of Theo and took my bag of Red Vines off the top. I pulled one out of the bag and took a big bite. Wordlessly, Theo reached out his hand, and I placed one in his palm as well. My constant consumption of sugar and red dye infuriated my mother, which only made it more attractive to me.

"Are they all going to fit?" I asked, eyeing the clearance display where we were standing. It used to be just an endcap at the end of the aisle, but over the past couple of years, it had grown steadily. Now half the aisle was marked with yellow and red signs labeled CLEARANCE! and LAST CHANCE!

Theo looked over at me. I could read his expression, and I knew we were thinking the same thing. We were young, but not *that* young; he had just graduated high school a couple of weeks before, and I was about to be a senior. We knew that everything in the store could be purchased cheaper and more conveniently elsewhere. We knew that the ever-growing clearance section wasn't a good sign for a small business. We knew that our parents had been working longer hours and spending more time in the backroom with the door closed, speaking in hushed tones.

Theo ran his hand over his freshly buzzed head. He habitually cut his hair once per year, on Memorial Day weekend. I preferred his April hair, which was long enough to flop over his forehead and curl at the nape of his neck. "I'll make them fit," he said, going back to my question. "I'll have to do some rearranging."

"There's no more coming after these," I assured him.

He nodded, and I watched as he started shuffling boxes around. "Go get me another rack," he said. He was always direct, even a little bossy, but not in a way that bothered me. I had no problem refusing his orders. If I followed one of them, it was because I chose to. "The gray one with the—"

"Got it," I said, knowing exactly what he was talking about. It had been in the backroom collecting dust for ages. "Be right back."

I strolled down the aisle toward the back of the store, bypassing the bathroom and entering the single swinging door that marked the backroom. There used to be two doors, but one of them had fallen off its hinges a couple years before, and nobody ever fixed it.

The backroom was small, but strategically organized to maximize storage space. The two walls perpendicular to the door had built-in shelving for backstock. At the end of the aisle, a right turn brought you to an alcove where bigger items, like the rack I needed, were kept. The office was back there, too, behind a door that had once been painted white but was now chipped enough to resemble chocolate chip ice cream.

I turned the corner and saw that the office light was on. Figuring it was Randi, I started talking as I stepped inside the small space. "Hey, I took all that stuff out to clearance and—" I stopped when I saw that it was not Randi, but my brother Brock, sitting at the computer desk. "What are you doing in here?"

Brock had his hands poised over the keyboard. From the doorway, I couldn't see what was on the screen. He didn't stop what he was doing; he kept tapping, not looking at me. "Just checking some things."

I narrowed my eyes at him. Although the three of us—Brock, Theo, and I—did some clerical work for the store and often closed out registers at the end of the night, we rarely had an occasion to be in the office alone. Especially on the computer. The only time I had ever used that computer was the previous summer, when I bought concert tickets while Theo distracted our parents up front.

"What things?" I asked him, crossing my arms.

Brock lifted his eyes to meet my identical ones. We had very little in common, but we did look like siblings. "Don't worry about it."

I walked further into the office and stood behind his desk chair. Brock promptly closed out whatever he had been looking at. "What are you hiding?" I pressed, leaning over to grab the mouse with him. I pulled the page back up and promptly deflated. It was just a spreadsheet, covered in numbers pertaining to sales and inventory. "Oh. Boring."

"I told you not to worry about it," he grumbled, batting my hand away and taking the mouse back.

I rolled my eyes and started walking away. Brock and I had never been close. I wasn't sure if it was the age gap, our diametrically opposed personalities, or the fact that Theo and I naturally became attached at the hip while he was a bit of a third wheel. The distance between us had only widened once Brock cut back on his shifts at the store. At twenty-two, he was mostly working construction to pay for his one-bedroom apartment down by the train tracks.

"You ever coming over for dinner again?" I hollered at him, using my foot to unlock the wheels on the gray rack.

"Yeah, I will soon," he said, not very convincingly.

"I think it's only fair that you suffer with me sometimes."

"I suffered for eighteen years. I've earned my freedom."

I still remembered how jealous I was when Brock moved out. I was thirteen then. Things between Mom and I had started going south about a year before, and cracks were starting to show between her and Dad, too. I sat on the porch steps all morning, watching Brock load up his car and wishing we had a better relationship. I thought that if we did, he might have invited me to go with him.

I started to wheel the rack back to the floor, but a thought stopped me. I poked my head back into the office. "Why do you think they haven't gotten divorced?"

Brock looked up from the computer again and exhaled hard, nostrils flaring. "Because they own a business together, Nina." He said this like I was a complete moron for even asking. "You can't just walk away from something like that with no backup plan."

I thought of Cecil and Randi, Theo's parents, whose own livelihood was wrapped up with my parents'. "I wonder—"

I heard the one swinging door whip against the wall, and then heard Theo's voice. "Hey, Sass. Where's my rack? I don't want to be here all night."

Abandoning Brock and our dead-end conversation, I walked out of the office just in time to see Theo turning the corner into the alcove. He came to a stop right in front of where our bin of toys used to sit. "Dude," he said, noticing Brock. He craned his head to look into the office. "What are you doing in there?"

"I'm leaving," came Brock's snapping voice, "because you two can't mind your own fuckin' business." A moment later, he emerged, slamming the door to the office shut behind him.

"Hey, man," said Theo, holding his hands up in surrender. "No judgment here. That's what incognito mode is for, you know?"

Brock glared at Theo. Not for the first time, it occurred to me that this whole dynamic—me and Theo, not related at all, ganging up on Brock, my only sibling—was kind of messed up. "Sometime, Hoyt," Brock said, "you're going to grow up a little bit and realize that shit isn't all fun and games."

"Brock," I warned.

Theo's eyes flashed. He wasn't a hothead, but he also wasn't anybody's doormat. "I think I've got a pretty good grasp on things, thanks."

Brock opened his mouth, but seemed to stop himself before any words came out. He shook his head and stepped through the narrow space between Theo and I, brushing against us both. Nobody said anything else as his footsteps retreated. Then we heard the back exit open and close, and we were left alone.

"I don't know what his problem is," I said.

Theo nodded to the office. "He was snooping."

"No, he was just looking at sales numbers or something. Something on a spreadsheet."

He leaned on the gray rack, propping his elbows on the top shelf. "So, snooping."

"I guess so," I said. "But I don't know why he'd be looking at that stuff."

Theo ran his hand over his head. He fixed his heavy gaze on mine. "I don't think things are going very well."

"I know," I admitted.

His eyes roved my face in that way they often did, as if he was trying to figure me out. It always made me feel like I was under a microscope. "You can't repeat this, okay?"

"Okay."

He glanced behind him, double-checking that we were alone. "My parents told me not to tell you, but..." He raised and dropped his shoulders in a shrug.

I nodded in understanding. Most people who had occasion to talk about me and Theo referred to us as *best friends* or *practically brother and sister*, and I could see why they would think that. Neither of us referred to each other that way, though. Our relationship was nothing like mine and Brock's, and my best friend was Sage Perry while Theo's was Quinton Damask. We were just...Nina and Theo. I found it exceedingly difficult to describe our relationship; all I knew was that it was the most important one in my life.

That's why I understood what Theo meant without him actually explaining it. Between him and I, the only secret was my occasional pining.

Theo cleared his throat. "Mom and Dad are starting to look into other options. Dad's been talking about trying to find work somewhere else."

A lump immediately formed in my throat. "Really?"

"Yeah."

In the same way that Theo had been my constant companion, the store had been the constant backdrop of my life. I didn't always like it—my mother and I had many arguments over how often I was expected to work—but

I did depend on it. The idea of us not running the store with the Hoyts was unfathomable to me.

"What would you do?" I asked Theo. Now that high school was over for him, our parents had put him on a full-time schedule at the store. He had been salutatorian of his class, though, and I wasn't completely clear as to why he was sticking around here. "Would you go to college after all?"

"Nah." For a moment, he looked torn. Then he gave his head a little shake, as if to clear it. "I'd find something. I could go work with Brock."

I laughed out loud and pushed at the rack, nudging him out of the way. "You two would murder each other."

Theo laughed too, and the mood was instantly lighter. He followed me back out to the floor. I could hear Randi's voice from somewhere in the store, telling a customer that we would have a new shipment of flip-flops in on Wednesday. We couldn't continue our conversation out here, but that was okay. I knew from experience that later, one of us would bring it back up, and we would continue as if we'd never paused the discussion.

"You and Sage going out to the farm tonight?" he asked.

"Yeah, I guess so."

The bell over the door sounded, indicating that a customer had entered the store. I was going to let Randi take care of it, but then she bustled by. "Get that, please," she tossed out in the general direction of Theo and I before disappearing into the back. Since Theo was doing clearance, I started heading that way.

"Hey," Theo hissed, and I turned back. In his best imitation of my mother, he drew his eyebrows together and sternly told me, "No food in front of the customers."

I made a big show of reaching into the bag, pulling out another piece of licorice, and chomping down on it like a cartoon rabbit. "Yum."

"Sass," he warned, visibly fighting a laugh.

I grinned at him. "Love you so much."

Theo shook his head and rolled his eyes, but he didn't miss a beat. "Love you so much," he responded, and disappeared around the corner with his rack.

Chapter Ten

Then

Shortly after nine p.m., I was packed into Sage's truck with two of our other friends, Peyton and Lori Ann. Sage was driving way too fast, but we were too busy discussing Lori Ann's fixation on Mitch Ellington to care.

"Okay, guys," said Lori Ann, twisted around in the passenger seat to talk to Peyton and me in the back. "Listen. I *know* Mitch is going to be there and I'm *going* to hook up with him tonight. We need to make a game plan."

The rest of us groaned in unison. "Child," said Peyton. She was sixteen, a year younger than Lori Ann, Sage, and I, but tended to be the mother hen of our group. Whenever she thought one of us was being stupid, she channeled that mom energy and talked to us as if we were children. "Find someone else. He's not gonna go for it."

"I know he wants it. Didn't you see the way he was watching me the other day when we saw him at Scoop Shack?"

"No, yeah, he was definitely checking you out," I admitted, and she put her hands in the air triumphantly. "But he's not going to do anything with you. Or anybody."

Mitch's dad was the pastor of the largest church in town. Earlier that year, his dad had launched a teen abstinence workshop and made Mitch the face of it. At our high school, the program was widely advertised with posters featuring Mitch holding up his hands to fend off a girl taking a step toward him, hands clasped in front of her, looking desperate. The fact that the girl was portrayed by his sister did little to improve anyone's feelings about the whole thing. In the end, I heard that they got eight participants—including the pastor's two kids. Mitch was hot, but not hot enough to wade into that mess.

Lori Ann disagreed. She had developed a huge crush on Mitch after they were partnered up in class a month before, and she hadn't been able to let it go yet.

"I can *corrupt* him," Lori Ann insisted. "I'll show him what he's missing."

"What's that?" Sage retorted. "Your B-cups?"

What followed was a symphony of shrieking that had my ears ringing by the time we piled out of the truck into the warm night. We were on the Redding property, the only place to be on weekend nights in Amity. Vince Redding had just graduated with Theo, and the parties he threw on his family's enormous ranch were always raging and never got busted—the advantage of having rich parents who basically owned the entire town.

Leaving Sage's truck with a line of similar ones near the gravel road, we began our hike across the grass. People we knew and people we didn't surrounded us: drinking from red plastic cups, dancing, screaming, making out. In the center of all the activity were several pickups belonging to Vince and his friends. One of them contained the speakers that blared music. Each of the others had a keg sitting on the tailgate and one of the boys standing beside it, filling plastic cups and passing them blindly into the crowd. We moved toward Vince, and he grinned at us. "Look who the cat dragged in!"

"Right behind you," Sage said.

Vince gave us an easy smirk and jerked his head, shaking his overlong blonde hair out of his eyes. "Gonna be a good night," he said.

For some reason, his eyes lingered on me after he said it. I met his gaze, reaching for the cup he held out to me. "Think so?"

"I gotta feeling," he said, a reference to the song currently playing, and then grinned at his own dumb joke.

As Vince handed off beers to the other girls, I took a sip of mine and looked around. Almost immediately, I spotted Theo a few yards away, standing near the bonfire with Quinton. He raised his cup to me in silent acknowledgment, and I raised mine back. I thought I saw his eyes drift over my outfit—a short skirt and spaghetti-strap tank, nothing special—but at this distance and in the dark, it was hard to tell for sure.

My friends and I wandered off to where people had started to dance, moving a respectable distance away from the speakers so our eardrums didn't blow out. We stood in a circle, hands above our heads, hips moving, beer sloshing over the side of our cups, sometimes listening to the music and sometimes just talking over it.

"Oh my god!" Lori Ann shrieked after a while, grabbing Peyton's arm. "Mitch! Look at Mitch!"

In unison, we all turned our heads to follow her pointing finger. I gasped in delight when I saw Mitch standing nearby, talking to Amy Baird. "Hey, she gets around," I told Lori Ann. "Maybe—"

We all watched in shock as Mitch grabbed Amy by the waist and began grinding on her.

"Oh," Lori Ann fumed, "oh, *hell* no. Not when he's been giving me the holier-than-thou treatment."

Peyton held up a hand. "Well, hold on—"

"He can tell me he doesn't want me to my face." She shoved her beer at Sage and bounded over to Mitch and Amy. We watched as she pushed her way between them and began yelling and gesticulating wildly. Mitch and Amy stared at her, taken aback.

"What's she saying?" Sage asked.

"I can't hear," I said. "Does anyone need a refill?"

Everyone shook their head, and I made my way back to the trucks alone. Most of the kegs had been abandoned by that point, so I picked one and pulled the spigot forward to pour my own drink. When I turned around, it was to a body hovering right behind me. I startled, spilling beer all over myself.

"Oh, shit," said Vince. "Sorry."

I tossed my empty cup to the ground and peeled my shirt away from my body. The stale smell of beer hit my nostrils, and already I could feel the stickiness setting in on my skin. "What the hell are you doing?"

Vince looked taken aback by my sharp tone. Briefly, I considered dumping some beer on him and seeing how he liked it. Then he recovered and turned on the flirtatious grin that had all the girls at school falling all over themselves. I didn't *dislike* Vince—well, until now, maybe—but I did seem to be one of the few that wasn't dying for a moment of his attention. "You can take it off," he leered. "Nobody here will mind."

"Oh, fuck off."

Done with this conversation, I went to step around him. Vince moved with me, blocking my way. "It was an accident, Nina. Jesus. I just wanted to talk to you."

I fixed him with a glare, my mild irritation growing more severe by the second. "Too bad. Bye."

Again, I tried to leave, and again, Vince stepped in front of me. This time he leaned forward, and in my effort to put space between us, I found myself pinned against the tailgate. Even though we were surrounded by people, a prickle of fear moved beneath my skin.

"I was coming over here to ask you to dance," he said. His laidback, easy grin was fixed in place, but it looked wrong inside of his hard expression. "Without that thing on your face, you'd be pretty hot."

I curled my hands into fists to keep myself from touching my birthmark. It had been a long time since somebody commented on it, at least to my face. There were times, like when my mother talked about how we'd get it removed as soon as we had the money, where the self-consciousness from my childhood came roaring back as if it had never left, but most days I didn't give it a single thought.

The finely honed sixth sense I had developed from years of being in Theo's orbit alerted me to his presence before his voice did. The tense muscles in my neck and shoulders immediately relaxed, and I stopped trying to come up with a retort for Vince. I simply waited, knowing I was safe now.

"What's going on?" Theo asked, stepping up beside us. He took a sip of his beer that would appear casual to most but didn't fool me. I watched as he noticed my soaked shirt. "You alright, Sass?"

"I'm fine," I said stiffly.

"We're just talking, man," said Vince. "All good here."

Theo regarded him coolly. "Really."

"Yeah." Vince tried to swing his arm around my shoulders, but I stepped out of his grasp. Theo immediately grabbed a handful of my shirt and used it to tug me into his side. His hand brushed my bare back, and I tried to pretend the touch didn't turn that spot red-hot.

That seemed to be the nail in the coffin of Vince's patience. His laidback facade dropped. "Imagine thinking you're too good for someone," he spat, "when you're a frigid bitch who looks like that."

Before I could blink, Theo's familiar presence left my side, and he and Vince were on the ground.

"Theo!"

He ignored me, or maybe he didn't hear me at all. Vince sprawled in the grass with Theo's knee in his gut. I stood by helplessly, wincing when I heard the sickening *crack* of fist meeting jaw.

"Fucking asshole!" howled Vince.

I watched Theo's arm rear back again, as if he intended to deliver another blow, and came to my senses in time to leap forward. "Theo! Stop!"

I grabbed at his elbow, and although I definitely wasn't strong enough to make him do anything he didn't want to, Theo let me pull him to his feet and away from Vince. As I got my bearings and registered the small crowd that had gathered, I noticed that it was mostly made up of Vince's friends. And they looked pissed.

Vince stumbled up to standing, clutching his face with one hand. He used the other to point toward the exit of the ranch. "Get the fuck out of here!"

Theo pushed at my shoulder, nudging me forward. Tension rolled off of him in waves. "Go."

I stood on my tiptoes and looked around. A few heads were craned in our direction, but most people hadn't even noticed the ruckus and were going obliviously about their business. "I don't see Sage."

Theo's hand shifted down to my hip. With his fingers digging into my stomach and his back pressed against mine, he pushed me forward, gentle but insistent. "We need to go, Nina," he said, and his authoritative tone had me briskly headed toward the edge of the field.

In his truck, I buckled myself into the passenger seat as he leaned across my lap to shuffle through the glove box. "What do you need?"

"Napkins."

I swatted his hand away so I could look for them, and he made a sound of discomfort. Frowning, I hit the dome light so I could see.

"What—" I started to ask, and then I caught sight of his knuckles, smeared with blood. "Oh my god, Theo. Here."

Holding his wrist with one hand, I found a couple of napkins and pressed them to his split skin. He hissed in pain.

"Sorry," I said.

"You're pressing too hard."

"I'm trying to stop the bleeding."

Theo let me clean up the worst of the mess, and he gently extracted his hand from my grasp. He held it up, studying the injury in the light, then opened the door to toss the bloody napkins into the grass.

"Litterbug," I said.

He snorted. "Vince can pick it up."

He pulled out his keys and started the truck, and I sighed in relief as the air kicked on and washed over my face at full blast. I let my eyelids fall, assuming that Theo was about to drive off. After a few moments where we stayed stationary, I opened my eyes and met his dark gaze. "What?"

"Are you okay?" he asked, soft but with an undercurrent of intensity.

"Yeah," I said, taken aback. "I'm fine."

"Did he touch you?"

"No. He bumped into me and made me spill beer down my front." I plucked at the wet shirt still clinging to my skin. Theo's gaze raked down my torso in a way that made me feel on display. "And then I wouldn't stay and talk to him, and he just got nasty."

"Asshole."

I sighed. In the dim light, I could barely make out his features. "You shouldn't have punched him."

Theo was still seething, every muscle in his body taut. I wasn't sure when I last saw him like this—if I ever had. "Yes, I should've, and I'd fucking do it again." Under his breath, he added, "Rich douchebag."

I absentmindedly touched my birthmark, running a fingertip along the ridge where it raised slightly off my skin. "Hopefully I'll be getting it removed soon."

He squinted at me, confused. "What?"

"My birthmark." I tapped it. "We don't have the money right now, but—"

"Why?" he interrupted.

I blinked. "What do you mean, why?"

"Why would you get it removed?"

"Why wouldn't I?"

Theo rested his elbow on the center console and leaned toward me. My stomach swooped as, for a split second, I was convinced that he was looking at my lips. That maybe he was about to kiss me. And Theo kissing me—I couldn't even fathom what would come after that. It would shake the foundation of my world.

Theo didn't lean in any further, though. Instead, he did something nearly as shocking—he raised his left hand and gently touched my birthmark. I sat, frozen, hardly able to breathe.

His fingers slipped away from my face, falling back into his lap, but his eyes stayed locked on mine. In the silence of the truck, with the dark night surrounding us, it felt like we were in a bubble. I'd been in bubbles with Theo my entire life—when we were on the play mat in the backroom, when we were laughing at some inside joke while the adults nearby rolled their eyes (my parents) or smiled at us (his), when we fell into the same humdrum routine we'd completed a thousand times, each of us knowing the other's next move as well as we knew our own.

Theo swallowed. I watched the flexing of his throat, entranced. "Because—"

"Hey!"

I startled at the interruption to our peaceful moment. When Theo shifted away from me, I could barely make out the outline of Vince over his shoulder, standing outside the window. He smacked the glass with the palm of his hand. "I thought I told you to get the fuck out of here!"

Theo yanked the truck into reverse. "Hold on, Sass."

I did as he said, gripping the seat beneath me as we careened backward. I could see Vince in the glow of the headlights, still yelling, arms gesticulating wildly. I wondered how much he'd had to drink.

"Are *you* drunk?" I asked Theo, suddenly wondering if that was why he'd lost his cool and gone after Vince. Theo was extroverted and gregarious, getting along with pretty much everybody. When other boys fought at school, Theo was often the one wedging himself between them to break it up. He didn't *seem* drunk, but I'd also never seen him show a hint of a violent streak before tonight.

Theo cranked the wheel and started toward the main road at a steady clip. "No," he said. "I had one beer, probably an hour ago. I'm fine to drive."

When we reached the edge of the Redding property, Theo slowed down, looked both ways, and pulled out onto the two-lane highway. "Home free!" he hooted as he stepped on the gas, bringing our speed up to about five over the limit. I laughed, relaxing into my seat as we put distance between us and the farm.

"I'm putting on music," I said, reaching for the radio dial.

"Go for it."

The radio was tuned to Theo's preferred alternative rock station, but I switched it to the country station that broadcasted from a few towns over. It was the same station that played constantly at the store.

Predictably, Theo groaned. "How do you not get sick of this shit?"

I sat back, propping my feet up on the dash. The adrenaline from the confrontation at the party had started to wear off, my heartrate returning to normal. "I like it."

"All the songs sound the same."

"All the *newer* songs sound the same," I corrected. "This is George Strait. Everyone loves George Strait."

"Do they?" Theo asked, but didn't let me answer. "What time does Queen Kelly want you home?"

"My curfew's still midnight."

He tapped the digital clock on the dash. "Almost two hours left."

My phone buzzed in my pocket, and I pulled it out to read the message from Sage. It sounded like word had gotten around about the fight, and she wanted to know where I had gone. I typed out a response, telling her that I was fine and with Theo. "What should we do?"

We reached a four-way stop, where a right would take us back to our neighborhood. Theo put on his left turn signal. "I've got an idea."

***

I yelped as I hopped out of Theo's truck and landed on a slick patch of grass, my feet nearly flying out from under me.

"Shh!" Theo hushed, laughing, even though we were four miles outside of town and hadn't passed another car the whole way here.

"Sorry." I giggled, stumbling after him as he started up the hill. He reached for me automatically, and I grabbed the hand he offered, letting him pull me along as we climbed through the dark and the brush to the old footbridge. Theo reached the crest of the hill first. With his feet flat and secure on the concrete, he kept my hand in his and used the other to steady me by the elbow as I climbed up beside him.

"Nobody here," he said, and although I had already guessed that, the confirmation sent an anticipatory tingle up my spine.

I walked out onto what was known locally as Train Bridge, taking my first steps gingerly as always. Nobody had ever been hurt out here, as far as I knew, but the bridge was old and beginning to crumble in places. "I hope we didn't miss it."

"It won't come until ten-thirty, eleven."

I checked my phone. If he was right, we still had plenty of time.

In the dark, I walked out to the middle of the bridge and sat down at the side facing north, where the train would be coming in from. There was a gap between the bridge and the bottom of the metal railing that was just wide enough for me to slide my legs through, and I did, letting them dangle over the edge.

"Careful," Theo warned as he came to sit beside me.

I wrapped my hands around the vertical rails in front of me. "I'm not going anywhere."

"Good."

I looked down toward the track, although it was too far down for me to see in the dark. I could barely make out my sneakers dangling in the air. Theo moved so he was leaning up against the rails, too, our hips and thighs pressed together, his feet swinging next to mine.

"When were you here last?" I asked.

He thought for a moment. "When we all came out last fall, I think. Us, Sage, and Quinton."

"Me too," I said, thinking back to the night in question. It had started out like this one, at the Redding farm—although nobody had been in a fistfight. "Lori Ann came, too."

"Oh, yeah."

I gave him an annoyed look, not that he could see it in the dark. "Why are you pretending you don't remember?"

"Because I'm not pretending? I forgot about her until you mentioned it. I've hung out with her, like, three times in my life. I can't even remember her last name right now."

I snorted. "Okay. Your protesting is a little much."

"Nina, come on. What the fuck are you talking about?"

I ran my fingers lightly up and down the metal rails. They were disgusting, absolutely covered in years of whatever nature had to offer, and yet something about the grit of dirt under my nails appealed to me. "I just think it's weird that you wouldn't remember flirting with her the entire time."

"What?" Theo sounded incredulous. "I was not."

I stared down at my dangling feet, unsure why this conversation was bothering me so much. To me, the memory was crystal clear: Theo skirting around Lori Ann, resting his palm on her back. Theo sitting down next to her even though there was room next to me, leaving me strangely lonely. Lori Ann doing a pretty accurate imitation of the quirky chemistry teacher at our school and Theo bursting into raucous laughter that echoed through the night.

"Whatever." I busied myself with picking at the frayed hem of my denim skirt, and then found myself saying, "She's into Mitch right now, anyway, so you'll have your work cut out for you."

"Nina."

"What?" I asked innocently.

Theo made a frustrated noise. "I don't give a fuck about Lori Ann, okay?"

"Oh-*kay*," I snapped, unable to mask my own irritation.

An awkward silence fell, something so rare between us that I didn't have the foggiest clue how to handle it. We were sitting close enough that I could feel the tension in his body. I began to wonder if I really had misread things—not that it should matter; I only meant to tease him, anyway, and wasn't even sure how we had ended up bickering.

To my surprise, Theo broke the silence with a burst of laughter. I looked at him, confused.

"Jesus, Sass," he said, "you *reek*."

It took me a moment to register his words, and then I started laughing, too. Just like that, we were back where we belonged: in perfect sync.

I pulled my shirt away from my body. It was mostly dry now, but it did smell. "Do you have an extra t-shirt in the truck?"

"I'm not sure. Maybe."

"I can't wear this home. If my mom is waiting up and smells it, she'll never let me out of her sight again."

Theo nodded in understanding. "You can have my shirt, if I don't have another one."

"So you'll show up half-naked back at your house?" I asked, appalled. "What would Randi and Cecil say?"

"They'll never know. They don't wait up."

I tilted my head back. You could easily see the stars in town—it wasn't like Amity was a buzzing metropolis—but out here, the stars stood out sharply against the inky black sky. I focused on one in particular that was a little bigger, a little brighter, than the others. "I always forget your parents aren't control freaks."

"I'm also eighteen," he said gently, "and out of high school."

"They didn't give you a bunch of rules before, either." Something occurred to me then, and I turned to him. Theo had been oddly reserved about the reason he decided to stay in town after graduation. It wasn't like he didn't have the grades for college, and I knew for a fact that he had been accepted into the University of North Carolina. I'd always assumed that Randi and Cecil would want him to go, but maybe not. Maybe they were like my family and the money just wasn't there. It would make sense; they did all have the same source of income.

"Are they the reason you're not going to college?"

A moment passed. "No," he said. "No, it's not because of them."

I waited, but it seemed like that was all I was going to get for now. My stomach twisted with discomfort at the thought of a secret between us. We didn't have those. At least, we didn't used to.

In the distance, I heard the first rumbles of the approaching train. It was so quiet out here that you could hear it from miles away; it would still be a few minutes before it reached us. Even so, my body began to hum with anticipation.

Without discussing it, Theo and I wriggled around until we were laying on our stomachs, faces near the railing on one side and feet tucked beneath the opposite one. This was the best position to be in when the train came through, because you could feel the vibrations from head to toe while still getting the full force of the wind in your face. I liked to close my eyes and pretend that I was on a roller coaster.

"What about you?" he asked, his voice hushed. "If the store closes, what will you do after high school?"

I inhaled deeply. Hearing it laid out like that—*if the store closes*—as an actual possibility caught me off guard, even after discussing it in veiled terms that afternoon. Theo had always been a straight-A student, but I brought home Cs and the occasional B. So many kids we went to school with were chomping at the bit, ready to find a way out of Amity. I wasn't one of them. I wanted to get out from under my mom's thumb, for sure, but I didn't imagine myself going far. Just to my own little place across town.

After he decided not to go to college himself, Theo and I had occasionally pondered the idea that we might eventually take over the store and run it together. With that possibility seeming to move further and further out of our grasp, I didn't have an answer to his question.

I turned my head to the right at the same time he looked to his left, and my breath caught in my throat as I realized how close our faces were. "I'm not sure," I admitted.

Even in the dark, I could see the intensity of Theo's pupils zeroing in on mine. "We'll figure it out," he said.

A shrill whistle pierced the air, and when I looked back at the track, I could see the train in the distance, its headlights just rising over the horizon. I wrapped my hands around the railing and wiggled excitedly. "It's coming!"

Theo threw his left arm over my back and pulled me snug against him. He always did this when the train came by, as if afraid I'd blow away.

Except for last time, I thought bitterly, *when he sat by Lori Ann.* I tried to remember if he had held onto her, too, but I couldn't.

I decided to believe that this gesture was just for me, whether that was true or not.

"Ready?" Theo asked as the train rushed toward us, the headlights close enough now that I had to squint against them.

I closed my eyes. "Ready!"

Beneath me, the boards of the bridge began to rattle. Wind rushed through my hair. Theo's fingertips dug into my ribcage, and the roar of the train grew ever closer. I was good at imagining out here, tricking myself into a bigger adrenaline rush than being on Train Bridge really warranted. My stomach turned just like it would at the top of a roller coaster, right before the big drop.

I knew the moment the train hurtled by beneath us because the air pushed upward with such force, it made me feel weightless. The rattle of the train's wheels and the roar of its engine surrounded us; I thought I heard Theo say something, but I couldn't hear him over the noise.

"What?" I yelled, opening my eyes, and in the next second he was cupping my chin and putting his mouth on mine.

I stiffened in surprise, sitting frozen inside the rush of the train going by, but Theo either didn't notice or didn't care. I had kissed other boys before, but never experienced the kind of gentle firmness that Theo possessed when he kissed me that first time. I didn't know what to do with that any more than I knew what to do with the fact that *Theo was kissing me*, and so I froze, raising one hand to touch his wrist but otherwise giving no response.

And just when I registered what was happening, when I began to move my jaw to kiss him back, his lips were gone. He stared at me, looking as shocked as I felt—as if *he* hadn't been the one to deviate from our well-established norms.

The last car of the train passed beneath us. The adrenaline of an imagined roller coaster was gone, replaced with the buzz in my veins left behind by Theo's kiss. Even as the rumble of the train grew distant, we stayed right where we were, afraid to move now that the earth had.

"What are you doing?" I asked.

He ran his tongue over his bottom lip, and I found myself watching closely. "Nothing."

"What do you mean, nothing?" I was incredulous, my voice borderline shrill. "You kissed me."

Theo exhaled, a hint of alcohol still lingering in his breath. "Yeah."

With the train gone and the night silent once again, I found no reason to stay splayed out on the boards with splinters poking into my skin. I held onto the rail for balance as I clambered to my feet. My heart beat fast, my pulse throbbing in my neck. Theo got up, too, but where I felt frenzied, his movements were slow and measured.

I moved to the other side of the bridge and leaned back against the railing. With a few feet between us, I found myself better able to think. "Theo—"

"You've never thought about it?" he interrupted. His own hands reached slightly behind him to grip the railing on his side. "About kissing me?"

I looked away, considering. The previous fall, around the time we had last been out here, I had an all-consuming crush on Kyle George. He wore ripped jeans and leather jackets and had a full head of thick dark hair that he was constantly swiping out of his eyes. When I was into Kyle, he was all I thought about. I watched him from across our biology class and practiced signing 'Nina George' in the margins of my notebook. I studied his mouth and tried to imagine what it would feel like moving against mine, his hair twisted in my fingers. After I finally got up the nerve to talk to him, I spent every waking hour plotting our next conversation, convinced that I was a single witty one-liner away from receiving a kiss that would transform my life forever.

I eventually did get a kiss from Kyle, and it was far from earth-shattering. There was too much tongue, too much spit, and he grabbed my ass approximately five seconds into it. I made out with him for only a minute or so before pulling away and so I could make up a lie about needing to go help at the store. In biology the next day, we ignored each other, and that was that.

Thinking about kissing Theo was definitely something I'd done over the previous few years, but it was different than with Kyle. It wasn't surrounded by anxiety, like I was on this mission I didn't know how to complete, and it didn't consume me. The idea would enter my head fleetingly and at seemingly random moments: watching him help the elderly Mrs. Bryant get a shoebox down from a high shelf. Doing my homework at the sales counter as he looked over my shoulder, giving me tips. The first time he kissed a girlfriend in front of me and I unwittingly wondered what it would feel like to be in her place.

When I first developed my crush on Kyle, we had no relationship. I barely knew him. It wasn't just the thought of kissing a cute boy that I was hung up on; it was the fact that Kyle was a blank slate, an image I could mold. But with Theo, we already *had* a relationship—one with deep, deep roots—and kissing was not a part of it. So I would have my occasional thoughts about kissing him and then I would shove them aside, because what else was I supposed to do?

"Maybe a few times," I admitted. "I guess you have too."

"Sass." Theo pushed off the rail and took a step toward me. His tone was low and as serious as I'd ever heard it. "It's *all* I think about."

My heart leapt into my throat. I opened my mouth uselessly. He kept walking toward me, and I put my hands up, starting to feel flustered from his words and his proximity and the way he was looking at me, so intense even in the low light of the moon. "I don't even know what you're saying," I spouted. "What the hell are we even still doing out here? The train's gone, let's just go back to—"

I cut myself off when he leaned forward, leaving only inches between us. I thought he was going in for another kiss—and despite my indignation, I was *absolutely* going to let him kiss me again—but instead he planted his hands on the railing on either side of me, caging me in. The heat of his body surrounded me, and I felt a bead of sweat roll between my shoulder blades.

Theo was only a little bit taller than me, so when he dipped his chin slightly, I found myself looking directly into his eyes. "You want to know why I was flirting with Lori Ann that night?" he asked, still using that low, serious tone.

"Thought you didn't remember that."

"Trust me, I remember. It was when you were obsessed with that Kyle kid. All that day at work, you'd been telling me that you'd caught him looking at you during class, and you were sure he'd ask you out soon. You wouldn't shut up about it."

"So what? You decided you were into Lori Ann?"

Theo laughed softly. "No. I was never into Lori Ann. I was pretending because I was jealous." He reached up to move my hair behind my ear. "I'm into *you*."

"Oh," I said dumbly.

"*Oh*, she says." For someone so intent on turning my world upside down, Theo's demeanor was remarkably casual. A little smirk played on his lips. "This is the part where you either tell me to get lost or that you're into me, too."

He seemed awfully confident that I wasn't about to shoot him down, and I found myself wanting to knock him down a peg, just to feel like I had some semblance of control here. "What if I do the first one?" I asked, a challenge in my voice.

"Then we'll go. I'll drop you off at home, and tomorrow, it'll be like this never happened."

Could I do that? Could I go to the store and hang out with Theo and not think about the biggest adrenaline rush of my life? He seemed to think he could, but I wasn't so sure. More than that, I wasn't convinced that I really *wanted* to.

"And the second one?" I asked, working hard to sound like I didn't care about the answer.

The humor fell from Theo's expression, and then he was in my space, pinning my hips to the railing with his own. I put my hands on his chest out of instinct; he held my waist and nuzzled my cheek. "That's the one you're going to pick," he told me softly.

"I haven't decided yet."

"Yes, you have." Theo dragged his nose along my jaw and dropped a kiss under my ear. It was barely anything, just a feather of a touch, but it felt like a burst of fire right there on my skin. "You didn't want to talk to Vince earlier, and you let him know it. If you didn't want to be here like this, we'd be back in the truck by now."

I couldn't even argue, because as usual, Theo knew me through and through. I let out a breath, and with it went my last bit of trepidation. "You're right."

"I know I'm right."

Theo kissed me again, and this time, I gave as good as I got. He tilted his head, and I tilted mine the other way. He opened his lips and my tongue was right there, ready for a taste of him. He wrapped a hand in my hair and I responded by twisting the collar of his shirt around my fist, holding him right there in front of me, where I wanted him. Where he belonged.

Eventually I had to break away to take a breath. I tilted my head back, trying to get a lungful of fresh night air. I was planning to get right back to it, but Theo ducked his head. I stared up at the stars and made some embarrassing noise as his mouth moved down the sensitive column of my neck. When he reached my pulse point, he sucked lightly, and I gasped at the unfamiliar bolt of desire that shot through me.

Then he was taking my face in both hands, gently pulling me back to look at him. We stared at each other for a moment, and then he leaned in to give me one more kiss—this time, over my birthmark.

"You're so beautiful," he whispered against my skin.

It was the first time I'd ever been told that.

It was the first time I'd ever felt it.

Nobody had ever called me beautiful before—not a stranger, not my father, and definitely not my mother. I had always been hyperaware of my birthmark, the way new people would do a double take when they saw it and then try not to look my way again. It wasn't just my birthmark, either—it was my mousy brown hair and overly pointed nose and the dull hazel of my eyes. Even though I had never forgotten how wonderful it felt to be six years old and have Theo call me pretty, that was kid stuff. *Beautiful* was a different level.

"Stop," I said, pushing on his chest. It wasn't forceful, but he moved anyway, giving me the space I needed to duck out of his embrace. "Don't say things you don't mean."

I started down the rocky path back to the car. Theo stumbled after me. He reached for my hand, but I crossed my arms over my chest. I'd take my chances on falling.

I was almost to the truck when he cut in front of me. I stopped so I didn't run into him, keeping my glare intact.

"You know earlier?" he asked, breathless. "When you asked why you shouldn't get your birthmark removed?"

"Yes."

"I didn't get to answer."

"Well, what were you going to say?"

He kept his hands to himself this time. Good. I'd be able to think better. "That you shouldn't change any part of you."

A gust of wind blew my hair across my face. Impatiently, I swept it out of my eyes and behind my ears. "I'll do what I want, thanks."

His eyebrows shot up. "What *you* want? Or what Kelly wants?"

I paused. It had never occurred to me that I *wouldn't* want to get it removed. Didn't I want a face that blended in, that wasn't worth a second glance? To overhear myself being described as 'the girl with the brown hair' instead of 'the girl with the thing on her face'?

"I want to stop being stared at," I said. "I don't want to hear any more pity from people who act like having a birthmark is the worst thing that could ever happen to me."

Some sort of understanding passed over Theo's features. "Okay. I won't bring it up again," he said, "as long as you promise me something."

"What?"

His hand slid up my arm, over my shoulder, and then curled around my nape. Instinctively, I licked my bottom lip, and I saw his gaze snag there for just a moment before he raised his eyes to meet mine.

"Don't ever accuse me of lying to you," he said. Hurt laced his tone; it was the first time I realized how my knee-jerk reaction had cut into him, and my heart fell under the weight of the guilt. "You're the one person in the world that I've never, ever lied to."

"I know," I murmured. "I'm sorry. I've never lied to you, either."

Theo's expression cleared, and he slung his arm over my shoulders. "Come on. Curfew's coming soon."

"Wait," I said, planting my feet when he tried to tug me toward the truck. "The kissing."

The corner of his lips rose in his familiar smirk. "Yeah?"

"Was that a one-time thing, or...?"

I wasn't sure who I was fooling earlier. If he said yes, I would be devastated.

He didn't. Instead, he just tugged me closer and gave me a playful, smacking kiss. "Does that answer your question?"

I tried to bite back my grin, but I suspected that it was a failed effort. "I guess so."

Chapter Eleven

Now

I know I shouldn't be doing this.

But having common sense and listening to it are two separate things, and by the time I swing my mother's car into a space at Hoyt Landscaping, the choice has been made.

About half an hour further inland than the coastal town where Mom and Travis live, Theo's company is housed in a nondescript brown building on the same lot as a paint store and a body shop. All three of the businesses look rundown, like they've been there for decades. The lots aren't paved, and there are only a few other vehicles around.

I climb carefully out of the car, checking that the heels of my shoes are steady in the gravel before I let go of the door. I'm wearing black cropped pants and a white button-down, and I take a moment to adjust my French tuck, making sure it looks perfect. My sunglasses go to the top of my head, and I bring my handbag close to my body.

This time, I won't be caught off guard by Theo's presence. I look good, I feel good, and I know what I came here to say. I'm in complete control of the situation.

With my head high and shoulders back, I take a purposeful step forward and immediately lose my balance. I pitch forward, stumbling over my own feet, only to find myself facedown in the dirt and gravel a second later.

"Ow!" I flounder on the ground, trying to find some equilibrium after my quick descent. "Son of a bitch!"

An engine rumbles and grows closer. I manage to sit up on my knees just as a Hoyt Landscaping truck comes to a stop a few feet away from me. I hold my breath as the driver's window rolls down, prepared to see Theo on the other side.

But it's not Theo.

It's his dad.

"You alright there?" Cecil calls down to me.

Just like Theo didn't recognize me when we first met again, I can tell that Cecil doesn't, either. He looks concerned, but not surprised or shocked. To him, I'm just some random lady on the ground for no reason.

I rise—carefully—to my feet and smooth my hands down my front, trying to brush the dirt off my white shirt. "I'm good, thank you," I say primly, as if he didn't just come across me shouting obscenities into the ground.

Cecil squints at me. His dark hair is threaded with gray now, but he still looks remarkably like his son. "Are you here for Hoyt?"

"I'm not a client," I tell him, adjusting my sunglasses on top of my head. "I'm here to see Theo."

I watch Cecil's expression morph into astonishment as the dots connect. He stares at me for a few seconds—trying to reconcile the face he sees now with the face he knew, I'm sure—and then lets out a low whistle. "Well, I'll be damned. It's Nina Lynn."

My answering smile is genuine. The Hoyts never treated me as a bother or a burden, and years ago, I grieved their loss from my life as well as Theo's. "Hi, Cecil."

"Now I know why Theo's been walking around with his head in the clouds all day. When did y'all get back in touch?"

I move my left hand, subtly but purposely, letting the diamond catch the sun. Cecil looks taken aback when his gaze snags on my ring, and that annoys me. Did everybody expect me to spend my life waiting around for Theo? "We ran into each other last week. He's been working a job at my wedding venue."

He recovers quickly, plastering a smile on his face. "Well, that sure worked out. Congratulations, Nina. You've got a lucky guy there. Let me park this thing and I'll walk you in, alright?"

I nod, and when Cecil pulls forward, I see that Theo has emerged from the building. He stands on the pavement just outside the door, and for a moment we stand there, looking at each other across the small lot.

Despite my well-rehearsed speech, the first words I find are, "Do you wear that polo every day?"

Theo glances down, plucking at his shirt. "Pretty much."

"Do you ever wash it?"

One side of his mouth raises in that smirk that's so familiar, it makes me ache. "I have more than one, Sass.

Where's Queen Kelly? Not looking over your shoulder today?"

I shift uncomfortably. "The Catskills with her husband, remember? They left this morning."

The slam of a door captures our attention. Cecil emerges from the fleet of work trucks parked near a large shed, and now I can see that he's wearing the polo, too. "Why didn't you tell me Nina was coming?" he calls to Theo, walking up to us. "Your mom would have liked to say hey."

"Sorry. It slipped my mind." Theo's voice is smooth. I pointedly raise my eyebrows in his direction, wanting him to know that I'm fully aware he is lying. Ignoring me, he turns to tug the door open. "Come on. We'll show you around."

There isn't much to show. The lobby is clean, gray tile, with an unmanned reception area and a single plastic chair in the corner. Theo walks me down the single hallway, pointing out his office, Cecil's office, and the break room, which is unoccupied except for a man eating a candy bar.

"I'm listening for the phones, boss," he says, making no move to get up.

I haven't been able to ascertain who is actually in charge here, so I glance over at Cecil and Theo, waiting to see who responds. It's Theo who speaks to the guy. "That's fine, Wade. God knows you can hear 'em back here."

"Ain't that the truth," Cecil adds. "We've gotta figure out how to turn that ringer down."

Wade looks at me, his eyes lingering on my figure for a beat too long. "Who's this?"

A muscle ticks in Theo's jaw. "This is Nina Sullivan. Soon to be Nina…"

It takes me a moment to realize what he's waiting for. "Hartley," I say with a quick, obliging smile at the stranger. "It'll be Nina Hartley."

There's something strange about hearing it spoken aloud, my first name with Daniel's last, and a heavy, uncomfortable silence falls over the room. Cecil looks at his shoes. Theo's stare burns a hole in the wall.

Seeming eager to be free of the tension, Wade clears his throat and rises from the table, flicking his candy wrapper into the trash. He nods in my direction. "Nice to meet you. Congrats. I'm headed back up front, boss."

This time, Cecil answers. "I'll follow you."

The two of them go, leaving me alone with a tense Theo. I look down at my shirt, checking for any dirt I missed earlier. Brushing at a small spot near my belly button, I remind him, "You brought it up."

"I know."

"All I did was answer."

"Yeah." Theo takes the cap off his head, runs a hand through his hair a couple of times. "I know. Just weird to hear you use a new last name."

My eyes fall to the logo on his shirt. He doesn't elaborate, and I don't ask him to, because I know what we're both thinking. It's not me with a different last name that's strange—it's the fact that the name won't be Hoyt.

"Let's talk in your office," I suggest.

Theo nods mutely and leads me back to the door that bears his name. On the other side is a small but tidy room. His desk is neat, occupied only by a computer and legal pad. There's a TV mounted on the wall. A thick oak frame beneath it catches my eye. I step closer, swallowing a gasp when I see Theo's name in fancy script on a diploma from the University of North Carolina.

I look at him. He's standing beside his desk, not behind it, watching me with a guarded expression. "You went to college."

"Someone told me I should."

I decide not to take that bait. "For business?"

"Yeah." Theo moves over, perches on the edge of his desk. "While I was there, I made a friend who did landscaping work for extra money. He brought me along on a few jobs, and I liked it."

"So this is your company? Or Cecil's?"

"We're partners. Neither of us works for the other," he says, a clear undercurrent of pride in the words. "Dad worked in retail management after Walk a Mile closed. It was a decent job, but when I graduated, we decided to do the family business thing again."

It makes perfect sense that while my family fell apart in the aftermath of everything that happened, the Hoyts flourished. They never acted like separate people who happened to live together, the way my family sometimes had. They were a unit, a package deal, the ideal nuclear family in black-and-white shows. Honestly, in terms of business—in terms of everything—becoming involved with my parents was probably the biggest misstep Cecil and Randi ever made.

"Do they still live in Amity?" I ask.

"Sure do. Same house and everything. I live up there, too."

"That's a bit of a drive."

Theo shrugs. "We get a lot of work near the coast. This is just about halfway between there and home. It's not too bad. Dad and I don't go out on every job anymore."

I shift my bag on my shoulder. My feet are beginning to hurt in these impractical heels, but as much as I want to sink into a chair, I don't. I'm afraid that if I sit down, if I make myself comfortable with Theo nearby, I'll never want to leave.

"Alright, Sass." Theo's long fingers curl over the edge of the desk, and I find myself watching as they flex against the wood. "Tell me why you're here."

We didn't text for long last night—only long enough for me to say that I wanted to talk in person and for Theo to send me the company's address. Then I lay awake into the early hours of the morning, planning the speech that is currently caught in my throat.

I fold my hands in front of me, just as I do at Daniel's work events when I'm bored with the conversation and trying not to fidget. The star on Theo's shirt winks at me. I fix my gaze on it, swallowing hard.

"Are you grounding yourself right now?" he asks before I can get a word out.

And it makes me want to scream in frustration, because yes, that's exactly what I'm doing, and it's not fair that he can still read me so easily after all this time. He abandoned me to build a new life from nothing. Where does he find the audacity to act like he has the right to know me the way he used to?

I force my eyes to meet his, trying to retain some semblance of dignity. Raising my chin in his direction, I start on what I came to say, my words coming out in slow, measured syllables: "I came to tell you that we need to draw boundaries here. I'm getting married, Theo. We can't be the way we were."

Theo blinks at me, seemingly waiting for more. When it doesn't come, he says, "You came all the way here to tell me that?"

I twist my hands in front of me. "Yes."

He pushes himself up from the desk, takes a step toward me. "So you texted me first and drove to my office...to tell me that we need to keep our distance."

I clear my throat, raise my chin with feigned confidence. Even that is dwindling by the second. "I thought—"

"Here's what I think," Theo interrupts. Another step forward, and we're close enough now that I really should be moving away, but my feet are cemented to the ground. "I think you wanted an excuse to see me, but now that you're here, you don't know how to handle it. So now you're trying to put down this boundary, even though it's not really for me—it's for yourself."

"You don't know me anymore."

There's a hint of smugness in his features when he says, "Really."

"Yes, really. It's been ten years, Theo. A lot has changed."

"Well, you're right about that part," he says, and his eyes are on the spot where my birthmark used to be.

Huffing, I take a step backward, reaching behind me for the doorknob. "I have my life. You have yours. Let's leave them be."

I'm about to walk out the door when Theo says my name, quiet but urgent, and I have no choice but to look back at him.

"I'm going to give you one more chance to tell me that Daniel makes you happy," he says. "Tell me that, and I'll leave you alone."

I search for the words we both need to hear, but they aren't there.

Nodding slowly, Theo takes a step back, letting me breathe. "Got it," he says. "I'll see you around, Sass."

And I don't know what to do besides leave.

Chapter Twelve

Now

The next day, I find myself back at Hoyt Landscaping.

I don't tell Theo ahead of time because I don't know that I'm going to do it. When I hop into my mom's car that morning, my only plan is to grab a coffee. But after I get my latte, I find myself bypassing the turn to her house and heading toward the highway.

I spend the entire drive telling myself to turn around, to go somewhere else—*anywhere* else—but I've learned by now that somehow, my connection to Theo is still the strongest in my life. Before I know it, I'm parking in that gravel lot and walking inside with my tail between my legs.

Wade is at the reception desk. He's speaking into the corded phone, and when he sees me, his eyes flash with surprise before he holds up a finger. I nod while positioning myself in clear view of the hallway.

It works. A couple of minutes pass before Theo emerges from his office in his usual outfit. He walks purposefully toward the door, stopping in his tracks when he sees who's blocking the way.

"Hey there," he drawls. "How's that boundary working out for you?"

I can only hope that my hundred-dollar foundation hides the flush in my cheeks. "Well, I—"

But Theo brushes past me, swinging a ring of keys on his index finger. "Walk and talk, Sass."

I watch him walk away until it's clear he isn't going to stop, and then I scurry after him, my pride having been left elsewhere. "Wait. Where are you going?"

"Out to a job."

He holds the door open for me while I clunk outside in my heels. I look around the lot, but it's empty aside from us. I look at him skeptically. "By yourself?"

We start toward the trucks parked over by the shed—or, more accurately, he starts that way and I follow. "There's a crew out there already," he tells me. He takes his baseball cap off, runs a hand through his hair, and replaces it with the bill turned to the back. "The client is pissed about something. I've gotta smooth it over."

"Oh." I stop, watching Theo walk between two identical trucks. "Okay, I'll go, I just—I was out and I thought—"

But instead of opening the driver's door of the truck on the right, as I expect, Theo turns to the truck on the left and tugs on the handle of the passenger door. He holds it open, expectant eyes on me.

"What?" I ask dumbly.

Theo motions toward the truck. "You coming or not?"

It hits me that, yet again, I have lost control of this situation.

If I ever had any to begin with.

In lieu of an answer, I walk carefully to the door, determined not to faceplant in the gravel again. Theo's eyes track me the whole way. I turn my back on him and put the toe of my shoe on the sidebar, hoisting myself up.

"Be careful," he orders.

I try not to react as I feel his hand press into the small of my back. He guides me inside, only pulling back when my butt is secure in the leather seat, and I look up at him. "Thanks."

"Sure."

The door shuts in my face.

***

We're silent for the entire twenty-minute drive. Theo is waiting for me to break first, which is only fair, considering that I'm the one who showed up unannounced at his place of business. Briefly, my mind flits to what would happen if I surprised Daniel at work. I've never done it, because I know better, but I have to stifle a snort as I imagine how pissed off he would be.

Words evade me until we pull up to a million-dollar home in a gated neighborhood. Two of Theo's company trucks are already there. Four guys stand on the sidewalk, equipment abandoned around them, casting nervous glances back at the house. "Looks like my mom's house," I say without thinking.

"Oh, so you both found rich guys."

It sounds like the opposite of a compliment, and the words lodge in my chest like a pill that didn't go down quite right. "That's not their defining feature."

"It was when you were telling me about yours."

"I told you his *job*," I snap, even though my frustration isn't truly with him. "It's a normal thing to bring up when you're introducing somebody. I should have led with how wonderful he is, I guess."

Theo grabs a pair of sunglasses off the dash and slips them on. "Well, you never were good at lying on the spot. You coming?"

My back teeth ground together. "I'll wait here."

He hops out of the truck and closes the door behind him, thankfully leaving his keys in the ignition so the air can stay on full blast. I watch through the window as he strides up to his crew. Theo claps the shoulder of the man closest to him, and I see lots of gesturing to the yard and the house as they converse.

The longer I look at Theo in his well-fitting jeans, his employees drawn to him like moons to a planet the way everybody always has been, the more discomfort lodges itself in my chest. In search of something else to focus on, I pull my phone from my purse and wake the screen.

"What?" I say out loud when I see a missed call from Daniel. The timestamp shows that the call came through half an hour ago, around the time I was waiting for Theo in the lobby. I check the time and find that it's ten-thirty now; he called me from work, then, which isn't something he would normally do.

I call him back, but it goes straight to voicemail. I zone out during his brisk, businesslike message, startling slightly at the sound of the beep. "Hey," I say uncertainly. "I'm just returning your call. Hope everything's okay." I let a beat pass. "Love you."

When I look out the window again, I see Theo up on the porch talking to the homeowner, a tall, middle-aged man dressed like he should be sitting in a corner office. Theo's crew is standing with their backs to me, their faces turned toward the house at the top of the hill. We all watch as the client goes from angrily waving his arms around, to folding them over his chest, to tilting his head back with laughter, to shaking Theo's hand with a smile on his face.

"Unbelievable," I mutter as Theo jogs down the porch steps. He goes over to the crew and speaks to them for a minute, and then he is headed back toward me. Our eyes meet through the windshield. Of course that cocky grin is already in place.

"So you can still get everyone eating out of the palm of your hand," I say as he hops back into the truck. "Must be nice."

"It comes in handy."

"What was he mad about?"

Theo stares down at his phone for a minute, typing out a text. I hear the *whoosh* indicating that the message has sent, and then Theo drops his phone in the cupholder. "He says we broke a pipe in the yard. The guys told me it was already cracked, but there's no way to prove it. I'm getting it taken care of."

I furrow my brow at him. "So you're taking the blame for something you didn't do?"

"Not really," he says. "I told him I trust my guys, but as a courtesy, I'd pay to have a plumber that we work with sometimes come out and fix it today."

He shifts the truck into drive and starts maneuvering down the winding road. I look at my phone, see that Daniel hasn't texted or called back, and slide it under my thigh. "Customer's always right, huh?"

Theo jerks his thumb back over his shoulder. "More like, the customer has an enormous yard and pays me a shit ton of money to maintain it. I'll spring for the damn plumber."

It seems obvious from the type of clients Theo has, but years of uncertainty about our families' store prompt me to ask, "So you're doing well?"

We reach the gates of the neighborhood, and the woman at the security post lets us through. Theo gives her a wave as we drive by. "Yeah. We're doing real well."

Beyond financials, it's so obvious that Theo is in his element. He was always meant to run the show, be his own boss, and here he is, heading up a successful business at twenty-eight. Meanwhile, I've spent my twenties following other people—first Mom, then Daniel—and aimlessly floating through life. It's now been several years since I last worked; I applied for a few retail openings when I first moved to New York, but nobody called me for an interview. Turns out, a girl with no college degree and a checkered employment history is a miniscule fish in a pond of that size.

Around that same time, Daniel had begun to speak to me more about his work—in particular, the role his colleagues' wives played in their circle. He mentioned that most of them didn't work, which was convenient when it came to company events, social gatherings, and last-minute business travel. The more he talked, the sillier it seemed to spend my days at any of the low-paying jobs that I was qualified to do when I was already living rent-free in a luxury apartment on the Upper East Side.

So ever since then, I've just...existed. I briefly tried to make myself useful with housework, but Daniel preferred me to leave that to the woman he'd been paying for years to clean the apartment and prepare his meals for the week. Otherwise, it's just been me and the city. Most of the time I feel like I'm waiting around for a cue from Daniel on what to do next—be here, wear that, make sure you smile at the important people.

I'm thinking about how many guests at my wedding will be more acquaintance than friend—even my bridesmaids are Daniel's sisters and a couple of women I've gotten to know through his coworkers—when my mind finally registers the fact that we're not driving back the way we came.

I look over at Theo, who is the picture of relaxation with one wrist draped over the wheel and his elbow out the window. For a moment, he looks so much like his teenage self that I can't breathe.

When I recover, I ask him, "Where are we going?"

"Amity."

"What?" Panic rises in my chest. "I can't go to Amity."

"Why not?"

"Because I haven't been there since—"

I cut myself off, and a loaded silence falls between us as we each finish the sentence in our minds.

I haven't been there since we left together.

Theo clears his throat, the sound cutting through the tension in the air, and says, "You showed up at my work and got in my truck, Sass. I've got stuff to do."

"Is it for the Reddings?" I ask, since they're the only people in Amity who could possibly occupy the same tax bracket as the man whose house we just left. At least, it used to be that way.

He snorts. "Over my dead body."

The air of relaxation surrounding him has evaporated; now his jaw is clenched, gaze hard, as he stares out the windshield, and I wonder if he, too, is thinking about the day Rick Redding showed up in our parents' store. We didn't know that his appearance was the beginning of the end—of the store, of us, of life as we knew it.

"Think of how many properties they own," I say. "It would be smart to align yourself with them."

Theo raises his brows in my direction, his face etched in disbelief. "You think I should make nice?"

"From a business standpoint—"

"Maybe I'll change my mind when we get an apology for what they did to our families." He casts me a chastising look. "Not everything is about money, Nina."

"I never said it was."

Theo eyes my sleek tote, my lightweight cashmere sweater, the hoops in my ears, the spot where my birthmark was. "Sure."

With that word—a single syllable, laden with meaning—hanging in the air, he pulls onto the highway. We pass the sign indicating that Amity is twenty miles away, and my stomach twists itself into a knot. I'm not prepared to return to my hometown today, but that doesn't seem to matter—I'm already on my way.

"So are you going to tell me what happened to your boundary?" Theo asks after a few miles. He drawls out the word *boundary* with a touch of sarcasm. "Don't you have things to do? Linens to pick out? Money to count?"

"Everything is picked out and counted." I'm snippy, but there's no real bite. "I was...in the area."

"Really." He clearly knows that I'm lying.

"Yes," I insist, "and I...felt like we left things in a weird place yesterday."

Theo tilts his head, pretending to think. My hackles preemptively rise.

"Oh, yeah," he says in faux realization. "Yeah, you mean when I wanted you to tell me that your fiancé makes you happy, and all you did was stare at me and then walk off?"

I press my lips into a tight line. "Yes. That."

"Right, right. That *was* a weird thing to do on your part."

"I'm sorry I don't have a ready-made defense for my relationship," I shoot back. "I'm not used to being interrogated about it."

Theo breezes past a white van going ten miles under the speed limit. "It just seems like it would have been pretty easy to say, 'yeah, he makes me happy,' if you want me to leave you alone so bad. But since you can't keep up your own *boundary*—"

"Stop saying *boundary* like that."

He ignores me. "I don't think you really want one."

I think of the missed call from Daniel and feel a jab of guilt. I've never confided in anybody about Theo—not my mother, not the people who pass for my friends these days, and not even Daniel. Whenever Daniel has asked about my childhood, I've avoided bringing up Theo by implying that my family owned the business on their own. But now I have to wonder what Daniel would think if he knew the whole story, if we knew where I am and who I'm with.

Not wanting to dwell on it anymore, I clear my throat and change the subject. "Can you please tell me where we're going?"

"I already told you." Theo glances over his right shoulder, checking his blind spot, and then signals to get back into the right lane. "We're going home."

Chapter Thirteen

Now

One moment, we're on the winding state highway; the next, we're coming around the bend and there is our hometown: the high school on the left, a cluster of fast food restaurants on the right, a crumbling stone sign welcoming us to Amity.

We're quiet as we drive down the main drag. I stare out the window, and even though it's still early in the day, I'm emotionally exhausted. I don't have the energy to fight off the memories that come to me as we pass the dentist, the dollar movie theater, the DMV. My heart rate picks up a bit when we pass the entrance to the strip mall where our families' store was. The storefront isn't visible from the road. I start to ask Theo what business operates there now, but the words jam in my throat, and I decide I'm not quite ready to know.

We enter the residential part of town, and Theo turns into a neighborhood of split-levels that were built when we were in middle school. As a kid, I thought that the people who lived in the new development must have been rich—and compared to my family, I suppose they were. But now I can see that the houses are close together, the yards are small, and subtle signs of disrepair—a missing shutter here, a crooked mailbox there—are beginning to mar the block.

Theo pulls into a driveway and cuts the engine. The grass is long, the front porch lined with overgrown shrubs. I wrack my brain, trying to remember who lives here, and come up empty.

Before I can ask, Theo has hopped out of the truck and started pulling things out of the back. Huffing, I leave my purse in the passenger seat and climb down unsteadily on my heels. A pair of work boots hits the pavement in front of me. I look up at Theo, squinting into the sun. "What are those?"

"Boots for you," he says from the bed of the truck. He reaches up to curl the brim of his hat. "You can't wear those deathtrap shoes while we work."

I make a sound of disbelief. "I don't work for you."

Theo spreads his arms, gesturing to our surroundings. "What else do you have to do? You just gonna sit there and watch me?"

"That was the plan."

The corner of his mouth ticks upward, and too late, I realize that I've unintentionally recalled our past—because Theo *absolutely* knows that my teenage sexual awakening was directly related to the sight of him stretching to put things on shelves, bending over to pick up boxes, and leaning against the register with that dumb smirk on his face.

Mercifully, he decides not to bring it up. I watch as he unloads a push lawnmower and weed eater and drops them in the front yard. Then he breezes past me, jerking his head toward the front door. "Let's go."

I trail behind him, taking my time climbing the front stairs. It's bothering me that I don't know who lives here. I haven't spoken to anybody from Amity in ten years, and all I can hope is that it isn't somebody who I knew well, somebody who might ask questions as to why my family left town so suddenly.

Theo raps on the front door twice. Almost instantly, a chorus of barking and movement sounds from inside.

"Hush, hush, hush. Lulu, get back!" comes a woman's voice. It's vaguely familiar, but I can't recall who it belongs to until the door swings open and I'm greeted by a herd of corgis being shooed away by Mrs. Wilson, the owner of the town's general store and a regular customer at Walk a Mile.

She's a decade older than the last time I saw her, but the only difference I see is the more pronounced wrinkles at the corners of her eyes when she beams at Theo. "You're early! I thought you were coming this evening, or I would've had the dogs put up."

I cast Theo a sharp look, only to find him stifling a smile. "We were out and had some time."

Mrs. Wilson steps onto the porch. After reaching back to nudge away a dog who tries to follow her, she pulls the door shut. "Well, no worries. I'm just glad you're here. I feel like I'm singlehandedly bringing down the neighborhood property values with this yard."

"Give us an hour and you'll have the best curb appeal on the block," Theo says.

I watch as she notices me for the first time. Her eyes travel from my shoes to my outfit to my face. I can see her trying to place me, but once again, the absence of my birthmark renders me a stranger to someone I grew up knowing.

Mrs. Wilson crosses her arms and turns on Theo. "Aren't you going to introduce me to your friend?"

He frowns, feigning confusion. "Introduce you? Who forgets Nina Sullivan?"

Mrs. Wilson's eyes pop open wide, she gasps, and then her arms are around me and I'm staggering backward in surprise. "Nina Lynn! Oh my goodness. Where have you been?"

This is exactly why I didn't want to come back to Amity: I don't know how to begin to answer that question. My eyes meet Theo's over her shoulder. He must see my desperation, because he jumps in to save me. "Frank got a job offer he couldn't refuse, and then after high school she moved to New York. She's just helping me out today."

I give him a grateful look, and he bows his chin in acknowledgement.

"New York!" Mrs. Wilson draws back but holds onto me by the shoulders. "I bet you've got some stories to tell. But you've kept in touch with Theo?"

My throat constricts. "Of course," I manage.

"Good, good. I—" She catches sight of my left hand, and we're treated to another dramatic gasp. "You two have been holding out on me!"

Theo's face goes white, and I feel my own stomach lurch. Mrs. Wilson doesn't seem to notice as she snatches my hand, turning it so the diamond sparkles in the sunlight. "Oh, goodness gracious. Look at that diamond. Nina, did I see you at Dale's service? It's all such a blur. Were you two together then, or—"

"No," Theo interrupts gently. He reaches between us and takes my hand out of Mrs. Wilson's, looking at neither of us as he lowers it back to my side. "We're not together. Nina still lives in New York with her fiancé."

Mrs. Wilson's face falls, and she looks uncharacteristically chastened. "Oh. *Oh.* Well, leave it to me to jump to conclusions." She pastes a smile on her face. "Congratulations, Nina."

"Thank you."

A heavy silence envelops the three of us. Theo clears his throat. "We'll get to work."

"Of course," says Mrs. Wilson, although she eyes my outfit doubtfully. "I'll go in and make some tea for y'all."

"Appreciate it," Theo says before turning away and tromping down the stairs.

I stay right where I am, though, as something that was said earlier registers in my brain. "Mrs. Wilson," I say carefully. "Did you ask if I was at Mr. Wilson's service?"

"I did. Were you? I'm sorry I can't remember. He passed so suddenly, and I was such a wreck. I barely remember the funeral at all, to be honest with you." A sad smile flits over her lips. "The thing I remember the most is how the church was overflowing. Some people had to watch the service on a laptop in the lobby."

I didn't know Mrs. Wilson's husband as well as I knew her, but since they owned the general store, everybody in town could pick either one of them out of a crowd. In their store, he could be found stocking shelves, bagging groceries, and passing out free fruit to little kids. He was one of those people who was such a fixture, it seemed impossible to imagine a world in which they weren't occupying the space that could only be filled by them.

"I wasn't there, actually," I tell her. "I didn't realize he had passed away. But I'm—I'm so sorry."

Against my will, my voice cracks a bit. It's a show of vulnerability like I haven't allowed myself in years, but when Mrs. Wilson's face softens, I find that I don't mind too much. "Thank you, Nina. That means a lot."

She disappears inside, and I walk over to where Theo is slipping on work gloves. He looks at me, his expression unreadable, and I find myself asking, "When did Mr. Wilson die?"

"A little over two years ago. Heart attack."

I glance at the house behind us. "Did they always live here?"

"No. They used to live out near the gas station, remember?"

"Oh, right."

"She sold their house pretty quickly after the funeral, and she stopped working at the store. Her kids are running it now. She told my mom it was too hard to be there without him."

"I suppose I can understand that," I say, thinking about how long I've spent trying to avoid any mention, any memory, of Theo.

His gaze bores into mine, and I know what he's thinking before he says it.

Even so, I'm not prepared when he steps closer to me, leaving barely a foot of separation between us, and says, "Me too. It's hell living in this town, Sass. I see you everywhere."

I raise my chin toward him in challenge. "Then why do you?"

"Because," he says, like it's obvious. "I see you everywhere."

His words are saturated with brutal honesty, his eyes unapologetic as they fix on me. Intensity crackles in the small space between us, and I find myself wondering how he's done it. How he's managed to live here, bombarded by memories, and thrive anyway.

I couldn't have.

That's why I ran.

Theo seems to be waiting for me to say something, and when I don't, he moves away. He stoops low to grab the weed eater off the ground. "You don't have to help. It'll be less than an hour. I'm sure Mrs. Wilson will let you sit inside."

"No," I say, surprising myself. I go back to the driveway and kick off my heels. My bare feet are met with hot asphalt, and that long-forgotten feeling spurs me on as I grab the work boots Theo left out. They're way too big for me, but I can deal with it for an hour. I slide them on, then begin removing the hoops from my ears. "I'll help."

For a second, Theo stares at me. And then his face begins to split into a grin—not the cocky smirk, but the sincere, beaming smile that used to be the biggest ray of sunlight in my day.

"Great," he says. "Let's get to it."

***

Later, when Mrs. Wilson's lawn is mowed, her shrubs pruned, everything perfect down to the smallest leaf, I collapse in the passenger seat of Theo's truck. My clothes are filthy, sweaty strands of hair frame a face full of smudged makeup, and my limbs ache. It's been a long time since I did any physical activity more taxing than half-hour jogs on the treadmill in Daniel's building.

It's been even longer since I felt this exhilarated.

I watch through the windshield as Theo jogs down Mrs. Wilson's steps, tucking a check in his back pocket. He crosses in front of the truck and grins at me, and it's only then that I register the fact that I was grinning first.

"Damn," Theo says, swinging himself up into the driver's seat and turning the key in the ignition. I stick my face in front of the nearest vent as cold air rushes out. "If only Queen Kelly could see you now."

The mention of my mother does nothing to dampen my mood. She isn't here. Neither is Daniel. In fact, every pressing matter in my real life seems far away from this situation where I feel both reborn and restored.

"She used to get so mad if I came home from school with dirty clothes."

"I remember once, you realized on the way home that you had a big smudge of something on your knee, and you made me rub it out of the fabric with my spit."

"I think you volunteered." I say, laughing. "Disgusting."

As my voice fades, the only reply is silence. When I look back at Theo, he's just staring at me.

"What?" I ask, feeling myself shrink.

His swallow is visible in his throat. "That's the first time you've laughed around me," he says quietly. "Since you've been back, I mean."

"Oh." I look away, remembering how the forgotten sound of his laugh had rendered me speechless, too. "Maybe so."

"No maybe about it." Theo shakes himself from his haze and puts the truck in reverse. "I was starting to wonder if you were just going to stomp around and glare at me forever. Do you want to get lunch?"

I glance at the clock on the dashboard. I am hungry; it's nearly one o'clock, and all I've had today is a coffee. Unfortunately, I'm also grimy and gross. "I can't go out in public like this."

We pull out of the driveway, and Theo starts back toward the main road. "Why don't we go to my parents' for a while?"

I balk. "What?"

"Dad is at work, but Mom will be there. You can take a shower and borrow some of her clothes. She'd probably make us something to eat, too."

We come to a stop sign. A left would lead us back to town, and a right would take us toward our old neighborhood. I can see Theo's hands fidgeting on the steering wheel as they itch to turn it toward me.

"I can't show up at your parents' house after ten years to use their shower and eat their food," I protest.

"Mom knows you're back in town. She wanted me to bring you by, but I said I didn't think you'd come—you know, with the *boundary* and all." I give him a flat look, and he snickers before turning serious again. "We don't have to. But I promise, she would love to see you."

Would she? Catching a glimpse of myself in the side mirror, I study my ruined but clearly expensive top, the face that cost tens of thousands of dollars to get. I remember the last time I heard Randi's voice—stressed, upset, watching her livelihood slip away because of something my family had done.

I can't think of a single reason Randi Hoyt would want me in her home.

But Theo seems sure of himself, and we're a solid hour away from my mom's house, and I really would like to take a shower. "Okay," I say finally. "But will you at least text her and warn her?"

"Sure." He grabs his phone from the cup holder, types something out with one thumb, and holds it up to me as proof. The message is concise: *Be there in five minutes. I'm bringing Nina.* As I'm reading it, her reply comes through: YAY!

I sigh, resigned to the fact that this is happening, and nod my assent.

Theo takes the right turn. I settle back in my seat and watch the houses go by on either side of us. We pass the park, our elementary school, the library. When I see the first cluster of older homes that mark the entrance to the neighborhood we grew up in, I breathe in sharply.

"You okay?" asks Theo.

"Yes."

The tension in my body coils tight as we approach, then pass, the turnoff for my childhood home. We turn the corner, and there is Randi, waving wildly from the end of her narrow driveway.

When we park, she rushes to my side of the truck. I climb out gingerly, my sore feet crammed into my heels once again, as she watches with her hands clasped over her mouth. I'm mentally grappling for what to say, but there's no need: as soon as I find my balance, Randi ignores the complete mess of my clothes and pulls me into a hug. "Nina Lynn," she sighs. "Oh, Nina, I've missed you, honey."

"Hi," I say weakly. My knees feel like jelly. Running into Theo that first day at the country club was enough of an emotional shock, but this entire day—coming back into Amity with him, seeing Mrs. Wilson again, having Randi welcome me with open arms despite what my family did to hers—has me feeling like I need to lie down.

She pulls away, grasping me by the shoulders, and looks at my face. She's the first person from my old life to not act surprised at what she sees there. I can only assume that Cecil or Theo told her, and I try not to think about what words they might have used.

You don't even look like yourself, Theo told me.

And in this moment, I can admit that he was right. I don't look like the person I was when I left here, and I don't feel like her, either.

At least...until today. Today, I feel like I've uncovered something inside me that I thought was gone forever.

"Sass went out on a job with me." Theo comes up to receive a hug from his mother. "She wasn't really prepared, as you can see."

"You never did let anything stand in your way," Randi says, regarding me proudly.

"I told her she could get a shower here." He takes his baseball cap off and uses his shirt sleeve to wipe sweat from his brow. "I might take one, too."

"Oh, absolutely." Randi ushers us up the driveway like a mother hen. "Nina, you can use the master bathroom. I have shampoo, conditioner, body wash, everything you could need."

"Great."

"And I'll find some clothes for you, too. It won't be anything as nice as what you've got on, but—"

"That's okay," I interrupt, becoming uncomfortably aware of the fact that my outfit may well have cost more than the mortgage on the Hoyts' house. "Whatever you have would be perfect."

We go inside the house, and I'm struck by how nothing has changed. There is the same oak table by front door, mail and keys strung across it; there is the navy-blue couch, pink throw blanket draped over the middle cushion. There is the family portrait above the fireplace, featuring a younger Cecil and Randi with a preschool-aged

Theo. His toothy grin seems to jump straight out of the frame and into my chest, nestling in a dusty corner of my heart.

Theo heads to the guest shower, and Randi shows me to hers. I could stay under the warm stream all day, but I'm only comfortable being naked in the house I still think of as Theo's for so long. I get out as soon as I've rinsed the drugstore-brand conditioner from my hair and the peony-scented body wash from my skin. Strangely, although I've grown used to long showers with a litany of high-end products, it's the freshest I've felt in a long time.

After donning Randi's shirt and joggers and combing out my hair, I wander back down the hallway. There's movement in the kitchen, but the sound of Theo's voice coming from inside his old bedroom makes me pause. I peek around the doorway, and he's standing there with his back to me. One hand holds his phone to his ear and the other perches on his hip. My eyes drift from his bare feet to his clean sweatpants and fitted tee to the drops of water trickling down his neck.

Before I can think it all the way through, I'm walking into Theo's room. He turns to me as I approach, his eyebrows hiking up as I brush past him and start looking around. The room looks untouched from what I remember. There's the dresser under the window, the twin bed perpendicular to it, the old oak desk in the corner. On the bed is the same plaid bedspread he had in high school, and although I'm not so presumptuous as to peek in his closet, I'm reasonably certain that I would find a stack of cartoon-printed sheets on the shelf.

"Thanks," Theo says. "Let me know how it goes."

I turn around as he ends his call. "Who was that?"

"One of my shift leads. I'm going to stop by another job this afternoon, if you don't mind."

"Sure."

His gaze drifts up my body, lingering on my make-up-free face. "Feel better?"

"Much." I glance around the room. "You don't still live here, right?"

"No," he says with a short laugh, "but my house is out on the edge of town, so sometimes I just crash here instead of going all the way home."

I find myself wondering about the space Theo has claimed for himself. I envision a cabin, deceptively compact on the outside but full of useful nooks and crannies on the inside, sitting on a couple of acres. I wonder if he keeps his lawn to the same standards as his clients', or if he takes a more relaxed approach to his own property.

I step over to the desk. There isn't much there: just a legal pad, a coffee mug full of pens, and a neat stack of books with the spines turned out. The one on top is called *Economics for the Twenty-First Century*. I pick it up and show it to Theo. "This looks like something Daniel would read."

"Daniel would read the textbook from my introductory econ class?" Theo asks doubtfully. "He should probably already know that stuff."

I send him an unamused look. "You know what I mean. He likes to read biographies and books about finance."

"I like a good biography," he says, and I resist the urge to respond, *I remember*. "Who's he reading about now?"

I try to recall the last book I saw on Daniel's nightstand. "Rockefeller, I think."

Theo snorts. "Of course."

"What's the last biography *you* read?" I challenge.

"Amelia Earhart."

I busy myself with putting the textbook back on the stack, taking an excessive amount of time to line the corners up exactly the way I found them. "Hmm."

"What have you been reading?"

"Nothing," I say, turning back to him. "You know I don't read books."

He shrugs, his arms crossed over his chest in a way that conforms his sleeves to his biceps. A drying lock of hair falls over his forehead. "If you're willing to change your face for your fiancé, picking up a new hobby isn't too much of a stretch."

"If you must know," I tell him, "I had the work done before I ever met Daniel."

That seems to legitimately surprise him, which pleases me. "Really?"

I make a derisive sound. "Why do you think he looked at me in the first place?"

"Nina, don't say shit like that," Theo bristles.

"Well, I—" I cut myself off when my eyes snag on the corkboard above the desk. Dangling from a thumbtack is a black satin scrunchie—one I thought I lost a long time ago. Snatching it, I turn on Theo. His face immediately pinks, and I feel a perverse sort of pleasure. Finally, I have the upper hand. "Theodore Hoyt."

"What?"

I let the scrunchie dangle from my index finger, trying not to sink too far into the memory of being pressed up against Theo, pulling the scrunchie from my messy hair after it had been ravaged by his hands. "Explain yourself."

"Is that yours?" he asks, feigning innocence. "I was never sure where it came from."

"Right." I desperately want to hold the scrunchie to my nose, to see if it still smells like anything familiar—the woods, Theo, this house—but the desire to maintain my dignity wins out. "You never asked your other conquests if they left it behind?"

My intention is to tease him, but as soon as the words cross my lips, I regret them. It's the first time I've given any thought to the existence of other women in Theo's life. Of course he has been with others—he's a young, attractive, successful business owner. I've certainly been with other men, am currently engaged to one, and shouldn't care one way or the other.

Knowing that doesn't wash away the sour taste in my mouth. I'm about to put the scrunchie back where I found it when Theo startles me by snatching it from my grasp. He leans in close, his fresh smell surrounding me. His eyes capture mine in an arresting gaze, and I find myself frozen in place, staring up at him.

"None of the rest of them matter," he says, his voice low. "And you were never a conquest."

And as I watch, Theo tucks the scrunchie in his back pocket and saunters out the door.

Chapter Fourteen

Now

"Where did you take poor Nina to work for free?" Randi asks when we've settled around the kitchen table, eating tuna salad on toast and sipping iced tea.

Theo reclines lazily in a chair and cocks a brow at his mother. "Poor? Did you see that thing she's lugging around on her hand?"

Randi gives him a sharp look. "Theo."

Determined as Theo seems to get under my skin, Randi has not brought up my engagement—which I assume is intentional, and it's also the way I would prefer it. I jump in to answer her question. "We were at Mrs. Wilson's."

"Oh, how is Bonnie?" Randi asks. "I worry about her."

"She seems fine, Mom." Theo lifts his toast to his mouth. "Especially when she saw who I brought with me."

"I'm sure." Randi smiles at me, rolling her glass gently between her palms. "She still asks about you."

"Really?" I ask, surprised.

"Of course," she says, as if it should be obvious. "She was so worried about you when your family left. We all were."

Even as Randi takes a casual sip of tea, I go still, taken aback by the mention of our departure. "Don't they know what happened?"

Theo and Randi exchange a quick look. I expect Theo to answer, but it's Randi who does, her voice soft. "Of course not."

I sit back in my chair, absorbing that. Aside from Theo, the other reason I never planned to return to Amity was that I assumed everyone knew what my mother had done. Even when I was a kid and our families were running the business together, it was the Hoyts that people liked. Randi and Cecil could have aired all our dirty laundry for the whole town to see and nobody would have taken my family's side—and I wouldn't blame them.

"I'm sure people have asked," I say.

"They have, but it's none of their business." Randi gives me a soft smile. "I hate the way things ended between us and your parents, Nina, but Cecil and I wouldn't dream of making it worse by contributing to the gossip mill. We've missed you so much." At that, she casts Theo a meaningful look, and he ducks his head to grab another bite of toast. "You won't find a person in town who isn't thrilled to see you."

It's at odds with every assumption I've ever held, but today I've been swept into hugs from both her and Mrs. Wilson, each of them acting as if no time had passed at all. And Theo—even as he's regarded with me with a bit more skepticism, he's taken me back into the fold, too. He let me see him at work. He brought me back to his childhood home. He's sitting across from me right now, eating the same tuna salad he used to trade away whenever it was packed in his school lunches.

I walked away, and when nobody followed, I thought that meant they didn't care.

But maybe they've just been waiting for me to turn around.

I clear my throat, ensuring my voice is free of emotion before I respond. "I didn't plan to come back."

Randi's face turns soft, her gaze tinged with sadness. "I know, Nina. Believe me." She reaches both hands out, laying one on Theo's arm and the other on mine. It's the kind of maternal gesture that has always come naturally to her—unlike my mom, whose actions seemed stiff and forced on the rare occasions she attempted to be comforting. "Losing the business was hard, but my biggest regret has always been what happened with you two. It *devastated* Cecil and me. And Theo—"

Abruptly, he pushes his chair back from the table and gets to his feet. "I'm full. I'm gonna throw my dirty clothes in the truck. Sass, I'll be outside whenever you're ready." He drops a kiss on top of Randi's head and walks out of the kitchen, never once looking at me.

Randi sighs and gives me a sad smile. "He had a very, *very* hard time after your family left," she tells me quietly. "As much as we missed you, I know that it was a thousand times worse for him. I can't imagine his pain."

We hear the front door open and close. I glance toward the front window in time to catch of glimpse of Theo's back as he jogs down the porch steps, and I remember what it was like to be seventeen, constantly peeking outside, full of desperate hope.

Unable to meet her eyes, I'm still looking outside when I admit, "I can."

***

By the time we go to a couple of other job sites and solve a mulch emergency, afternoon is turning to evening. When we pull into the parking lot of Theo's office, the sun is just beginning to descend in the sky, and the businesses look like they've closed for the day. Theo drives his truck toward where my mom's car was parked earlier, slowing when we pass a sleek black sedan idling near the grass.

Theo leans over to look out my window, his warmth hovering at my shoulder. "Who the hell is that?"

"I wouldn't know."

The car's taillights turn off, and the driver's door opens. We watch as a man steps out, unfurling his long limbs from the cramped space of the car. When he turns, I let out a loud gasp. "Oh, fuck."

"What?" Theo demands.

Daniel's eyes meet mine and immediately go stormy. He's dressed like he came straight from work, which doesn't make sense. As he stalks toward the truck, I'm completely frozen, unable to comprehend how he could possibly be here.

He steps up to my side of the truck and gives two hard raps on the window. Theo rolls my window down a couple of inches, and his fingers graze my shoulder as he stretches across my lap. "Hey, man. What can I help you with?"

I surreptitiously shrug off Theo's hand, but Daniel has already noticed him touching me. His gaze goes even darker, and my stomach twists into a knot. Daniel presses his face up against the window and glares down at me, completely ignoring Theo. "Nina. Get out."

"Excuse me?" Theo snaps.

Daniel flicks a quick glance at Theo, as if he's nothing more than a fly on his sandwich. Then he turns his attention back to me. "Come on," he says, and startles me by yanking open my door. "Now."

My mind is lagging, trying to catch up with what is happening—how Daniel is *here*, in a car with Wyoming license plates, standing next to Theo's truck.

Theo doesn't seem to be suffering from any shock. He crowds in even closer to me. "Who are you?"

"I'm Nina's fiancé," he practically spits, "and I had to leave work and fly down here because you're running around with her."

"I've been running around with her my whole life," Theo says, which only renews the vigor in Daniel's glare.

Finally, I find my voice. "How did you know where I was?"

"Your mom can track her car from her phone," Daniel says, and I close my eyes. *Stupid.* "She said you were here earlier this week, and she looked today and saw you'd come back."

"This is Theo," I say. "We grew up together. We—"

"Yeah. Kelly told me."

"Nice to meet you," Theo says with faux cheer. "How was your flight?"

Daniel rolls his eyes before turning his ire back on me. "We can talk about this later, Nina. I don't have time for this bullshit right now. Let's *go*."

I look at my fiancé. I don't move, and I don't say anything because I have nothing to say. I could try to convince him that this isn't what it looks like, smooth things over like I always do…but I'm simply not interested. Today has drained my already limited reserve of emotional energy. I don't have anything left.

With Theo's firm, tense presence behind me, I cross my arms over my chest. "Why didn't you just call me?"

"I did. You didn't answer."

"So you jumped on a plane and came down here?" I ask doubtfully. "You rented a car instead of asking me to pick you up from the airport?"

Daniel's jaw clenches. "Your mom seemed to think I was going to catch you doing something."

"Doing what? I've been here planning our wedding, Daniel."

He snorts. "Yeah, when you're not hanging out with a guy who fucked you."

Before I can react, Theo is out of the car, storming around to my side of the truck. He roughly pushes against Daniel's shoulder, forcing him to step back from me, and then grabs the collar of his starched shirt. Daniel is taller by several inches, but that doesn't stop Theo from yanking Daniel close and snarling right in his face: "You aren't going to talk to her that way."

"Theo—" I say, but Daniel holds up his hand, and I clamp my mouth shut.

"This isn't any of your business," he says to Theo.

"Your ass is on my property, so it seems like my business." He turns his attention to me and says, "You've got a real winner here."

Daniel yanks himself out of Theo's grip. He runs his hand over his now-rumpled shirt collar, trying to smooth it out. His glare intensifies. "Nina. Let's. Go."

I knew I shouldn't have come to see Theo, and I did it anyway, and here's the consequence. *You're engaged*, I tell myself, staring at Daniel. *This is your fiancé. This is your life. Go.*

But even as I unbuckle my seat belt and pull my purse over my arm, hesitation saturates my every move. I keep my gaze directed toward the ground, avoiding the two pairs of eyes boring into me. We are cloaked in tense silence as I plant one heel, then the other, carefully into the gravel.

Then Daniel's patience seems to run out. In two quick strides, he closes the distance between us. He grabs me roughly by the elbow, his fingers digging into my skin as he yanks me forward. Legitimate fear strikes my chest, and then I feel Theo at my side.

"Get your fucking hands off her," comes his sharp demand, and in the next second, I'm released from Daniel's grasp. Theo shoves him back but doesn't follow. Instead, he plants himself in front of me. "She's not going with you, dickhead. Leave."

Daniel's face is beet-red. Over Theo's shoulder, he fixes me with his steely glare. "He speaks for you now?"

Theo glances back at me before shifting almost imperceptibly to the right. He's still guarding me, but I know the message he's sending with the movement: if I want him to let me through, he will.

I can still feel the phantom press of Daniel's fingertips in the skin of my arm. I search his face for a hint of regret, but every feature is locked into that hard, impenetrable expression. He's never grabbed me like that before. Maybe he never would again. But the residual adrenaline from split second of fear is still pounding through my veins, and in that moment, I make a decision.

I step out from behind Theo. He inhales sharply, his hand still partially extended, ready to get between me and Daniel. We happen to glance at each other at the same time, and the moment our eyes meet, the tension ebbs out of Theo's body. He nods, I relax minutely, and I turn back to Daniel.

"No," I respond to Daniel's question. "He doesn't. But neither do you."

And I tug off my engagement ring.

Daniel blanches, his lips moving soundlessly for several moments. "You're fucking kidding me."

I look down at the ring, held between my thumb and forefinger. It glints in the fading sunlight, its center jewel downright gaudy in a way I've never noticed before.

"I'm not kidding," I say. "This isn't going to work out."

Daniel's face contorts, somehow grows even redder, and then he's screaming at me: "You're white fucking trash, Nina Sullivan. You come from nothing and if you leave me, that's right back where you're headed."

He continues on, cursing, waving his arms, as my conscious mind lifts from my body and watches the surreal scene from above. Buttoned-up Daniel standing in a dusty parking lot with a mussed suit, completely flying off the handle. Theo nudging me in the side, murmuring, "Get back in the truck," under his breath. Me ambling into the passenger seat as he hurries back to his side.

The truck is still running, and Theo shifts it into drive. Before he takes his foot off the brake, though, he pauses. "You sure about this?"

"Yes."

We begin to move, and I belatedly realize that I'm still grasping the ring. I stick my hand through the narrow space at the top of the window and let it fall to the ground.

"Nina!" Daniel shouts again, but his voice is already fading. I look in the mirror and find him standing there with one hand on his hip, the other clutching his phone, as if he's about to call my mother and tattle on me. "I'm not taking you back if you don't get out of that truck right fucking now!"

I roll the window up, and his voice disappears. Theo pulls out onto the road, and I let out a breath that's louder than the blasting air conditioner. Feeling numb, I stare out the windshield at the asphalt rolling beneath us. "I just ruined my life."

"Nah," Theo says. "You just got it back."

Chapter Fifteen

Then

I had snuck around with boys before, but whatever thrill I got from that was nothing compared to sneaking around with Theo.

It was jarring, the change from thinking of Theo as unattainable to craving his next kiss. My mind wandered to him constantly—especially at the store, where I often felt his eyes on me. I never had to wait too long: whenever he had the chance, he was tugging me out the back door, into the alcove by the office, even down behind the counter with a customer standing ten feet away.

The first time I turned the tables by shoving him into the single-stall employee bathroom, he leaned back against the sink and beamed at me. "I like you like this, Sass," he said as I plastered myself against him.

"Me too," I murmured, tugging his face down to mine. It wasn't just the new side of my relationship with Theo that had me feeling so giddy; it was that the rebellious urge that had always been inside of me, trying to claw its way out, was now unleashed.

I was the one who was intent on keeping things under wraps. Theo's parents were the opposite of mine: they trusted him, had no interest in micromanaging his life.

"They wouldn't care," he'd told me. "And if they did, they'd just be excited."

The problem was my mother, who absolutely *would* have an issue with us being together. The conversation where she told me to impress *the right kind of boys* stuck permanently in the back of my mind. Mom would have been thrilled if I were dating someone like Vince Redding. In fact, if she had been at the party that night, she probably would have chastised me for turning him down and running off with Theo instead. The fact that Vince was a jerk wouldn't have mattered: his family had money, connections, and power that our family didn't.

It had been about a week of kissing in secret when I showed up to work earlier than I ever had. I was notorious for rushing through the door minutes before—or after—my shift began, breathless with an excuse about my old beater of a car not wanting to cooperate. That day, I arrived a full thirty minutes early. Theo was opening with me, and we were supposed to be alone until noon.

I practically skipped into the store from the back, then came to an abrupt halt. Theo *was* there, standing behind the cash register with his palms flat on the counter. Across from him, as if they were customers checking out, were both of our dads. Cecil was wringing his worn baseball cap in his hands. My dad had his arms crossed, tension tight in his shoulders.

The chime of the front door stopped the group in mid-conversation, and in uncanny unison, they all turned to look at me. Theo ducked his head, wincing; my dad sighed, and Cecil turned his eyes to the ceiling.

"You're early," Dad said. "Come here."

I glanced at Theo. He didn't say a word, but I could see it in his apologetic eyes: they knew something.

I slipped behind the counter, pausing to shove my bag in one of the cabinets. Then I stepped up to Theo's side to face our dads. Too late, I realized that this probably wasn't the best move. Too late—I was already there, because standing beside Theo was second nature to me.

I swallowed my nerves, fought to seem casual. "What's going on?"

Dad and Cecil exchanged a look, and then my dad spoke. "The Reddings," he said. "They own this whole stretch of storefronts, Nina Lynn, you know that?"

My heart plummeted to my feet. I did know that, but I hadn't thought about it in a long time. Not even when I was pissing off their son and getting him punched in the face. "Yes, sir."

"They've raised our rent," he said bluntly. "By a lot. And I was talking to Julie next door at the salon, and she said she hasn't heard anything about a rent increase. Then I went to the hardware store to ask Keith, and his rent isn't getting raised, either, but he heard there was some incident between you two and Vince Redding at a party last week."

"We're just asking for the truth," said Cecil. "We're going to fight them on targeting us for a rent increase, but—"

"We *might* fight them on it," Dad interrupted, "but we might not have the means to. This store is hanging on by a thread, and you two might have just cut it completely."

My mouth was so dry, I didn't think I could have spoken even if I had words. Theo cleared his throat. "I got into a thing with Vince," he said, shifting his body so he was standing just slightly in front of me. "This is my fault, not Nina's."

"What happened?" Cecil asked Theo, seeming more concerned than upset.

I glanced at Theo, which I immediately regretted when I caught him doing the same thing. We made eye contact and promptly looked away, but it was too late: my dad drew in a deep breath, and I knew we were toast.

"Over Nina?" Dad demanded. "You risked our livelihood over a *girl*, Theo?"

Cecil opened his mouth, but Theo cut him off. "I defended *your daughter* from a guy who was physically preventing her from getting away from him," he said. He stood tall, shoulders squared, and it wasn't until that moment that I truly realized Theo was no longer the boy I'd grown up with: he was a *man*, a capable, confident one whose hands I wanted on me that very instant. "I understand this has caused a problem, and I'll work for free if that's what it takes to help us make rent. But I won't apologize for punching that jackass."

Cecil looked like he was fighting a smile, and even my dad's eyes softened around the edges.

"Are you okay?" Dad asked me.

Nice of you to finally ask, I thought, but saying that to my dad would have invited a whole new host of problems. "I'm fine."

"He touched you?"

"No, he was just standing in front of me."

Dad nodded, his jaw working. "Stay away from him," he told us. "Stay away from that farm and from Vince, alright?"

"Yes, sir," I said at the same time Theo said, "We will."

He studied us, and we stared back at him. I kept my face carefully blank, silently urging him to believe that we had nothing left to share.

It was Cecil—always the gentler one, the good cop to my dad's bad cop—who stepped away first, giving my dad a light smack on the shoulder. "Let's bring out that stock so the kids can run it."

Dad nodded and walked off with him. I heard the murmur of their voices, low and serious, but couldn't make out their words.

They disappeared down an aisle, and I looked at Theo. "Oh my god," I hissed.

"I know."

"I completely forgot they owned the store."

"I thought about it," he admitted. "Afterward. I hoped it wouldn't cause a problem."

Guilt clawed at me. I sank into the chair behind the counter, the same one that had hosted my many time-outs as a kid, and pulled my knees to my chest. "You didn't say anything."

He leaned back against the counter, crossing his feet at the ankles. "There was no reason for both of us to worry about it."

Picking at a loose thread on my jeans, I glanced around us. It was the backdrop of my life, even more of a home to me than our house. The Hoyts were here. *Theo* was here. The idea of the store being gone was incomprehensible to me. "What if we have to close because of this?" I asked quietly. "What have we done?"

"You didn't do anything wrong. Vince was harassing you."

"You should have let it go."

"No," Theo said. His tone wasn't sharp, exactly, but it left no room for argument. "I couldn't listen to him talk to you like that and let it go. Hell, maybe next time Kelly comes after you, I'll tell her to shove it, too."

I couldn't help my laughter, even as I told him, "Don't. That won't help anything."

He reached over to chuck my chin. "I know it won't."

I leaned my head back against the wall and looked up at him. "You can't work here for free."

Theo shrugged with nonchalance that I saw through immediately. "Sure I can," he said. "I live with my parents. I'll be fine."

"Don't you want to save up and move out?"

He hesitated for a second before he replied. "Yeah. Eventually."

"Maybe in the fall, you could go to UNC after all," I said. "You can take out loans."

He shoved his hands in the back pockets of his jeans and looked away, staring out the glass doors to the parking lot. "Nah."

We sat in silence for a few moments. I heard Dad and Cecil come out of the back room, probably setting out the stock they wanted us to take care of. I caught a few words of their conversation and relaxed a little when I realized they were talking about football, not our massive screwup with Vince. Their footsteps and voices faded, leaving us in quiet once again.

There was some sort of tension between Theo and I that had appeared when I brought up college, and I didn't like that. I scratched at the skin beneath my birthmark. "Remember the other day, when we both said we'd never lied to each other?" I asked, and waited for Theo to nod in the affirmative. "I feel like you're lying to me about this."

"I'm not lying," he said. "I'm choosing to keep some things to myself. Like I did when you were into Lyle—"

"Kyle," I interrupted, knowing full well that Theo messed up his name on purpose.

"—and instead of telling you that I really wished you'd forget him and be with me instead, I kept that to myself because it seemed like the right thing to do."

"Is it because of the money?" I asked. "I know student loans suck, but there probably isn't going to be a business for us to take over, Theo. I really think you should—"

"Nina." Theo let out a heavy sigh. "Stop."

I did.

He glanced behind him, making sure we were truly alone. There weren't cameras in the store, since it was a small town and we knew most of our customers. When he saw that the coast was clear, he closed the gap between us. His hands came up to cradle my face, and all I could do was stare at him, transfixed by the way he was looking at me.

"I have a reason for staying here," he said quietly. "It's not anything bad. The acceptance is still good; I just deferred for a year. I'll tell you why, but I'm not ready right now. Okay?"

And even though that did nothing to assuage my curiosity, he looked so intent and sincere that I nodded, my head bobbing up and down in his grasp. If there was anyone in this world I trusted, it was Theo. "Okay."

He kissed my mouth, and I melted into him, reaching up to hold onto one of his wrists.

Then the bell above the front door jingled.

Theo practically leapt backwards, trying to put distance between us. Dread settled in my belly as I glanced over, because I knew it wasn't time to open yet, and I knew there were only three people in the world who could be walking through that door right now: Randi, Brock, and my mom.

I looked over, bracing myself, and let out a breath when I realized that it wasn't my mom. The relief wasn't as big as it could have been, though, because standing inside the door was Brock—and from the look on his face, he'd seen everything.

"Huh," he said, as if he'd just learned a mildly interesting fact about bumblebees. "Who knew."

Chapter Sixteen

Now

When we turn the corner at the end of Theo's long, private drive, I can't help but be surprised at what I see. The two-story farmhouse isn't a mansion, but it's certainly not the humble cabin I envisioned. From what I can tell in the dark, it looks recently constructed, with a wraparound porch, an attached three-car garage, and chimneys on either side of the gabled roof.

We park in the garage, which is also occupied by shelving, some boxes, and a riding mower. I have long given up on wearing my heels; I climb out of his truck barefoot, letting the shoes dangle from my fingertips, and watch as he hoists my bags from the back. I quietly follow him through the interior garage door.

"I'll show you the guest room first," he says, leading me through a spacious kitchen and a cozy living room. I want to stop, to sink in these new surroundings and square them with the new image of Theo I've been piecing together in my mind, but he keeps moving, turning up a flight of carpeted stairs and making me follow.

"Did you build this house?"

"From the ground up," Theo says proudly.

We emerge onto the landing. The hallway stretches in both directions, but Theo takes a right and steps into the first open door. "Flip the light on, will you?"

I feel along the wall for the light switch and do as he asks. The walls are plain and beige, the twin bed covered in a solid navy-blue duvet. The oak nightstand is empty aside from a small orb-shaped lamp. There's no evidence, really, that the room has ever been used.

Theo puts my two suitcases down at the foot of the bed. As if reading my mind, he says, "I think you're going to be the first person to sleep in here who isn't drunk off their ass."

"Oh."

"Don't worry. I changed the sheets." He gestures to the closet in the corner. "There's a few hangers in there if you want to put stuff up. There's a bathroom down the hall and I don't really use it, so feel free to take over in there."

"I won't be here long." I let my shoes and purse drop to the carpeted floor. "Just until I figure something else out."

"Well, as long as you need," says Theo.

I cross to the closet and peer inside, acting as if I haven't noticed the pity in his eyes. In those surreal, adrenaline-fueled moments after I tossed Daniel's ring out the window, I didn't ask if I could stay with Theo. He didn't offer. But it was tacitly understood that I would be coming home with him, and so I directed him to my mom's house, and we set off to grab my belongings.

I was haphazardly tossing things in my suitcase when Mom called for the first time. When I didn't answer, she called a second time, and a third, and then left a voicemail. I didn't bother listening to the audio of her scathing disapproval—I just turned my phone off and went back to Theo's truck, which he drove to his house without any further discussion.

Now that the adrenaline of dumping Daniel has worn off, I'm left staring at the stark truth I don't want to face: I haven't had a penny of my own money in years. Every credit card I have access to belongs to Daniel or Mom. My name isn't on the lease for the apartment we've been living in together. Being with Daniel these past few years made it so that I've always had a safety net. Now that it's gone, I'm freefalling.

"I have a friend in New York." My mind starts racing, trying to think of where I can possibly go from here. "I haven't talked to her in a year or so—her fiancé was friends with Daniel, but she caught him cheating and they broke up. If I called her—"

"Sass."

There are a few empty hangers in the closet, like Theo said. I grab them in one hand and toss them on the bed. "Last I heard, she was living in the East Village. I think she'd let me sleep on her couch. Or, well, I could use the money I have in my checking account to find a short-term rental and—"

"Sass."

I step around him, reaching for one of my suitcases. "Brock and Dad live in Arkansas now. I don't talk to them much, but maybe—"

"*Nina.*"

His tone is firm, bordering on sharp. I draw back, empty-handed, and snap, "What?"

"As long," he repeats, stressing each word, "as you need."

I try to keep the tension in my body—an act of stubborn, willful resistance—but his hazel gaze disarms me. Understanding passes through the air between us, and all I can say is, "Thank you."

Theo nods, and I hoist a suitcase onto the bed. I fling it open and begin pulling out the clothes that I hurriedly tossed inside an hour ago. Even as I busy myself with laying the clothes flat on the bed, I'm still very aware of Theo's presence next to me.

When all the clothes have been laid out and I'm ready to transfer them onto hangers, Theo is *still* staring at me. I slowly turn to face him. "Yes?"

"Did Daniel ever hurt you?"

I blink. "What do you mean?"

"He left a bruise on your arm," Theo says, and I look down to see that there is, in fact, a small dark spot blooming on my skin. "And he said some pretty messed-up shit."

I pick up a green silk top and mindlessly run my hand over the wrinkles. It'll need to be ironed, but I won't worry about that now. "He's never grabbed me before," I tell Theo, being honest. "And I've never seen him fly off the handle like that, either."

Theo nods, but his expression is still troubled. "He's not coming near my house. If you decide you want to work things out—"

"I don't," I interrupt. It's as much for my benefit as his, because even though I know I've done the right thing, there will always be that part of me that yearns for stability, security, and—unfortunately—my mother's approval. "I'm not going to be with someone who hurts me."

"Good. You shouldn't."

There's an undercurrent of skepticism in his words, though. I resent the fact that we're still so in tune with each other—that we both know there's something the other isn't saying. It would be so much simpler if we could both take this conversation at face value, say goodnight, and move on.

I toss aside the shirt I'm holding and turn on him, crossing my arms over my chest. "Just say it."

"What?" Theo feigns confusion.

"You tell me. I'm a doormat? A sellout? I know it's something like that."

"No," he says, the word a slow drawl. "No. I'm worried about you."

"I'm *fine*."

With a frustrated sigh, he threads his fingers together and rests them on top of his head. "All of this just doesn't seem like you, okay? I know it's been ten years—"

"Yes, it has been," I snap. "We've been apart for a long time. This might be a surprise to you, but I haven't been making my life choices based on whether eighteen-year-old Theo would've approved."

"No," Theo says sharply, "I think you've been making them based on whether *Kelly* would approve."

I bite my tongue to keep the *fuck off* inside, since I'm standing in his guest room with nowhere else to go. But my voice still drips with venom when I say, "I'm tired. I'd like to go to bed now."

"Okay." Theo seems to sense that he's pushed me to my limit and that now would be a good time to back off. "I'll leave you to it."

I turn back to the bed and resume shoving my clothes on hangers as quickly as possible. Theo's footsteps retreat, and the door closes gently behind him, leaving me alone.

Later, when I'm laying in bed watching the ceiling fan rotate above me, my phone buzzes with a text from Theo.

I'm glad you're here, it says.

I give it a few minutes before typing out a reply. *You know Queen Kelly would NOT approve.*

She sure wouldn't, he replies. *That's how you know you're in the right place.*

***

Theo's guest bed is exhilaratingly soft—or maybe I'm just excessively tired. Either way, I sleep like a rock through the night, and when the first beams of sunlight wake me, I stumble to the window and yank the curtains closed. Then I collapse back onto the mattress, letting it swallow me up, and remain dead to the world for another few hours.

When I wake up again, the LED clock on the nightstand reads 11:37. I groan into the pillow but force myself out of bed and down the hall to the bathroom. As I wrangle my hair into a bun and apply a light layer of makeup, I listen for any clue as to what Theo might be up to. The house is quiet, though, and when I go downstairs, I find that all the lights are off and he is nowhere to be seen.

In the kitchen, I get a glass of water and then slide onto a stool at the center island. I sit there for a minute, sipping my water and staring out the kitchen window at Theo's backyard—rolling emerald, no fence, perfectly maintained—before heaving a sigh and powering on my phone.

The notifications come in one after the other, my phone vibrating several times in quick succession. When it's done, I take stock of the damage: Six texts. Five missed calls. Two voicemails. All from my mother—apparently, Daniel meant it when he said he was done with me.

I scroll through her texts.

What is going on?

Answer your phone.

Don't throw your life away like this.

Did you get cold feet? Theo Hoyt is not worth sacrificing your future. Call me and let's talk about it.

I snort at her feeble attempt to sound understanding.

Are you planning to just leave my car out there in the middle of nowhere?

Nina Lynn Sullivan, call me back RIGHT NOW.

I roll my eyes and pull up the voicemails. The first one, which she left while I was back at her house packing, is a firm scolding: "I just spoke to Daniel and he told me what happened. I have no idea what you think you're doing here, but he's very upset with you, and at the very least, you owe him an apology. Really, you ought to be doing whatever it takes to fix things with him. This is childish behavior. It's time to start acting like an adult."

The second voicemail is from fifteen minutes after the final text, and it's short: "I'm done with this. You're on your own, Nina Lynn."

"Crazy bitch," I mutter as I delete the messages.

There is no communication from Daniel, and since I have no desire to change that, I set my phone to the side and study Theo's kitchen. It's neat and orderly: the counters clear of crumbs, the fridge bearing two plain silver magnets that hold nothing. There's a small, older TV tucked into the corner next to a high-end mixer; it's the only thing that doesn't blend with the sleek, modern theme.

I wander into the living room, which is clean but not quite as meticulous as the kitchen. There's a dark sectional facing the big-screen TV, a couple of throw blankets tossed haphazardly on the back, and a fireplace on the right side of the room. On the coffee table are several remotes and a tin of dominos, which triggers the memory of sitting in the backroom with Theo as he taught me how to play.

There's a bookshelf beside the fireplace. It mostly has books on it—and there's the Amelia Earhart biography he mentioned—but one shelf is full of picture frames.

They're packed in densely, three or four deep, and I have to step closer to study them.

Most of the pictures are of Theo, Cecil, and Randi; some have other relatives in the mix. A picture of Theo in a suit catches my eye, and it takes a minute for me to realize who's standing beside him: Quinton, his best friend from high school. It's definitely recent; neither of them look like the teenagers I remember. They're beaming at the camera, each holding a glass of scotch, and, upon closer inspection, I see a silver band on Quinton's ring finger.

"Wow," I say out loud, and I wonder who he married.

I nudge that picture to the side in order to see the one behind it, and as soon as I do, my breath catches in my throat. It's a picture of Theo and I when we were kids—eleven and twelve, maybe. Theo stands on a stool in an aisle of the store. I sit on the floor in front of him. Theo's foot is lifted in the air, as if he's about to step on my head, while I smile cluelessly at the camera.

Beside it is another picture of us. We're younger in this one—maybe early elementary school. We sit on a bench at the park, each holding a blue slushie. We're beaming with our mouths wipe open, dye coloring our lips and teeth.

I swallow, unsure what to make of the fact that Theo has framed pictures of us on display in his living room, and it's only then that I take notice of my birthmark. It's visible and obvious in both photos, but it's not engulfing my features like I always imagined—like my mother always told me it did. The birthmark is one part of my face, and not even the part I noticed first.

"Snooping?"

The voice comes out of nowhere, making me jump out of my skin. I whirl around to see Theo standing in the doorway.

"You scared the shit out of me," I accuse, trying to catch my bearings.

"Noticed that."

He's not wearing his work polo today; instead, he's dressed in a fitted white t-shirt and athletic shorts, his baseball cap currently facing the front.

He looks *really* good.

"Have you been at work?" I ask.

"Yeah. I usually go in for a few hours on Saturday morning. I got your mom's car towed while I was there."

I make a startled sound, a cross between a laugh and a gasp. "What?"

Theo shrugs. "Told the guy my cameras out front aren't working and I don't know who it belonged to, but it had been there for days." He doesn't give me a chance to respond before turning to leave the room. "Come in here."

After another glance at the photos, I follow him out into the kitchen, where the island is now covered with plastic grocery bags.

"I stopped by the store on my way home," Theo says. "If there's anything else you need, we can go back later."

Skeptically, I eye the pile of bags on the counter. "It looks like you already bought one of everything they had."

He shrugs. "Pretty close."

"I won't be here long," I feel compelled to remind him.

"Yeah, I know," he says dismissively. "This is my normal weekly grocery order, Sass. Don't get a big head."

There's no way one person could eat all this food in one week, but I let him deflect. We begin unloading the bags, and it isn't long before I realize that in front of us is a parade of every food I liked when he last knew me. Cheese crackers. Mini powdered donuts. Portabella mushrooms and fresh green beans. Butterfly shrimp. Strawberries. Peanut butter granola. And...

"Red Vines!"

Theo looks amused at my excitement. "I figured those were a safe bet, even if you don't like this other stuff anymore."

"I haven't had them in forever." I reach for the package and look up at him. "Can I have one?"

"Of course you can," he says. "I bought them for you."

"Right." I tear open the package and pull out a piece. I bite into it, and as soon as I get a hit of the cherry flavor, I want more. I scarf it down—unladylike, for sure—and barely let myself breath before shoving a second piece right behind it.

Theo looks at me like he wants to say something else, then shakes his head, seeming to decide against it. "What about this other stuff?" he asks. "Is this enough for you to eat for a while?"

I almost laugh. "My diet for the past few years has been mostly salad. This is plenty."

His eyes drift over my figure, and I try not to give any indication that I've noticed. "Salad?"

"The official meal of rich guys' wives and girlfriends everywhere."

"You look like you've barely gained weight since high school."

"It's not about what you look like," I say sagely, and eat another Red Vine. "You have to give the appearance of being on a diet at all times."

Theo opens the fridge and begins shoving food inside. "That's the stupidest shit I've ever heard."

It had never seemed stupid to me when I was trying to blend in at Daniel's work dinners, but here, in Theo's kitchen, shoveling licorice into my mouth, I have a hard time disagreeing.

We finish putting the groceries away, falling into an easy rhythm that reminds me of days at the store and which honestly should not be so natural after all this time.

Then Theo leaves again—to mow his parents' lawn, he says—and I wave my half-empty bag of Red Vines at him. "Thanks again."

He smiles at me—not a smirk, but a genuine, soft smile. "Not a problem."

Chapter Seventeen

Now

For the rest of the weekend, I putter around Theo's house while he works outside. I might have suspected him of avoiding me, except that it's obvious he keeps up with his several acres of land. I keep waiting for my phone to buzz with a call or text, but it's absolutely silent. Evidently, my mother and Daniel were serious when they said that they were done with me, and I don't hear from anyone else, either: not his family, none of my bridesmaids. Nobody.

On Monday, while Theo is at work, I call the country club from beneath the covers of his guest bed. Matilda answers the phone, and when I tell her that I need to cancel our booking, she responds—rather coldly—that my mother has already called to take care of it. Then I call the boutique, the florist, the baker, and it's the same story: everything has been canceled and refunded.

My wedding is officially off.

And, it would appear, nobody cares.

It's not like I have any moral high ground. When Leona, Daniel's cheating friend's fiancé, ended their engagement, she was immediately cut from our social circle. Others in the group had looked the other way when the same thing happened to them, but Leona made a different choice: she moved out of the big apartment, got a job, and started over. I wasn't any better than the others; I didn't keep in touch with her. I joined in the gossip behind her back.

And yet I told Theo that maybe I could sleep on her couch. How presumptuous.

I'm such a bitch.

A little after five, I see Theo's truck pull into the garage from where I'm sitting on his covered back porch. The polite thing it do would be to go inside; instead, I stay put and wait for him to find me.

When the door from the house snicks open, Theo steps out, two bottles of beer dangling from his fingers. "Found my hiding place?"

I glance around. The porch is like a whole other room, with wicker furniture and a hammock. There's an enormous, expensive-looking grill in one corner. Thin mosquito netting keeps the bugs out, and a screen door allows entry to the backyard. "What kind of hiding place has see-through walls?"

"The kind that's in the middle of nowhere."

I stay lazily slouched on his sofa, my feet propped up on the small table in front of me. Theo steps over my legs and sinks into the chair on my other side. He sets the beers down on the table, produces a bottle opener from his pocket, and flips the caps off both. He picks one up and slides the other toward me.

I stare at the label on the beer. It's the same cheap brand we used to drink in high school, and I don't think I've had it since then. "You still drink that?"

Theo shrugs, takes a long gulp. When he swallows, his throat bobs over the collar of his polo, and I suppose I'm out of fucks to give, because I openly stare. "Sometimes," he tells me. "What do you drink now? Three-hundred-dollar bottles of wine?"

The last bottle of wine I can remember Daniel ordering for us at a restaurant was north of four fifty, but I decide not to disclose that information. "I think my days of three-hundred-dollar anything are over."

"Back to your white trash roots, I guess."

It's a joke with a trace of bitterness. Belatedly, I realize that Daniel's insult was directed toward both of us, not just me.

I pick up the drink that Theo set in front of me and take a tentative sip. The beer is cold and crisp, and I find myself tilting my head for a longer pull.

"*Very* white trash of you," Theo remarks.

I rest the bottle on my thigh. "Quit saying that."

"Just trying to fit in."

"He's an ass," I snap. "He doesn't know what he's talking about."

Theo props his socked feet up on the wicker table between us. "How did you even wind up with this guy?"

I pick at the damp label with my manicured nails. They're starting to chip, but I won't be able to get them redone anytime soon. "I met him in Hilton Head a few years ago. He was there for a bachelor party, and I was on vacation with Mom and Travis."

"And Kelly played matchmaker?" Theo guesses.

"No. He approached me."

It was the same year I'd had my rhinoplasty and excision. Even though everyone around me kept saying how great I looked, I was unsure. I'd thought that the surgeries would make me more comfortable in my own skin, but every time I looked in the mirror, all I saw was a stranger.

Then Daniel was there, in a button-up shirt and pressed chinos, sidling up to me at the beachside bar and asking to buy me a drink. He didn't ask much about me, and I didn't offer; I was happy to sip my mojito while he told me about growing up in the suburbs of New York, moving into the city for college, and working in finance. Then he asked me back to his hotel room, and from there, I was swept into his world.

"What did you like about him?" Theo asks.

My answer needs no deliberation. "That he didn't ask questions."

"That sounds like another way of saying that he didn't care to get to know you."

I shift on the couch, tucking my feet beneath me. "I dated people before him." *And after you,* is the unspoken end of that sentence. "Even if we were just messing around, eventually they'd feel comfortable enough to ask about my birthmark. Then it would turn into asking about my family, which was a completely shit situation by then, and it was only a matter of time before I'd have to start—"

I stop myself. Theo is watching me closely, and I exhale hard, averting my gaze to look out at the mature pine trees that line the northern edge of his property. They've been here for generations, just like Theo's family. Just like mine.

"Daniel took me as I was," I elaborate. "I never had to tell him about things that I wanted to keep to myself."

"He seemed real understanding about it when he was yelling at us the other day," he drawls sarcastically, and then taps his cheekbone. "What about that?"

Reflexively, I lift a hand to trace my scar. "What about it?"

"Did he ever ask where it came from?"

"Eventually."

"And did you tell him the truth?"

"Nope."

"So you were prepared to marry a guy who didn't know the most basic things about you," Theo says, equal parts puzzled and scornful. "You were going to go the rest of your life without showing your husband a picture of you as a kid or bringing him back to your hometown? Or talking about any of the shit you went through as a teenager?"

I find myself grinding my back teeth together. "He never asked."

"That's my point, Sass. Why—"

"It's *my* point, too," I snap at him. "So we weren't madly in love or whatever, but not everyone is like your parents. Daniel made it so that I didn't have to worry about much of anything, and I never had to talk about you. To me, that was plenty."

Predictably, Theo's expression softens. I don't want his pity, and I don't want to delve any further into the fact that getting over him was the hardest fucking thing I've ever had to do, so I barrel onward. "And anyway, I think you gave up the right to have an opinion on any of this when you dumped me on the side of the road."

Just as I intended, his annoyance returns. "For god's sake, Nina."

"Oh," I say innocently, hiking my eyebrows up my forehead. "I'm sorry, is that not what happened?"

With a frustrated groan, he takes off his hat and grips it between his hands, curling the brim. Tension and humidity thicken the air. "Things weren't all that great for me, either."

I know what he means—Randi alluded to it the other day—but I'm not ready to be kind. "You were fine. You went to college, you started your own business, you live in this enormous house—"

"Nina."

"What?"

"Stop running your mouth for two seconds."

"*Excuse* me?"

"This stuff I've done that you're going on about—everything I did after you left—think about it a little bit harder."

I turn my palm upward. "What? What about it?"

He leans toward me, and I find myself distracted by the slight protrusion of his tongue when he enunciates, "*Think.*"

We stare at each other, him expectant, me just fucking confused. Eventually he looks away, letting out a short, humorless chuckle. I watch as he shoves his hat back onto his head. He gets to his feet, empty beer bottle in hand, and nods at mine. "You done with that?"

"Yeah."

He picks it up, strides past me, and walks into the house.

"Where are you going?" I call after him.

The screen door opens, and Theo pokes his head back out. "Leaving you to think," he says, and then he's gone again.

Chapter Eighteen

Then

"Peyton says that Lori Ann and Mitch are making out."

I gasped, shuffling across the back seat of the truck so I could see Sage's phone. "Really?"

She tilted it toward me. I could barely read Peyton's message as Sage's thumbs flew, typing out a reply that was full of capital letters and exclamation points. "What about Amy?"

"I think that was a one-night thing."

Quinton was in the passenger's seat, and he turned around to look at us. He wore his hair in something resembling a mullet—it was chopped close at his ears with the ends brushing his collar in the back. "Isn't Mitch the abstinence kid?"

"Yeah, but I don't think he practices what he preaches," I said, pulling a Red Vine from the bag in my lap.

"What his father preaches," Theo corrected from the driver's seat.

"Right."

"You're lucky I love you," Sage told me. "I can't believe I'm missing this."

"It must be real hard for you," I said, "having to spend your evening drinking on the water."

The beer was in the bed of the truck, along with a cheap inflatable boat that Theo brought along. We were going down to the pond, which was nothing special but was at least big enough for the boat and deep enough to swim in. It was only a couple of miles from my neighborhood—as kids, we ended up there often when we were outside playing—but still relatively isolated, set far back from the road and nestled among the trees.

As was generally the case on weekend nights, most people we knew were at the Redding farm. Theo and I couldn't go, so we decided to hang out at the pond and convinced our best friends to come with us. Quinton didn't really mind, actually, but Sage hated being away from the action that would fuel the gossip mill for the week.

We reached the pond, rolling through the brown, trampled grass where others had driven before. Just as we expected, we were the only ones there.

Sage and I spread out our picnic blanket on the bank of the pond while the boys grabbed the cooler. The beer was in the very bottom, beneath some gas station deli sandwiches and a thick layer of ice. Since the police department turned a blind eye to the massive amounts of underage drinking going on at the Reddings', they compensated by patrolling the streets closely on weekend nights. We hadn't seen any cops on the way here, but if they showed up, our plan was to throw our bottles into the pond.

We each grabbed a sandwich and a drink and spread out on the blanket. I situated myself at a healthy distance from Theo, only to have him scoot over and wrap his hand around my hip. I winced reflexively, not used to being like this in front of other people. Ever since Brock walked in on us a few days ago, I'd been especially on edge.

Sage and Quinton could be trusted, though, so I mentally ordered myself to relax and leaned into him. He leaned toward me, and I lifted my head in anticipation of a kiss. Instead, he swerved his head to the side and took an enormous bite of my sandwich.

"Hey!" I shoved him away. "You have your own!"

Theo grinned at me with a full mouth. It was disgusting—there was a mayonnaise-soaked piece of lettuce stuck to his front teeth—but because it was Theo, it managed to be endearing as well.

"Gross," said Sage. "Your sandwich has boy cooties."

"I hope you don't act like that at the store," Quinton added. "If you do, your cover's gonna be blown pretty quickly."

Theo unwrapped his sandwich and held it out to me. "Here. Let's make it even."

I took a bite—not like the one he took, since I wasn't an animal, but enough to make my point.

He gave me an affectionate smile that gave me tingles before turning back to our friends. "We've barely glanced at each other in the store since Brock caught us."

"To the point where *that* might be getting suspicious," I said. "It's not like that's how we acted before."

"Yeah," agreed Theo. "You're right. They might think we're mad at each other."

Sage squinted against the sun, sitting low in the sky. "Have you two ever been mad at each other?"

"I was pretty mad at you," Theo told me, "when you stepped on my phone and broke it in middle school."

"That was your fault for leaving it in the floor!"

"Definitely your fault," Sage concurred.

"I was mad," I said, determined not to be outdone, "a couple years ago when Henry Green came into the store looking for me, and you told him I'd been in the bathroom for fifteen minutes. He had been flirting with me for weeks, but we never spoke again after that."

Theo threw his hands up. "It was the truth!"

"I was in there *fixing my hair*, which you knew and conveniently didn't tell him."

He shrugged. Quinton was snickering under his breath. I glared at him, and he stifled it with a pull of his beer.

Sage set aside her half-eaten sandwich and stretched out on the blanket, lying on her side with her head propped in her hand. Her toes poked at my thigh. "Sounds like another Lori Ann situation," she said in a sing-song tone.

I glared at her and then looked at Theo, unsure if he would care that I told her about his jealousy. There wasn't a trace of irritation on his face; rather, he was nodding. "It was," he said. "I wanted her all to myself."

There was a question on the tip of my tongue: *how long?* Because the Henry incident was during the fall of my sophomore year, and Theo had definitely had girlfriends since then.

When he looked back at me, though, his expression gave me pause. It wasn't one I was used to seeing from him, as laidback and upbeat as he was. Theo looked vulnerable, as if there was a spotlight shining on his most personal thoughts. My words died in my throat.

"Do you have the bottle opener?" Quinton asked Theo, effectively changing the subject.

He tossed it over, and the conversation turned back to Mitch and Lori Ann, to what a dick Vince was, to our plans for the rest of the summer. Quinton would be leaving for college in August, and he spoke about it as if he was going to the West Coast. In reality, he would be attending a relatively cheap state university that was about ninety minutes from Amity. About half of the kids we knew who went there were back by Christmas, and my suspicion was that Quinton would be one of them.

Still, Theo played right into the conversation. He groaned about Quinton leaving him behind, hyped up all of Quinton's plans for his supposed last summer in town, and then dramatically threw his arm around me. "At least Sass isn't going anywhere," he said. I leaned into his side, a silent reminder that he was right: there was nowhere I'd rather be than right by his side.

Talking about Quinton going to college did reignite my curiosity about Theo deciding not to. His grades were much better, after all, and he had been accepted into a much more selective school. We finished eating and stripped down to our swimsuits, but when we headed to the dock, I hovered a few steps behind Sage and Quinton.

Theo seemed to know that I was trying to talk to him alone, so when the others went sprinting down the dock, he stayed at my side. "What's up?"

I watched Sage and Quinton jump into the water, their shouts filling the air. They weren't paying any attention to us. "I was just wondering if you were ready." When he looked confused, I clarified. "To tell me why you aren't going to college."

"Why I deferred for a year," he corrected.

"Right."

Theo smiled gently at me, and I knew his answer before he said it. "I can't tell you yet," he said. "But I will. I promise."

I put my little finger in his face. "Pinky swear."

He wrapped his around mine and held on tight. I smiled at him, showing that we were okay. Although I burned with curiosity—with a need to know if this mysterious reason had anything to do with me—I trusted Theo, and whatever his reason for not sharing this with me, I knew that it had to be a good one.

Theo's expression became mischievous. Keeping our pinkies twisted together, he slipped the fingers of his free hand just under my bikini strap. His touch on my bare shoulder made my stomach swoop. "This is cute," he murmured.

My mouth twisted. "Cute?"

His eyes lifted to mine. "You don't like me calling you cute?"

I shrugged. He had never made a habit of commenting on my appearance, positive or otherwise, which was part of why I accused him of lying when he said I was beautiful out at Train Bridge. But after that, along with a week of feeling his hands trace my face, of watching his eyes spark with heat when he looked at me, *cute* felt like a downgrade. Like he just looked at me and saw the little girl he'd grown up with, rather than someone to be desired.

"It's a little...kiddish?" I said uncertainly.

Theo dropped both of his hands. Even out there in the warm June sun, I felt inexplicably cold without his touch. Then it was back, on my hips this time, and so was that fire. His eyes followed his hands as they traced a line along the waistband of my pink bikini bottoms, up my stomach, to the band of my top. One of his thumbs brushed the underside of my breast—accidentally, I thought, although I couldn't be sure—and I fought to control my breathing.

"You're not a kid," Theo said huskily.

"I know."

"Do you like hot better?" he asked. His hands settled on my lower back, dangerously close to my butt. I didn't mind it one bit. "Gorgeous? Sexy? They all fit, Sass. Just tell me which one you want to be."

What I wanted was to say something that made his world shift the same way mine just had, but I couldn't. I had no words of my own; just his, echoing through the humid air.

"Hey!" Sage yelled. Her voice startled me, and I instinctively jerked away from Theo. She was splashing near the edge of the pond, her dark hair plastered to her head. "Either get a room or get in here!"

Theo hoisted himself onto the dock, then reached back for my hand. I let him pull me up to stand beside him. He jogged in place for a few seconds. "Alright," he said, rolling his shoulders back. "You ready?"

"Ready," I said, and then we were off, sprinting down the dock and throwing ourselves off the end of it. My hand stayed twisted around Theo's as we went airborne, and in that split second that we were suspended above the water, I had time for a single coherent thought: *I never want to come down.*

Chapter Nineteen

Now

"Ow, ow, ow, ow," I hiss, leaning over the sink and plunging my wrist under a stream of cold water. "Shit!"

As the water flows over the angry red skin and the pain begins to ebb, I glance around the kitchen. The counters are strewn with dirty dishes. The sheet pan chicken and vegetables that look like they've been through the pits of hell are smoking on the stovetop.

Luckily, it's too early for Theo to get home from work. I still have at least an hour before--

The garage door rumbles open.

"Shit!" I say again. I look around wildly, as if there's any chance of me cleaning up this mess before Theo gets inside. I end up staying right where I am, and when Theo comes in from the garage, it's to a wrecked kitchen and a guilty grimace.

"Sass?" He kicks his boots off by the door. "What's burning?"

I point at him in blind panic. "You're home early!"

"I'm sorry for not clearing that with you ahead of time," he deadpans. He heads for the stove, but changes course when he notices what I'm doing. "Did you hurt yourself?"

I turn my arm over and study the scorch mark on my wrist. "I'm fine."

Theo steps up close behind me. I inhale sharply, surprised by his proximity, but he's oblivious as he peers over my shoulder. His long fingers curl around mine, and he turns my wrist so he can better see the burn. "Ouch."

"It's fine," I insist, even though it really does hurt.

He strokes his thumb along the skin, and the sensation is like he's applied a layer of aloe. Together, we move our hands back beneath the faucet. I watch the water cascade over us, the protective curl of his hand around mine. My shoulders drop their tension, and without thinking about it too much, I lean back against him.

"Sass." It's a sigh. Almost a reproach. Even so, he doesn't pull away. "What are you doing?"

It's a valid question, and one I don't have an answer for. I flick the faucet off and turn into Theo, the throb of my injury nearly forgotten when I press my forehead to his chest. For a split second, he stiffens—then his arms come around me, and I breathe out in relief, lacing my fingers together at his lower back.

"I don't really know how to cook," I confess into his shirt.

"Yeah? And you thought you'd learn today?"

"I was trying to make myself useful," I gripe. "It was all going really well until I forgot to set the timer."

Theo hums his understanding. "Rookie mistake. How did you get burned?"

"I was washing the dishes," I say, flicking my arm back to indicate the sink, "and then I smelled smoke. I was in a hurry and I only pulled the oven mitt over half of my hand."

An exasperated groan rumbles in his chest. "You've got to be careful, Nina."

The kitchen is a complete disaster, smoke still heavy in the air, but Theo only scolds me for not taking care of myself. I'm not sure of the last time I was made to feel like a priority—like *the* priority—to another person. It may well have been ten years ago, in this town. In these arms.

I can't allow myself to become wrapped up in Theo again, and my brain is sounding the alarm that this is dangerous territory—but it doesn't *feel* dangerous when he's holding me like this. It's warm and familiar, something I thought was lost forever, and the memory of grieving him keeps me right where I am.

Theo must know what I'm thinking, or maybe he's just feeling the same, because his grip on me suddenly tightens. My feet are lifted off the ground; I press my face into his neck, my palms against his back, and hold on tight. It's been a couple of weeks since we first saw each other again, but somehow, *this* feels like the real reunion. We clutch fiercely, desperately, anchored by raw emotion and a bond that runs deeper than our conscious memories.

"Nina," he breathes, cupping one hand around the back of my head. "I thought I was going to die when you left."

"Don't even say that."

"I mean it." My shirt has ridden up, and the calluses on his hand scrape against my hip when he squeezes even harder, his words falling into my hair. "I didn't *want* to die. I spent the rest of that summer trying to find you, and I couldn't, and I hated myself for it. I should have answered the fucking phone. I should have kept on driving."

"No," I whisper against his skin. I may have been blaming him for the past ten years, bitter that he evidently didn't need me as much as I needed him, but I know now that I was wrong. He didn't abandon me. None of it was easy for him, either. We were so impossibly young. "It's okay."

Theo bends at the waist, placing my feet back on the ground. I brace myself to separate, but he only draws back enough to look me in the eyes. His are a little bit wild. "I would lay in bed at night, trying to figure out what else I could do. Where else I could look. I couldn't sleep or eat. There was this feeling in my chest—this... this *knot* that never went away."

"Like when I was in the hospital," I say softly.

He closes his eyes briefly, lets his chin fall. "It was *exactly* like that."

"That's how I felt, too."

For a long, loaded moment, we're connected in a shared gaze. Theo leans in closer, but even as my heart trips over itself, I know he won't kiss me. This is not a romantic interlude. The fact that we were involved for a month as teenagers is a significant, but small, part of our history. We may have been each other's first love—but for the seventeen years before that, we were each other's whole world.

Right now, it feels like we're rediscovering *that* part of us.

Pausing with his face a breath away from mine, Theo's hand comes up to touch my cheek, fingers curled over my ear, thumb at my chin. "When did your chest stop hurting?"

Those early days without Theo are a blur, but I know that by the time my mom demanded that I "do something besides wallow", I was at least coping well enough to appease her. Over time, I became an expert at suppressing every complicated feeling I had—about Theo, about my family, about myself—until I believed that they no longer existed.

"I don't think it ever did," I admit. "Not until now."

Theo gives a slight shake of his head. "Me either. And I didn't even realize it until you were standing in front of me again."

He does close the gap between us, then, but only to drop a light kiss on the tip of my nose. I receive it with butterflies in my stomach, and when he goes to pull back, I don't let him.

"No," I say, not remotely embarrassed to be locking my arms around his middle, holding him in place. "Not yet."

Theo goes along with it, giving me another hug and laughing quietly against my ear. "Tell me when."

***

Eventually, we get around to cleaning the kitchen. The rhythm comes to us naturally: by silent agreement, I load the dishwasher, he wipes down the counters, and we move around each other effortlessly. When Theo picks up the sheet pan and tilts it, none of the food budges. It's securely burnt on. He goes to the trash can and casually drops the entire thing inside. "Let's go pick up a pizza."

My blood pressure spikes. "In town?"

"You can stay in the truck," he says, fishing his keys from his pocket. "Come on."

It's been nearly a week since I called off my wedding, and I haven't left Theo's house since. But I know I'll have to emerge from hiding at some point; there's no reason to put it off any longer.

I make Theo wait while I change out of my slouchy loungewear, replacing it with cropped pants and a chiffon tank. On my way out to the truck, I grab my Red Vines off the kitchen counter. Theo automatically holds out his hand as I settle into his passenger seat. "Give me one."

"I guess I did destroy your kitchen," I acknowledge. I place a piece in his open palm and take a bite out of my own. "Maybe I'll try pasta tomorrow. I know I can boil water."

Theo backs out of the garage and heads down the long driveway. "Yeah," he says, holding his licorice in a fist and taking a bite. "About that. You don't have to earn your keep."

"Well, it's not like there's much else to do around here," I say, defensive. This feels unsettlingly like the conversation where Daniel asked me to 'stay out of the way' of his housekeeper. It's not that I particularly wanted to cook and clean—then or now—but in the absence of any real direction in my life, it was at least something purposeful to do.

And here, I don't even have the streets of New York to distract myself with.

"If you *want* to cook, cook," Theo clarifies. "Ruin every pan I have. I'm good with that. Just don't feel like you *have* to do anything."

"I'm not going to ruin all your pans," I snap.

"That wasn't my point."

I cross my arms and stare out the windshield, letting out a huffy sigh that even I recognize as bitchy. Immense frustration comes over me suddenly, and I can't pinpoint the source. "Okay."

We continue the drive toward town. Theo's window is open, his elbow hanging out the side, and there's a warm breeze blowing through the cab of the truck. Leafy canopies bow over the road, creating a kaleioscope of sunlight around us. It's the kind of night that brought me back to North Carolina for my wedding. There were lots of things I liked about New York, but on what was supposed to be the most important day of my life, I wanted to be surrounded by *this*. Not concrete and asphalt.

When Theo breaks the silence, he speaks slowly, each syllable falling on eggshells. "When the police picked you up, where did you go?"

"What?"

"You didn't come back to Amity," he says patiently. "Where did you go?"

I have never liked revisiting these memories, but as I do it now, I notice that the pang isn't quite so sharp.

I wonder if our earlier conversation helped with that. "Raleigh. By the time my parents picked me up from the police station, my dad had already called a guy he knew there, gotten a job—I'm not even entirely sure what he was doing; he was definitely being paid under the table—and found a house to rent."

"Raleigh," he says just under his breath, like a revelation not meant for me. "You were in Raleigh, and I was in Chapel Hill. We were so fucking close."

There's a lump in my throat. I can't get emotional twice in one day, so I swallow it down and continue. "Dad and Brock only lived with us for a year before my parents separated."

"What happened?"

I give him an incredulous look. "What do you mean? Without the business, they weren't obligated to stay together anymore."

Theo tilts his head in understanding.

"They moved out west together," I continue, "and Mom started working for this catering company. That's how she met Travis—at an event she was working."

"What about you?"

"I thought I told you. I met Daniel in—"

"No," he interrupts. "What did you do in Raleigh? Before that?"

"I worked in a department store until Mom and Travis got engaged, and when she moved in with Travis, I went too." I snort sardonically. "I was twenty-one, making minimum wage and living off my mom's boyfriend at the same time you were finishing college. At least one of us did something worthwhile."

"You were figuring things out," he supplies, always ready to defend me, even from myself. "What high school did you graduate from up there?"

The question lingers as we reach the edge of town and stop at a red light. Theo looks both ways, sees that nobody else is around, and casually rolls through the intersection.

"I didn't finish high school," I admit.

"What?" Theo asks. "Really?"

I nod, staring into my lap. Although I've always carried a little shame about being a dropout, it multiplied when I was going out with Daniel. He did *not* want his friends and acquaintances to know that he was dating someone without a high school diploma. Keeping it out of the conversation with his circle meant that I also stopped talking about it with anyone else. "I was too depressed to go to school," I tell him. "Nobody forced me. It wasn't like I was going to get to go back to *my* school, with my friends and teachers. So I just...never went."

He looks flabbergasted. Horrified. "Nina. That's not fair to you at all."

I shrug. "It's not like I needed a diploma to work in the mall."

"It's not about that," he says, indignation creeping into his voice. "Your parents should have helped you. They should have gotten you enrolled so you could finish. Even if—even if just to make some new friends."

"Yeah," I murmur. "Well. We don't all have parents like you."

Theo runs a hand through his hair and looks at me sadly. I can sense him wanting to say something else, even argue with me—except that he grew up with my parents, too. He knows the difference between his and mine.

"I'm sorry," he says, and I nod, even though there's nothing for him to be sorry about.

Chapter Twenty

Then

"You can't do it."

Theo looked down at me, one eyebrow cocked in challenge. "I've done it before."

"Not that I've seen."

He stepped off the curb that I was perched on. In his hand was a full black trash bag from inside the store, practically bursting at the seams. The dumpster was across the back parking lot—a good fifteen feet away. "If I make it," he said, "you let me sneak you out tonight."

Reflexively, I glanced over my shoulder, making sure the exit door of the store was still closed. It was; we were alone. I tossed the remainder of my Red Vine into my mouth. "If she catches us, I won't be allowed out of the house until school starts."

"She won't catch us," Theo said.

"Or we could just hang out at a time when nobody will care."

"What's fun about that?" he asked, eyes twinkling, and I got that familiar swoop in my stomach. He was right; although I always enjoyed being with him, it was a special kind of thrill to be in a cocoon made up of the two of us, with not a single other person knowing where we were or what we were doing.

Besides, there was no way he would be able to throw that giant bag of trash into the dumpster from where he was standing. I didn't believe for a second that he'd done it before. Theo was known to have misplaced bravado from time to time. "Alright. Go ahead and try."

"And if I make it, you'll sneak out with me tonight?" he clarified.

I leaned back on my hands. "Sure."

Theo turned back to the dumpster. He squared his shoulders, gripped the bag by the strings, and flung it.

I watched the bag arc through the air as if in slow motion. It caught on the edge of the open dumpster, half in and half out.

We stared at each other. Then I catapulted myself off the curb and started sprinting.

It took Theo a second to catch on. "Hey!" he yelled. His steps pounded on the pavement behind me. "Sass!"

I reached the dumpster first, arm outstretched, reaching for the bag. I managed to snag a corner and was about to yank it to the ground when strong arms closed around my waist.

"Theo!" I shrieked as he picked me up and spun. I wriggled in his grasp, but he held on tight. "Put me down!"

I looked back in time to see Theo use his shoulder to nudge the rest of the bag inside. "I win," he said. "See you at eleven."

"This doesn't count, you cheater!"

"Sure it does. It was mostly in, anyway."

"That's what she said," I muttered, and Theo guffawed.

He set me down but didn't loosen his grip. The contours of his front—chest, abs, *hips*—pressed into my back. His familiar scent, pine and just a hint of sweat, surrounded me. "Tonight," he murmured against the back of my neck, sending goosebumps across my skin, "I'm gonna—"

"Nina Lynn."

Theo's arms dropped like stones and we sprung apart. The warm anticipation of the rest of his sentence faded away, replaced with an icy rock in my gut.

It was my mother who stood by the back door, covering us both with a hard glare. As much as I wanted to look at Theo, the ground, or the sky, I knew that failing to make eye contact with my mother would only anger her further. When I met her gaze, I swore I could *see* how pissed off she was.

"There are three customers browsing right now," she said tightly. "It takes about ten seconds to put the trash out, Theo."

"Yes ma'am." He jerked his thumb over his shoulder. "All done."

Mom pointed at me, red nails bold against her pale skin. "And your break is over."

I walked over to her and bent to retrieve my Red Vines. In my haste to beat Theo to the dumpster, about half of them had tumbled from the package. I scooped them up hurriedly and made to throw them away, but another glance at Mom's face told me that heading back in Theo's direction was not a wise idea.

"I'll get on the register," I said.

Mom stepped in front of me, blocking the door. "Actually, I'm headed out. You're coming home with me."

"But I have two hours left in my shift," I said, startled. Usually when my parents were upset with me, that meant more time at the store—not less.

"Theo can handle it," Mom said. For the first time since she emerged, she relieved me of her piercing gaze, settling it on him instead. "Can't you?"

"Yes ma'am," he said again. Part of me wished he would stand up to her the way he stood up to my father, but I knew that he was being deferential for my sake. While my dad might have been quick to anger, he was also quick to move on. Mom played a longer game.

"Thank you, Theo." Her voice dripped with acid. She pulled open the door and held it for me. "Come on. And for god's sake, throw that candy away."

***

On the ride home, I refused to be the first to speak. It took a full five minutes for Mom to clear her throat, and I felt a surge of satisfaction at my minor victory.

"You cannot go down this road," she said at last, and I was surprised to hear that her hard tone had dissipated. If I didn't know better—and I did—I would have said that she almost sounded concerned.

"We were just messing around."

"Uh-huh," she said, unconvinced.

I didn't say anything, deciding that silence was my best option.

"I've always worried this might happen," she continued. "Ever since you were little. I should have stepped in sooner."

"We're friends," I insisted. "Like we always have been."

"Whatever you were doing out behind the store sure didn't look very friendly," she snipped.

"Well, it was."

We rolled to a stop at an intersection. I stared down at my thighs that were beginning to tan from the summer sun. Theo had kissed one of them the other day, just a quick smack while we reclined beneath a tree out by the pond, his head in my lap. Just the memory ignited that heat in my belly that was still new, but becoming more familiar by the day. I wished I were back there with him. Anywhere with him.

The only sound in the car was the ticking of the turn signal as Mom yielded to a red sedan. She liked to leave a lot of space between herself and other cars—one fender bender a decade earlier had made her permanently cautious—so she waited until it was halfway down the next block before following.

"You've seen your father and I struggle," she said. "Theo's parents, too. If they want to let him go down that same path, then that's their choice. But I don't want that for you."

"What about Brock?" I asked. "You don't want better for him?"

"Of course I do. He'll get there. He has a job outside of the store. Theo doesn't."

I stared out the windshield, watching the leafy green trees pass by. "Theo and I *like* the store," I said, my voice soft. Meek. In the same way Theo made me feel like I could do anything, nobody humbled me like my mother. "We've thought about—maybe—taking over someday, once you all retire."

Mom gave a derisive snort. "When we retire? How do you suppose we'll manage that?"

"I don't know," I said dumbly. "Social security?"

She shook her head. "Do you even know how social security works?"

I thought I did, but I wasn't confident enough to answer.

"It's based on how much you pay in," she told me. "it's a percentage of our profits—so, lately, not much at all. Not that the store will be around long enough to get us to retirement, anyway."

I glanced at her out of the corner of my eye. She sat rigid in her seat, hands tight on the steering wheel. Bringing up my transgressions right now was risky, but the need to know won out. "Do you know about the rent?" I asked slowly, as if trying to get the words past a land mine.

"You mean the rent going up because of you and Theo? Yes, I do. Honestly, Nina, you should know what a bad state we're in, since you've made yourself part of the problem."

I decided then that it was in my best interest to keep my mouth shut, and I did so for the rest of the way home.

By the time Mom pulled into our driveway, my seatbelt was off and I was ready to flee for my bedroom.

But after she cut the engine and used the remote to close the door, she didn't budge. And from experience, I knew that meant I shouldn't, either.

"Look," she said finally, and the accusatory tone was gone from her voice. She sounded...tired. Maybe even a little vulnerable. "We never planned for things to be this way. The shoe store was supposed to be a starting point. We imagined expanding, selling other products, investing in properties." Mom laughed without humor. "We thought that eventually *we* would own our storefront, and the ones around it. And here we are, getting the rent driven up instead."

Things were beginning to click into place for me. My parents' discontent with their situation, with each other—even before the store started struggling—made so much more sense. They didn't want to live a simple life running a small business. They wanted to be big fish in a small pond.

Essentially, they wanted to be the new Reddings.

"Brock will do fine in construction," she continued. "It pays well. He won't live in that apartment forever. But if Theo's only plan is to stick around the store, then that's not a plan at all."

"He's thinking about other things, too," I said defensively. "He just graduated, Mom. Let him figure it out."

"As far as I'm concerned, he's not my child, so I don't care what he does. But you *are*, and I'm not going to let him drag you along while he 'figures it out.'"

I should have doubled down on my insistence that we were nothing more than friends. Instead, I felt a surge of anger at her air quotes, her mocking tone, her complete refusal to see how important Theo was to me. "Nobody's talking about getting married."

"You will be soon enough," she countered. "I've been trying to tell Randi for years that you and Theo are too close. Too codependent. She's been no help; she thinks it's cute. If you aren't careful, you'll never be able to untangle yourself from him."

I looked at my hands, folded in my lap. I thought about being *literally* tangled up with Theo after we made out in his bedroom the other day: his legs twisted around mine, heart pounding beneath my cheek, his warm laugh washing over my neck. Feeling safe and free and, when his parents arrived home and I got to jump off the windowsill and into his waiting arms, exhilarated. "Would that really be a bad thing?" I nearly whispered.

"Yes," Mom snapped. "My god, Nina, I'm trying to help you see this *now*, when you can still do something about it. You certainly won't be able to in five years, when you're married and pregnant and living off whatever scraps he manages to bring home."

"And that's what happened to you, right?" Her eyes widened, but I plowed forward with the extremely questionable choice of vocalizing the math I'd done some time ago: the fact that Brock was an eight-pound baby born six months after my parents' wedding. "You got pregnant, so you were stuck with Dad?"

Mom's nostrils flared. In my entire life, she had never raised a hand to me. But for about half a second, I thought she might.

Instead, she pushed the button to unlock my door. "Nina Lynn Sullivan," she said, low and dangerous, "go to your room."

Chapter Twenty-One

Then

Tap. Tap.

The sound made me lose count of the glow-in-the-dark stars on my ceiling, and I huffed in annoyance. After tossing and turning for an hour, I'd flopped onto my back and started counting the stars that had been stuck above my bed since kindergarten. I knew from past sleepless nights that there were one hundred twenty-seven of them. Most of the time, I fell asleep before I got to fifty.

Tap. Tap. Tap.

I rolled onto my side and stared at the window. In the dark, I couldn't make out the face of the person outside, but I knew it was Theo. I'd sent him a text earlier, telling him not to come over. Even then, I had a feeling he wouldn't listen.

He jiggled the window. It was locked from the inside and didn't budge. "Sass," came his muffled voice. "Sass, come on."

I sighed, and, with a glance at my bedroom door to confirm that it was locked, crossed over to the window. I flipped the lock and shoved it up. There was no screen; it had fallen out years ago and never been replaced. I leaned my elbows on the windowsill and stuck my head out. "I'm not going anywhere," I hissed, keeping my voice down. "Queen Kelly's on the warpath."

He slipped his hands into the back pockets of his jeans. With me in the house and him standing in the grass outside, we were exactly the same height. "I know. Figured I'd come in."

"No!" I hissed. "I'm serious, Theo. I can't do this tonight."

Theo sighed. "If I just stand here, will you talk to me?"

I glanced nervously over my shoulder, but no sound came from the hallway. Our house was only about a thousand square feet; if anyone was still awake, I would know it. "Sure," I conceded, turning back to him.

He leaned in to smooth a flyaway off my forehead. "What happened?" he asked softly. "Does she know?"

I licked my lips as I mentally replayed the conversation I'd had with my mother that day. Even though I didn't technically tell her anything, it was clear by the time she sent me to my room that I had unwittingly shown her my hand. "I think so."

"I'm sorry, Sass." He gripped the top of the window frame and leaned in toward me. The movement accentuated his arms, his neck, the jut of his collarbone. "I shouldn't have been touching you like that at the store."

"It wasn't just you," I said.

Theo nodded slowly. The dim light of the streetlamp was all I had to see him by, but even with his face cloaked in shadows, I could tell that he looked troubled. "What do you think she'll do now?"

My fingers twisted together. "I don't know."

"That makes me nervous."

"Me too."

Theo gently pried my hands apart, to entwine them with his own. Our tangled fingers rested between us on the windowsill. "I wish they would just yell at us and move on."

"She didn't yell at me, but she was pissed." I hesitated, grounded myself by running my thumb over a callus on his palm. "Has your mom ever said anything to you? About me?"

His mouth twisted to the side. "Yeah," he said, but didn't elaborate.

"Recently? Or when we were kids?"

"Both."

I waited, but Theo was uncharacteristically reticent. Finally, I asked, "Do you think we're codependent?"

His eyebrows hiked halfway up his forehead. "Is that what Kelly said?"

"Yes. She said she told your mom that they needed to do something about it, but Randi didn't care."

Theo ducked his head to let out a chuckle. "'Course," he muttered, then looked back at me. "Do *you* think we're codependent? Need to take a little break from each other, find ourselves?"

I let out a light laugh. It was genuine, but a nagging thought kept it subdued. "Sometimes," I admitted, "I feel like I don't know who I am without you. It's like...I'm not just Nina. I'm half of Nina and Theo."

"Do you *like* being half of Nina and Theo?" he asked carefully, fingers pulsing in mine.

"I do. Especially now." I paused to study him. "Do you?"

Theo lifted one hand to my face, gently cradling. Fingertips pressed into my hair; his thumb stroked my birthmark. "Do you remember when you were in fourth grade and you were hospitalized with the flu?"

My brow furrowed in confusion. "Yeah."

"That's the longest you and I have ever been apart," he said. "Five days. Five days, and I could hardly stand it. Every night before bed, I would ask my parents if you were going to be at school or the store the next day, and every time they said no, I cried. Which was very embarrassing, by the way. I was almost in middle school."

He edged a little closer. My hands drifted to his chest, lightly gripping the fabric of his t-shirt. "On the fourth night," he continued, looking down at me, "my mom came to my room and told me that you were home from the hospital. I jumped up and said I wanted to go see you. She told me that you needed one more day to rest, and I absolutely lost it. Just crumpled up in a ball and started sobbing."

"Theo," I whispered, taken aback. I remembered reuniting with him: we usually met at the bus stop before school, but that day, he showed up at our house so he could walk me there. He gave me a hug and a declaration of "love you so much", insisted on carrying my backpack, and when we got to school, he followed me to my classroom and excitedly told my teacher, "Look who's here!" The rest of this, however, was news to me.

"I told Mom that my chest hurt, and it had for days. She said, 'that's because half of your heart is missing.' She said that it would stop hurting once I saw you again."

"Did it?" I whispered.

"Yeah," he whispered back. "I didn't believe her, but yeah. It did."

I closed the short distance between us and kissed him. He immediately tilted his head to deepen the kiss, and between us, he grasped one of my wrists and moved my hand slightly up to cover his heart. I pressed my palm there, relishing in the proof of what he just told me, choosing to believe that this heart really did beat for me.

We broke for air. Theo covered my hand with both of his, keeping it firmly against his chest. "Ever since then, I don't really think of us as Nina and Theo, like two separate people," he said. "I think of us as two pieces of the same heart."

"And that's not codependent?" I tried to circle back to my original question, even as my voice shook.

"What if it is?" Theo challenged. "Would that be so awful?"

It was the same thing I'd asked my mother earlier in the evening. I answered the way I wished she had.

"No," I said. "No. I suppose it wouldn't."

Chapter Twenty-Two

Now

"Hey."

I groan.

"Nina."

"What."

A hand closes over my shoulder and shakes gently. "Wake up."

"Whaaaat," I whine, flopping onto my back. It must be early; there's only muted light coming into the room, and the sky outside the window is still gray. Theo stands over me in his work clothes. "What do you want?"

"Mornin' to you, too."

"I'm sleeping."

"Do you want to go to work with me?"

I squint up at him. Slowly, I push up onto my hands, blinking a few times while I let my brain catch up. "Why?"

He shrugs, thumbs casually slung in his pockets, as if it's no trouble either way. "It seems like you might be bored of hanging around here."

He's right; I have been getting restless. The chicken incident from yesterday proves that much. However, I am also not in the habit of getting out of bed before ten. "It's *way* too early for this, Theo."

"I'll take a long lunch and come grab you later, then."

"But I don't have anything to wear," I protest—although, the more I regain my consciousness, the more enticing I find the idea. I've never been particularly outdoorsy, but hands-on, tangible work is what feels natural to me. Taking care of Mrs. Wilson's yard last week reminded me of that. "I don't want to ruin any more of my clothes."

"We'll take it easy. Just wear something comfortable." Theo turns his wrist, checks his smart watch. "I need to get going, but I'll be back at eleven thirty. Be ready."

He lopes out of the room, leaving my door ajar behind him. I sputter for a few seconds, then clamber out of bed and poke my head into the hall. His footsteps are retreating down the stairwell, but I call after him: "So you *do* want me to earn my keep!"

"No," he hollers back, sounding completely unbothered. "I want you to get out into the world again."

I let out another pitiful whine, then stagger back to my bed and belly flop onto it.

It's all a front, though, because when Theo's truck comes rumbling up the drive at eleven twenty-seven, I'm on the porch waiting for him.

To my relief, we bypass Amity and go into Goldsboro instead. First we stop to eat lunch at a bar and grill, where I order a side salad and water—until Theo stares at me long enough that I get flustered and add a grilled chicken wrap.

"Any sauce or dressing?" the waiter asks me.

"No thank you."

When it's Theo's turn to order, he says, "I'll have the sirloin burger with steak fries. And extra ranch on the side, please."

"You don't like ranch," I say when the waiter leaves.

"No," he replies, unrolling his silverware, "but you do."

"Restaurants in New York don't usually have it."

"Luckily," he says, "you're back in the land of more sophisticated tastes."

As expected, Theo immediately slides the giant cup of ranch over to me when our food arrives. I sigh, but as I look down at my pitiful, plain salad, I figure a little flavor wouldn't be the worst thing I have going for me lately.

When I take my first bite of ranch-saturated lettuce, an involuntary "ohhh" comes out of my mouth and sends Theo's eyebrows flying upward.

"Jeez, Sass," he says. "We *are* in public."

"Shut the fuck up," I mutter. Theo guffaws, and I can't help laughing a little, too, as I shovel another forkful into my mouth in a way that would definitely be frowned upon in both Michelin-starred restaurants and my mother's dining room.

After lunch, he drives a few blocks over to a supermarket. I'm expecting to get supplies for a job; instead, Theo leads me into the main part of the store, grabs a cart, and walks to the women's clothing section.

"What are we doing here?" I ask, eyeing the racks of garments priced at five, eight, twelve dollars. I haven't paid so little for clothes in three years—maybe even longer, since Travis used to give me a pretty nice allowance when I still lived with him and Mom.

"Get some clothes that you won't have to worry about ruining." Theo pushes the cart toward me, and I stick my fingers through the wires to catch it. "I need a couple of things from the garden area for this afternoon. Come find me when you're finished, okay? I'll pay."

My first instinct is relief, because while I really could use some clothes besides the stuffy ones I brought for meetings at the country club, I need to save every measly penny in my checking account for my next steps—whatever the hell those are.

Then, it's like a lightbulb goes off over my head. My life flashes before my eyes; not a compilation of my best memories, but rather the chain of events that took me from Amity to Raleigh to New York to right here. In my entire life, I have only made two decisions on my own that had any real consequence: running away with Theo and deciding not to marry Daniel. The first led to such heartbreak that I didn't dare step a toe out of line for ten years. The latter—the latter happened so suddenly, and yet I didn't feel an ounce of regret when I threw that ring out the window of the truck. Nothing has ever been as exhilarating as the sensation of my left hand in those first moments it was bared. It was freedom. It was a new start.

A new start in which I have continued to be completely dependent on another person.

The lightbulb above my head burns brighter as I arrive at the third major decision of my life: *I'm not doing this again.*

Theo steps forward, appearing alarmed. "What? What's wrong?"

"Nothing," I hedge. "But I'll buy my own clothes."

He shakes his head. "It's not a big deal. You can save your--"

"Not a big deal?" I laugh in a humorless way that sounds foreign to my own ears. People mill by us in the main aisle, and I push the cart further into the clothes, trying to get some space. My lunch—that Theo also paid for—sits heavy in my stomach. "Yeah. I'm sure it's not a big deal to you."

Theo squeezes into the cramped space, slipping between me and a table of graphic tees. "What the hell does that mean?"

"Theo." I lean an elbow on the handlebar of the cart and prop my other hand on my hip. A lady and her preteen daughter are browsing nearby, so I lower my voice to keep it between us. "We had the same childhood, but we wound up in completely different places."

He makes a big deal of twisting around to look at our surroundings. "Looks like we're in the same place to me."

"You know what I mean," I snap. "I'm not trying to be a bitch, okay? I know you and your family. I know you've worked hard. Nobody deserves success more than you and Cecil. And Randi, of course. But that doesn't mean it feels good to be your little charity case."

"Yeah, I famously spend my time searching for people who are down on their luck to live in my house," Theo quips, his sarcasm tinted with real irritation. "Come on, Nina. Charity is the hundred bucks I send to the children's hospital every month. Anything I do for you is..." He trails off, shaking his head as words escape him. "It's *you*."

I hear what he's saying, and I hear what he's not. There are a thousand little meanings wrapped up in that single stressed syllable, but if I dwell on them—if I dwell on all the things I want to say in return—I'm going to lose sight of myself. As usual.

"I know," I say, forcing my voice to soften. I move a little closer to him, making sure only he can hear me. "I'm just realizing, literally right this second, that my mother was right. Which sucks."

"It always sucks when Kelly's right," he agrees.

"I'm codependent." It feels like a huge admission, but Theo just looks at me, waiting for more. "I got used to it, growing up with you, and then I just stayed that way with whoever was around: my mom and Travis, Daniel, and now you again."

"Sass—"

"Actually, wouldn't codependent mean both people are dependent on each other? That's not it. You don't need me; you were doing fine before I came back to town, and you'd be fine if I left. I'm the one who would be shit out of luck without you." I thread my fingers through my hair and tug lightly at the roots, feeling unhinged. "How can I be twenty-seven years old and have *nothing*? No job, no career, nowhere to live, no money, no friends. I mean...what the fuck?"

Theo turns his hat backwards, taking his face out of shadow before stepping into my space. He wraps his long fingers loosely around my wrists and gently draws them out of my hair, back to my sides. "Okay," he says, placating. "Hold on."

"You knew me," I say. "When I was a teenager. I may have been codependent--"

"I think you're really overusing that word."

"—but I did have plans for myself. Right? We talked about the future. I didn't know exactly what I wanted yet, but I had ideas. Then we left Amity, and it's like..." I trail off, my eyes wandering over Theo's shoulder and landing on a shirt that reads *Shell Yeah!* That's what I've been over the last ten years. A shell. "Like I was so focused on not thinking about you, I didn't think about anything else, either."

Theo is still holding my wrists, his hazel eyes piercing as his thumbs press lightly against my pulse points. "Listen. I've said some things to you since you got back that I shouldn't have, about your birthmark and stuff, and I'm sorry. You were coping with no support from anyone around you. Nobody should fault you for that. Especially me." He slips his fingers down into mine, squeezing quickly before stepping back and taking his touch with him. "And shit, Sass. When we were teenagers, I felt like I was the one being clingy. I had deferred my UNC acceptance, remember?"

"That was stupid of you."

"My parents agreed. That was the silver lining of all the shit that went down, I guess—there was no reason not to go." He slips his hands into the back pockets of his jeans, looks around, and sighs. "Okay. So what I'm hearing is that I'm not buying you clothes."

"Right."

"Not because I don't want to," he verifies. "And not because I can't."

I blink, a little taken aback by that. Theo's success is obvious; he doesn't have to prove it to anyone, least of all me, and it's uncharacteristic that he would feel the need to. Theo has always brimmed with confidence; rarely have I been in a position to reassure him. But for some reason, I can sense that he needs it right now.

"I know," I tell him. "It's not about that."

He gives a resolute nod, and just like that, we're back on the same page. "Got it."

I reach out and touch a pair of pink corduroy shorts hanging nearby. They're seven dollars, and a month ago, I wouldn't have even worn them to bed. But they although they look cheaply made, they also look exceptionally comfortable, and I decide that they will be the first purchase—*my* purchase, with my own scarce funds—of my new life.

Chapter Twenty-Three

Now

After an afternoon of following Theo around a job site, my feet encased in new, cheap, comfy sneakers, we get in the truck and head back to Amity. I may be fifty dollars poorer than I was this morning; even so, I'm feeling better than I have in days. Maybe weeks. Possibly years.

I'm a little restless, too—like now that I've taken this first step toward being reliant on myself, I need to take another so I don't end up back at square one. As we drive through town, I stare out the window, as if the answer is going to jump out at me.

And then, inexplicably, it does—in the form of a giant Help Wanted sign in the window of the Wilsons' store.

"Hey." I nudge Theo with my elbow. "Pull over there."

His eyes follow the direction of my pointer finger. "To the Wilsons'?"

"Yeah."

I see the moment he notices the sign. Understanding, and then trepidation, seeps into his expression. "Sass, you know that if you go in there, you're going to see people you know."

He's right. It's the one thing I've been avoiding since I got here. I haven't spoken to anybody from Amity except the Hoyts and Mrs. Wilson, the three people besides Theo who were like family to me. But this town isn't big enough to hide in forever, and if I'm going to be living here, I'll have to face everyone eventually.

"It's fine," I say as Theo swings the truck around, coming to a stop at the curb.

"Hold on—"

I set my bag of clothes on the floorboard and unbuckle my seatbelt. "I'll be right back," I tell him as I hop out.

"Wait, Ni—"

I shut the door, muffling the second syllable of my name, and head toward the entrance. Bright red and pink flowers stand on display on either side of it. My steps falter slightly when my fingertips touch the door handle, but I recover so quickly that I'm sure nobody would have noticed—except Theo, whose eyes I can feel boring into my back.

When I pull the door open, the tinkling bell sounds exactly as I remember. I step inside and look around quickly; there's nobody around, which gives me a second to breathe and take in the store.

For the most part, Wilson General is exactly as I remember it. Now that I've lived in New York, I know that it would be called a bodega there. The building has enough room for the basics—a small section of produce, four tightly packed aisles of dry groceries, and some household and personal care products crammed into the remaining spaces. There's a fridge of milk in the corner, a chest of ice up by the register. Anyone could get by shopping here exclusively; for frills, or just a wider selection, you would have to go into Goldsboro.

I walk up to the counter, which is vacant. The cash drawer is slightly open—typical for Amity. We wouldn't have worried about that at my family's store, either.

"Coming!" a female voice calls out. It's vaguely familiar, the way I suppose most voices in Amity will be, and my bravado wavers. Theo's truck is still idling at the curb—I could run out the door, push this off another day.

But I stay where I am, hands falling into their natural position at my hips, as hurried footsteps come from one of the aisles. "Good evening," the girl calls again. "How can I help you?"

I turn around just as she emerges, and my breath catches.

Standing in front of me, wearing the Wilsons' signature green apron, is Sage Perry.

I can't remember the last time I saw Sage in person, because whatever we were doing, it was completely normal and unremarkable and failed to stick in my memory. It's not like we knew what was about to happen.

After I was separated from Theo, I talked to her on the phone a few times. Everything from those days is such a blur; I know I told her what happened, and that she tried to talk to Theo for me. His parents wouldn't let her. Then my mom confiscated my phone. Months passed before she returned it with a new number, and by that point, I had become so bitter about Theo abandoning me that I refused to reach out to him—or anyone else from Amity.

It takes Sage a beat to recognize me, of course, and when she does, her eyes bug out until I can see the whites. "*Nina?*"

I try to reply, and it sticks in my throat. I cough into my fist. "Hey."

She looks at me. I look at her.

Then she turns her head and screams across the empty store: "*Quinton!* Come here!"

"Oh," I say, quickly piecing together that this is what Theo was trying to warn me about before I got out of the truck. Oops. "Quinton works here, too?"

"No, he's a cop, but he comes in to visit me when he has down time. He's back there using the bathroom." She holds up her left hand and wiggles it. For the first time, I notice the diamond perched on her ring finger. "We're married."

"What?" I sputter. They were friendly in high school, but mostly because of me and Theo. Privately, she had referred to him as a 'redneck wannabe skater boy' more than once. "Really?"

Sage nods. She smiles, and even after all this time, I recognize it as her most sincere version. "We got together after you—you know. Left."

"Congratulations, Sage," I say, meaning it. "I saw a picture of the wedding in Theo's house, but I didn't know who the bride was."

I realize my mistake too late. Sage's eyes go even wider than when she first saw me. She grabs my arm as if we aren't practically strangers. "What the hell is going on? You've been hanging out with Theo?"

I sigh. "It's such a long story."

She gestures at the empty store around us. "I've got time."

Thankfully, Quinton comes around the corner then. He's in a full police uniform, gun and all. His hair is cut army-short, like in his wedding photo. I never would have recognized him at first—or second, or third—glance. "Hey—whoa. What?"

I wonder how many more times I'm going to have some version of this same conversation. "Hi, Quinton."

"Now I know why Theo hasn't wanted to go to the bar this week," he says, and his tone isn't exactly warm. I force myself to keep my mouth shut against the defensive words that threaten to come out. If Quinton wants to be upset with me for hurting his friend—and his wife—then that's fine. I can't blame him. "What are you doing here?"

I sigh, loud and long. "A lot has happened. I'll catch you up," I add, speaking directly to Sage, "but the reason I came in here is... I'm back in town, staying with Theo, and I need a job."

"Oh," she says, surprised. "Yeah. Of course."

"Sage," Quinton warns.

"What?" She crosses her arms and fixes him with a withering look. "That sign has been up for weeks and not a single other person has applied. Do you want me to have to keep working overtime?"

They have a brief staring contest that Quinton loses. "Can you come in tomorrow around nine to meet with Judith?" Sage asks me. "I'm the assistant manager, but she does the hiring."

Quinton glares at me, and briefly, I wonder if I should decline. Then I imagine walking back out to Theo and telling him that actually, I haven't yet reached the point in my life where I'm capable of taking care of myself.

"Sure," I tell them. "I'll be here."

***

That night, Theo surprises me by revealing that he still has his old truck. I haven't seen it because he uses it to haul things around on his property, and it's been parked behind some thick brush. I wait in the driveway as he drives it over the hill, my stomach fluttering when I see it again. It's the same truck he drove in high school, the one we took to work and parties and the gas station for dollar sodas. The one where we had sex for the first time—and most of the times after that.

Most significantly, it's also the truck that Theo was pushed up against as he was put into handcuffs. I think it heals a little part of me to see him casually steering it into his enormous garage, elbow out the window, grin on his face.

"Enjoy," he says when he tosses me the keys. I snatch them out of the air, swing them on my index finger. "No guys in the back, alright?"

"We'll see," I say coolly. "Lots of room to roll around back there."

I stay long enough to watch Theo's eyes spark at my not-so-subtle reference, and then I saunter away.

In the morning, I dress in a completely new outfit—sweatshirt, jeans, and sneakers—and drive myself to the general store. Mrs. Wilson's daughter, Judith, and I barely exchange two sentences before she hands me an apron and instructs Sage to train me on the register.

After thirty minutes, it becomes clear that I don't actually need register training, so I start learning the specifics of the store, facing shelves, and running stock. Quinton comes by around lunchtime to see Sage. He gives me the cold shoulder, refusing to even look in my direction. I keep my head down and let him be that way.

"Is this weird for you?" Sage asks me that afternoon, after Quinton has left and Judith is in the back. "No offense, but you look like you've become used to a life that's a lot more luxurious than this."

"What do you mean?"

She gestures toward her own head. "I mean...your hair looks treated. And you obviously had that surgery your mom always wanted to save money for."

"Yeah." I continue stocking bubble gum on the display in front of the counter, giving the task more focus than it warrants. "Well, I won't be retouching my roots anytime soon. But no, this isn't weird."

Strangely enough, I'm telling the truth—it's not weird at all. A few weeks ago, I never would have imagined that I'd be back in here. If I hadn't run into Theo that day at the country club—or come to my senses about Daniel some other way—I'd be at my mom's, putting the final touches on the wedding and stealing moments on the phone with my fiancé, trying to convince him to summon some enthusiasm.

Now that she's opened the door to the changes in my appearance and not been rebuked, Sage continues to probe. "Did you get your nose done, too?"

"I figured I might as well."

The bell over the door chimes, announcing the entrance of a customer. I automatically tense up, and when I look over my shoulder, I see a middle-aged man whom I recognize but can't name. He pays no attention to us; Sage calls out a greeting, then lowers her voice to speak to me. "What did Theo say about it?"

I snort. "What *didn't* he say?"

She hums sympathetically. "Was he upset?"

"I wouldn't say upset, exactly." I finish with the bubble gum and grab a box of chocolate bars. "I'm being a shitty friend—I've barely asked about you."

"I think whatever *you've* got going on is more interesting."

As much as I am trying to change the subject in my own interest, I'm not completely self-absorbed. Sage and I had been best friends since third grade. Not reaching out to Theo was one thing, but not reaching out to *her*...yeah. I'm a bitch. "Tell me how you and Quinton got together."

She tells me about how, after I disappeared and Theo went to college, she was left with more questions than answers about what had happened. Quinton went to college that fall, too, but decided it wasn't for him at the end of his freshman year. By the time he came back to town, Peyton and Lori Ann were leaving, and that left Sage without any of her closest high school friends. She started working for the Wilsons and hanging out with Quinton, who had begun to grow apart from Theo—something that surprises me to hear, since they seem good now. After a year of slowly growing closer, Quinton and Sage went to the state fair together. He kissed her on top of the Ferris wheel, and they've been together ever since.

I never would have imagined the two of them as a couple, but Sage is glowing and beaming throughout the entire story, and I allow myself to think that I helped make something good happen.

Chapter Twenty-Four

Then

"These are two for six dollars," I told Mrs. Wilson, nodding to the martini-patterned socks she had placed on the counter. "If you want to grab another pair."

"Hmm." She shuffled back over to the display stand and spun it with so force, I didn't know how she could see any of the choices. "Maybe."

"I think we have some with—"

"Ooh, corgis!" Mrs. Wilson squealed. She grabbed a pair and tossed them on top of the others. "You know, Dale told me no more dogs. But I did see a listing for some corgi puppies up for adoption in Wilmington, and we're down to five since Gertrude passed on last year. I was thinking about taking a trip down there next weekend and bringing one back. Better to ask forgiveness, you know?"

"Sure," I said. "That's how I approach everything with my parents."

She laughed, and I smiled, knowing that she wouldn't rat me out. After grabbing two more pairs—one with dachshunds, the other with tabby cats—she sidled back up to the counter. "Okay, no more!"

There were now three shoeboxes and four pairs of novelty socks in front of me. "You sure?" I asked.

"Child," Mrs. Wilson chided teasingly. She smoothed down her stick-straight white hair, which had somehow become tousled from her enthusiastic perusal of the sock display. "Don't go getting me in trouble with Dale. I need to keep him nice and buttered up for when I bring that dog home, you know."

"Right, right."

I pulled her items toward me and started keying in the prices. Mrs. Wilson took the opportunity to look around, then leaned conspiratorially toward me. "Your mama and daddy around?"

"No," I said. "They already left. Theo and I are closing."

Technically, Theo wasn't supposed to be closing with me—after the dumpster incident, my mom had changed our shifts around to keep us from working alone together—but she didn't need to know that.

"Where's he at?"

"Cleaning the bathroom, I think."

Her nose wrinkled in disgust. "Oh, you sure got the better end of the stick."

"Yeah." I giggled. "Well, he wants to keep me happy now that we're—"

Too late, I realized my mistake and stopped just short of spilling the beans. Mrs. Wilson was perceptive, though, and one look at the grin on her face told me that I wasn't fooling her any more than I was fooling my mother.

"Um." Flustered, I hit a key on the register. "Your total is eighty-seven twelve."

She handed me her card with a sympathetic look. I avoided her eyes as I swiped it, handed her the receipt to sign, and busied myself with bagging up her purchases.

"Well," I said, wanting nothing more than for this conversation to be over, "have a good—"

"Hold on a minute, honey." She pushed the signed receipt over to me and then shoved her bags to the edge of the counter so there was nothing blocking our view of each other. When she spoke again, her voice was hushed. "I won't tell your mama that you and Theo have a thing going on. I know she can be difficult."

My shoulders sagged in relief. I didn't even bother denying it; Mrs. Wilson had always been kind to me and cordial—but distant—to my mother. I trusted her. "Thank you. She already suspects, and she's not happy about it."

"Well, I was about to say," she continued, and something about her tone raised my hackles again. "It's gotten around that he punched the Redding kid for hitting on you."

"That's not really what happened. Vince was being a jerk," I said defensively.

Mrs. Wilson made a gesture as if she were swatting away a fly. "Oh, I don't doubt that. I've never cared much for him. But then some other kids saw you and Theo leaving together, and, well, you know how rumors get going."

Theo and I had arrived and left hundreds of places together hundreds of times, and until recently, it didn't mean a thing. Was I the literal last person to pick up on the fact that something had shifted between us?

"It's been all anyone can talk about at our small business meetings," she continued. "That, and the Reddings raising your rent. That's how your mama caught wind of it, I'm sure."

"I'm sure," I said hollowly.

"All I'm saying is, be careful if you want to keep it under wraps." Mrs. Wilson grabbed her shopping bags. "Those meetings are better than a reality show, I swear."

I laughed because I didn't know what to say, and Mrs. Wilson gave me a wave over her shoulder as she strode out the door. I put her receipt away and then looked at the clock, which showed that we only had ten minutes until closing time.

I doubted there would be any more customers, so I went ahead and pulled the cash drawer from the register. "Theo," I called as I headed for the back of the store.

"Yeah."

"Where are you?"

"Right here."

I came around the corner and found him slouched against the wall by the men's dress shoes, scrolling on his phone. "Did you clean the bathroom?"

"Yep. It's all done. You could eat off the floor in there." He looked up with an expression that was equal parts mischievous and sultry. "Go count your drawer. I wanna get you out of here."

"In a minute," I said curtly. The heat slid off his face like melted butter. "Mrs. Wilson was just in here—"

"I know," he groaned. "She talks so loud."

With the cash drawer propped under one arm, I planted the opposite fist on my hip as I glared down at him. "So did you hear her saying that the whole town knows we're together?"

"I heard her say there are rumors. Not the same thing."

"It might as well be the same thing, as far as my mom's concerned." Frustrated, I stalked past him and headed into the backroom. Theo's footsteps sounded behind me, and by the time I was plunking my drawer down on a table in the office, he was in the doorway.

"Sass."

I gathered the day's credit card receipts and began stacking them, making sure that they lay flat and faced the same way.

"Nina," Theo said, and then he was there, gently but firmly taking the receipts out of my hand. He put them down carefully before returning his attention to me. "I've been doing my best to keep things under wraps, like you wanted. But I don't really get why it has to be this big secret."

"Are you joking?" I snapped. "Have you *met* my mother?"

He sighed. "Look. I get that you and your mom have issues. And she pisses me off plenty, too. But she's not a movie villain, Nina. She's your mom."

"Easy for you to say," I muttered bitterly. "Your mom is proud of everything you do. All mine ever talks about is how I can change to become the dream daughter she never had."

Theo put his hands on my shoulders, leveling with me. "I'm not saying she's not flawed, okay? But what if we sat her down—Frank too—and we explained that our feelings are real, that this is a long-term thing, and we're not just hooking up or messing around. Would that help?"

I doubted he would be defending my mom if I told him all the terrible things she had said about him—how he would never be successful, how being with him would ruin my life—but I didn't have it in me.

Still, there was no way we could go ahead with this plan—if Theo and I went to my parents and used phrases like "our feelings are real" and "long-term" to describe our relationship, I was pretty sure that I would never be allowed out of the house again.

"Let me think about it," I told him. I slid my arms around his waist and leaned into him. And then, as penance for lying, I offered up a nugget of truth: "I think it's kind of fun to sneak around, anyway."

"It is," Theo agreed, stroking along the waistband of my jean shorts, "but not if it's stressing you out."

I hummed in acknowledgement, if not agreement, and let him sway me back and forth. "I think we've done a good job of being sneaky," I mused aloud after a minute. "Mrs. Wilson said the rumors started when we left that party together. Which I thought was weird—it's not like we haven't left places together before."

"Well," he sighed, "maybe I wasn't so pathetically obvious until now."

I pulled back. "Obvious?"

His eyebrows hiked up his forehead, and he looked almost as surprised as I felt. Uncertainty—so out of place on him—marred his features. "About being in love with you?"

My breath caught in my throat, completely caught off guard by that particular string of words. "What? You're in love with me?"

Theo ducked his chin to his chest, looking down at me. Before he got his yearly buzzcut, there would have been a lock of hair falling over his left eye; now, nothing. I wished, not for the first time, for his longer hair. I had never had the opportunity to run my fingers through it—except when I was fourteen and checked him for lice when he kept scratching his head, but that ceased to be a pleasant experience when one of them got lodged under my fingernail.

"Nina," he sighed. "You're ridiculous."

I let go of him and crossed my arms. "How?"

His smirk came out, just teasing the edges of his lips. "Didn't I say 'love you so much' the other day?"

"You've always said that."

"And I literally told you that you're the other half of my heart. What did you think that meant, exactly?"

"I don't know." I gnawed on my lower lip. I heard the air kick on, a cold blast washing over us. "My mind didn't really go there."

"Clearly," he said, sounding amused now. He reached out and gently pried my arms apart. "Come here, honey."

The endearment was new, but I spared it only a passing thought as I fell back into his familiar embrace. His hand curled around the back of my head, pressing it into his chest, and I hooked my fingers through the belt loops of his jeans.

I had always thought of falling in love as being some inevitable, but distant, part of my life. There were girls in my class who swore they'd marry their boyfriends right after graduation. A few already wore rings on their left hands. I figured they'd just happened to find their love young and that someday I'd understand that big, sweeping feeling that makes somebody know for certain who they want to spend their life with.

But that day, at seventeen, standing in Theo's arms in the middle of our parents' office, I realized the truth: I had never fallen because there was nowhere to fall. There was only the same steady ground I'd always stood on.

He had always been there, and he had always been mine.

I had always been his.

"I love you," I said on an exhale, my breath rippling his t-shirt. "I'm so dumb. I love you."

Theo held me tighter, ducked his head, laughed quietly into my neck. "I love you, Nina," he murmured.

"Love you so much?" I felt a little jolt—the good kind—as I used our childhood refrain in this new way.

He dropped a kiss just below my ear. "Love you so much."

Chapter Twenty-Five

Now

Working alongside Sage instead of Theo is strange, as if I've both traveled back in time and shifted into an alternate universe. But at home—at *his* home; I need to stop thinking of it as mine—we fall into an easy routine. He cooks; I wash the dishes. He mows the lawn; I water his ferns and hang potted impatiens on the front porch. He reads biographies in his wicker armchair while I recline in my hammock, munching on Red Vines and enjoying the fact that my mother has forgotten to cancel my phone service.

I know better than to get comfortable here. I know that at some point, I'm going to have to gather up my things and move along—out of his house, probably out of Amity. Out into the world, where I'll forge a path that wasn't paved for me by a man.

But today, after two weeks of working at the Wilsons', I've received my first paycheck. It came out to five hundred eleven dollars after taxes, and by depositing it, my bank account has gained a comma.

It's not nearly enough for me to get out of Theo's guest room. Even so, seeing that money hit feels ten times better than anything Daniel ever gave me to "keep myself entertained."

I'm buzzing around the front porch, cheerfully spraying water over my new flowers, when Theo calls. I balance the phone between my shoulder and ear and greet him with, "Guess what?"

"What?"

I grin at the way he says it, matching my enthusiasm. "I got paid today."

Theo whistles. "Look at you, moneybags!"

"Scoop Shack is still in business, right? Do you want to go after dinner? I'll even buy."

"We can," he says, "but I also told Quinton I'd go to the bar with him tonight."

My entire body stills. The hose is arcing water into the middle of the porch, nowhere near any plants. "Oh. Yeah, of course," I say, feeling stupid. Of course he has things to do besides hang around with me every night. He has lasting friendships, a business, a family. It's not his fault that I don't. "I might just go on my own, then. It's stupid humid today."

"Well, you can come with us," Theo says, as if I should have already known that. "I'll tell him to bring Sage."

Sage and I have been getting along at work, and I've filled her in on the basics of what brought me back to Amity. It isn't like with Theo, where we've had to navigate our cataclysmic ending and untangle layers upon layers of complicated feelings—work that isn't even close to done, and that fills me with anxiety whenever I dwell on it too much.

True female friendship, when you have it, is simple and constant: you can drift apart and come back together, and nothing will have changed in the meantime. I had forgotten what it was like.

Quinton is a different story.

"No, he still hates me," I respond. "I'll stay ho—here."

Theo sighs. "He doesn't hate you."

"I doubt he wants me around."

"What if I want you around?"

I turn the faucet off and begin coiling up the hose. "You don't have to sound so desperate."

His soft laugh fills my ear. "I'll beg if you want."

A flame ignites in my chest. My mouth dries out, and I stumble through a response. "I—yeah. Okay. I'll get dressed."

"Sounds good," Theo says, so damn *smug*, and the line goes dead.

***

Amity has a handful of bars, but the most popular one is called The Hutch. When Theo and I pull into the parking lot, it's already half-full, and I recognize Sage's car a few spots down from us. My heart rate is a little elevated, my body humming with anxiety, neither of which are helped by the fact that Theo eyes me appreciatively when I fall into step beside him.

"You look nice."

I glance down at my cutoff shorts and cropped tank. The memory of Daniel calling me white trash flits briefly through my mind before I shove it away. Initially, I had put on linen pants and a blouse; then I looked in the mirror and realized that I would get laughed out of The Hutch, or at least stared at, if I showed up like that. So I put on one of my new outfits instead, knowing that even if I wasn't used to showing midriff or most of my legs anymore, at least nobody would think twice about it.

Except Theo. He appears to have been thinking about it, continuously, for our entire walk across the parking lot.

"Thanks," I manage, slipping past him when he holds the door open for me, and I swear I can feel him looking at my ass.

We find Sage and Quinton at a high-top near the bar. The last time the four of us were together, we were sneaking cheap beer down by the pond; tonight, the waitress who takes our order doesn't even bother to card us. After she leaves, the three of them complain that everything on the menu has recently gone up by two dollars.

"You could never find alcohol this cheap in New York," I tell them.

Quinton's face immediately clouds over, Sage looks away, and Theo winces. I'm not exactly sure why this doesn't go over well—at this point, Sage and Theo are well aware of where I've been, and I assume one of them has relayed the details to Quinton. I didn't realize it was a taboo topic.

"I always wanted to go there," Sage says, leaning into it. "I've still never been."

"I liked it," I say, which is true enough. There was plenty to do, plenty to see. I needed a place like that to stay busy while I waited around for the pockets of time Daniel occasionally made for me. There were experiences I'd had in New York that could never be replicated in a place like Amity—experiences like being surrounded by people but feeling completely alone. "But it is expensive."

Quinton settles back in his chair, crossing his arms over his chest. He's not in uniform today. "What did you do up there?" he asks, and I can tell that he already knows the answer.

I trace my fingertip along a stain on the oak table. "I worked retail in Raleigh, but I couldn't find a job in New York."

He cocks a brow, unimpressed. "Really? Nothing?"

"I tried for a while," I say. "But I couldn't find anything, and my boyfriend at the time didn't—"

"Nina." Theo leans forward, shaking his head at me before directing a glare at Quinton. "You don't have to talk about it."

"Well, wait," Quinton says, still in that practiced, falsely congenial voice. "I'm curious. Your boyfriend...who became your fiancé, right? He had money, so you didn't have to work? Lucky break."

"Quinton, you promised you'd behave," Sage admonishes him.

"I'm sorry," he says, but he doesn't sound like it. Not at all. He turns his hard eyes on me, dropping the nice-guy act. "I just find this whole thing pretty damn convenient. You were shacked up in New York City with a rich guy, zero responsibilities, and all of a sudden you're back in Amity working for the Wilsons?" He pauses, drumming his fingers on the table. We sit in thick silence. "That doesn't make sense to me."

Beside me, Theo's shoulders are drawn taut, his jaw clenched tight. Half of me is grateful for his restraint; the other half wishes he would jump in.

"It didn't work out," I say vaguely. "I had nowhere else to go."

"Weren't you back here to plan the wedding?" he shoots back. "Sounds like it was working out fine until you ran into Theo and found out he's rich now, too."

My cheeks flame hot—with anger, with embarrassment, with frustration at being so wildly misunderstood. Sage covers her mouth with her hand, and it's the last straw for Theo.

"Quinton," he barks. "Shut the fuck up."

Ignoring both of them, Quinton zeroes in on me. When I broke up with Daniel, he was so angry. Seething. The look Quinton is leveling at me now... it's pure, cold hate. "Do you know what you did to him?" he asks, jerking his thumb toward his best friend, then his wife. "To her, too? Theo's family had to get a lawyer. Sage had no idea what was going on."

"I was a teenager." My voice rises steadily, each word louder than the last. "My parents took me to Raleigh. They took my phone. I couldn't do anything about it."

"You've been an adult for a long time," he shoots back, unmoved. "And still, you only came back once you found a new meal ticket."

"Enough!" Theo thunders in a tone that I have never, ever heard come out of his mouth. Sage, Quinton, and I stare at him in silent shock. "What the fuck is wrong with you?"

Over his shoulder, I can see the waitress heading toward us with a full tray. In a split second, I make the decision that I'm not going to be here when she arrives. I push my chair back, grab my purse, and ignore the waitress's startled expression when I brush past her. I fully expect to hear footsteps behind me; when I get all the way to the front door and haven't heard Theo's voice, I turn back around.

He's still at the table. I can only see the back of his baseball cap from here, but he's leaning across the table toward Quinton, jabbing the air with a finger. Quinton puts his hands up in surrender while Sage looks chastened.

I don't need defending.

I don't need forced apologies.

I turn my back on them and walk out the door.

Chapter Twenty-Six

Now

A quarter mile down the road, I hear the rumble of a vehicle approaching. I keep my arms crossed tightly over my chest, glaring into the space ahead of me as I tromp through overgrown grass in my flip-flops.

Beside me, Theo's truck slows to match my pace. The window rolls down.

"Leave me alone," I snap before he can say anything.

He leans across the passenger seat to talk to me. "Get in here."

"No."

"You're going to walk four miles home?"

I move a little quicker, making the soles of my shoes slap louder. "I don't have a home."

He doesn't correct me. The pit in my stomach deepens.

But he doesn't leave me, either. We continue down the road together, Theo rolling along at three miles an hour, me maintaining my unaffected bitch facade. The grass is making my shins itch, and my mood sours further at the realization that I'll be covered in bug bites in the morning.

Another pickup passes Theo in the opposite direction, and I glance behind me when an SUV comes up behind us. The lady behind the wheel rides his bumper for a few seconds before pulling around him and speeding away with her middle finger in the air.

"Laura Ellington just flipped me off," Theo says, sounding shocked.

I don't want to engage, but I can't help myself. "Who the hell is Laura Ellington?"

"She's married to Mitch Ellington."

Curiosity gets the better of me, and I look over at him. "From high school? The preacher's kid?"

"Yeah," he confirms, one wrist slung lazily over the wheel, the muscles of his arm on full display. In his entire life—at least during those times it intersected with mine—I don't believe Theo has put the slightest effort into looking a certain way. It's infuriating how casually handsome he manages to look all the time. "Well, actually, Mitch is the preacher now. He took over the church from his dad."

"You just got flipped off by a *preacher's wife*?"

The sound of an engine approaches us once again. Theo glances in the rearview mirror and flips his turn signal on. He pulls onto the shoulder of the road, coming to a halt beside me. I take the opportunity to step out of the grass and onto the asphalt.

"Please get in here," he says, sounding tired.

I'm tired, too—of walking, of arguing, of pulling away from him when every instinct I have screams at me to draw closer.

"Only to save you from the embarrassment of stalking me in a truck with your name on it," I say as I climb inside.

Ignoring me, Theo pulls out behind the car that just passed us. As soon as we're in that confined space together, all conversation of Mitch and his wife stops, and tension grows as our short-lived time at The Hutch comes back to the forefront.

"Quinton was way out of line," Theo says finally. "I told him that."

With my arms crossed, I shrug my shoulders. "It doesn't matter. You can stop pretending."

"Pretending what?"

"That you don't agree with him," I tell the dashboard.

"What?" he asks, incredulous. "What are you even—"

"'Oh, so you *both* found rich guys,'" I quote. This seems to only confuse him more, so I elaborate. "That's what you said about me and my mom. Gosh, I *wonder* where Quinton got the idea that I'm a gold digger."

"Nina." Theo puts a hand out as if to touch my thigh. I scoot away, pressing myself against the passenger door, and he lets it fall back into his own lap. "That is absolutely not what I think of you."

I snort. If my mother were here, she would call the noise *very unladylike*. "Whatever."

We pull up to a stop sign, and Theo turns left—the opposite direction of his house. It takes a few miles and a couple more turns for me to figure out where we're headed. I know that I could ask him to take me home, and he would; still, I stay quiet, secure in the knowledge that even if I'm not happy with Theo, I will always be safe with him.

Outside of town, we rumble down the gravel road toward Train Bridge. I wait for memories to assault me—there were lots of things we did out here, all by ourselves, after that first kiss—but I find that there aren't many parallels between then and now. For one, it's still broad daylight; for another, we're tense, not buoyant from the anticipation of having the time and space to explore each other's bodies.

We park at the bottom of the hill, the entrance to the bridge just visible above us. I watch Theo to see if he's going to get out, and he doesn't. He leans back in his seat, knees spread beneath the steering wheel. I slip my feet out of my sandals and bring my legs up to sit crisscross, and I wait for whatever it is he has to say.

"Quinton got over being mad at me a long time ago," he offers up eventually. "He's not over being mad at you yet."

"Why would he be mad at either of us?"

"Same reason you and I spent the last ten years upset with each other, I think."

I prop my elbows on my knees, my chin in my palms, and wait for further explanation.

"I really withdrew when I left for college. For four years, I barely came home, and I barely talked to anyone here, including Quinton. I didn't want to—" He lets out a breath. "I didn't want anything to do with Amity if you weren't here."

Theo pauses, letting that sit between us for a second. "Then Dad and I started the business, and it was time to make peace. I called Quinton the night I moved back, acting like everything was normal, and he lit into me. We had it out and patched things up. I finally talked to Sage, tried to fill in the blanks for her, so she got some closure. I was the best man in their wedding. It was all good. And then..."

"And then I showed up," I finish for him.

"You haven't done anything wrong."

I think about what Sage told me the other day—how confused she was after I left, how lonely after our other friends followed. How she and Quinton fell in love over a shared feeling of abandonment, while I avoided them all.

"I don't know if that's true."

From beneath his baseball cap, Theo watches me. "It's true, Sass. He doesn't know you like I do."

"Well," I say, "nobody does."

He smiles at that, seeming a bit surprised, and reaches over the console toward me. With gentle fingers around my wrist, he pulls my left hand away from my face. "Do you want to know what I think?"

"Yes."

Theo strokes his thumb over my knuckles, and I relax. My eyes want to drift shut; I'm tempted to sit here and let his touch smooth away everything that is unsettled inside of me. But his intense gaze keeps me anchored from under the bill of his hat, and I wait, a bit too eager for his validation.

"I understand why you were with Daniel," he tells me, his words soft. "I know I gave you shit about it, but I get it now, Sass. You grew up being told you were too much. You had your world ripped out from under you right before you became an adult."

He glances over, seeming to want permission to keep going, and I nod. So far, it all rings true.

"Daniel gave you stability. Simplicity. Maybe not delirious happiness, but I understand what you were saying before—that's not always the point." Theo glances down at our joined hands, squeezing mine once. "I should have known that."

A shift in his tone tells me that we're not just talking about me anymore. I shift in my seat, tucking my legs up beneath me and leaning toward him. "Who were you with?"

"Nobody that mattered. A couple of girls in college." He rolls his lips, averts his eyes. "One night stands here and there."

Hypocritical as it is—after all, I was *engaged* to somebody else not even a month ago—jealously burns in my chest. I glance up at the bridge, thinking again about the first time he kissed me. Has he ever brought anybody else out here? To the bridge, or any of the other backroads where we used to be alone together?

"Anybody I know?" I ask with forced lightness.

He glares at me as if it's a ridiculous question. "Of course not."

"Well, I don't know." I shrug. "It *has* been ten years."

Theo stares at me, and I stare back, daring him to blink first. His right hand still has a loose grip on mine; the left touches his door handle, as if he's thinking about walking away.

"Nina, I'm going to tell you something," he says finally. "Several things, actually. And I don't want you to freak out. I don't want you to run off and make me pick you up off the side of the road again. I expect nothing from you, honey. Okay?"

My battered heart skips a beat at that old endearment, then bangs against my ribcage when my imagination begins to run wild. I'm completely lost, clueless as to what he's about to say. "Alright."

Theo stares out the windshield for a moment, jaw working, searching for a beginning. "After you, I didn't date again until junior year of college. We were together for seven months and then she dumped me because I wouldn't bring her home to meet my family. She thought I was cheating on her. I wasn't," he clarifies, as if I'd ever think him capable of such a thing. "Amity is where *we* grew up together. It's where *we* fell in love the first time. I couldn't imagine bringing someone else to my parents' house, or to The Hutch, or to this fucking bridge."

The first time. My brain snags on those words, even though they seem to be beside the point. Is he implying that there will be another time for us to fall in love?

I look down at our hands, where he now grips mine with both of his.

Is that time already here?

"Hey."

I startle from my thoughts, looking up at him again. "What?"

He looks me in the eye, his voice serious and firm. "I have never brought another woman home. I've never introduced anyone to my parents. Yeah, once in a while, if I'd been drinking in Raleigh or Chapel Hill, or if I was on vacation, I'd hook up to scratch the itch. But it was always at her place or a hotel room—"

"I don't want to hear about where you fucked your endless parade of women," I interject harshly.

Theo's smirk makes a quick appearance. It ghosts over his face for a split second, disappearing just as quickly. "It wasn't an endless parade, Sass, my god. What I'm trying to say is that...I wanted to protect my memories of you." Hesitation slows his next words. "And any we might make in the future."

"What do you mean?" I ask, clipped, as my pulse picks up, the walls of every vein thrumming in time with my heart.

He adjusts in his seat again, turning fully toward me so that we're both leaning over the console. Our faces are close—either of us could easily close the gap between us. But I can tell we're getting to this big admission that I shouldn't freak out about, so I wait, watching him and barely daring to breathe.

"Starting the company was my idea," he tells me. "I'm glad my parents decided to go in on it. They're so proud to have a family business again. *I'm* proud. It's worked out really well for everyone, but in the beginning...it wasn't about that. It was just about you."

The pounding in my body stops, replaced with an eerie stillness.

"Me?" I whisper.

"You."

I shake my head, even as I glance at the star dotting the *i* on his polo. *Think about it*, he told me that day on the patio. *Think.* "I don't understand."

"I thought that if I ever found you and I had something to show for myself—that I could give you that stability we didn't have with Walk a Mile, provide for you like Kelly said I'd never be able to—you might give me another shot."

Theo—calm, confident, unflappable Theo—sounds vulnerable, even fragile when he tells me this, and then terrified as he waits for my reaction.

It's a lot to absorb, I'll give him that. But more than anything else, what I'm hearing is that he *understands*. He understands how the wounds of my childhood, of being the disappointing daughter and watching everything I knew dissolve in a matter of days, led me to a life that was just good enough. I didn't set out to be rich; I set out to be secure. I didn't want to replicate the love I shared with him; I looked for a weaker connection that wouldn't be so devastating to sever.

Theo sees me.

He always has.

Gently, I extract my hand from his, only to reach up and press my palm to his cheek. He inhales sharply at my touch—eyes falling closed, lashes resting on his cheekbones, close enough to count.

The bill of his cap bumps me between the eyes. I should take that as a sign not to lean in any further, and I do; then he plucks it off his head and tosses it into the backseat, and I let out a little sigh of defeat as our foreheads join.

"Thank you," I whisper, hoping he can hear all the meaning wrapped up in that single breath.

He nods, and with the movement, our lips brush. It's just the slightest touch, but it's enough for electricity to spark, and I'm not prepared for the lightning that zings down my spine and between my thighs. My mouth opens on a small gasp.

"What?" Theo asks. "What's wrong?"

"I—I can't." I start to draw away, but he stops me with a callused hand behind my neck. "I need to figure out what the fuck I'm doing with my life, Theo. I can't—"

"Okay," he says, immediately backing off. "Alright. I get it."

"Are you sure?"

Unbidden, I remember a time just a few months ago when I refused sex with Daniel because I had a cold. He hadn't pushed, but he had clearly been upset, ignoring me for the rest of the night and most of the next day.

But when I search Theo's face for disappointment, for anger, I don't see any. He just nods, moving his hand from my neck to my shoulder and stroking down my arm. "Of course, Sass. I want you to get what you need, even if that isn't me."

I want to tell him that he has it all wrong. I *do* need him—that's the problem. If I kiss him right now, there is a ninety-nine percent chance that I will fall in love with him all over again. I will go back to that big, beautiful house—*oh my god, did he build the house for me, too?*—and completely forget about the concept of standing on my own two feet.

Or my biggest fear of all—something will go wrong, and I'll lose him all over again.

I won't do it.

"Is there something else you need right now?" Theo asks in a pitch that's a couple notches below his normal. I follow his eyes into my lap, where I'm horrified to find that I've been squeezing my thighs together.

"No." I rush to uncross my legs, trying to ignore the fact that my underwear is damp and my cheeks are hot. "No, I'm good. We can just go."

Ever respectful of my *boundaries*—in my head, I hear the word in his voice, sarcastic lilt included—he nods and puts the truck in reverse, and we begin backing down the gravel road.

My regret is almost instant.

"Wait."

He slams on the brakes, and for two seconds that feel like two years, we stare at each other in the charged stillness.

Despite all the reasons I shouldn't, I'm the one who crosses the line.

Up on my knees, I maneuver myself over the console and into Theo's lap. His pupils dilate, his hands instinctively coming up to my hips as I straddle him. I'm hesitant to put my hands on him, but with the two of us crammed into the driver's seat, it's hard to spread my arms out. I let my fingertips glide up his chest.

"You can't kiss me," I tell him. "This can't be romantic."

"I won't kiss you."

I narrow my eyes at him. "And will it be romantic?"

"No strings attached, Nina." He strokes his thumbs along the bare skin at my waist. "I promise."

He still hasn't answered the question, but with this painful throbbing between my legs, *no strings attached* is good enough for me. I fold my fingers beneath the collar of his polo and hold on as I shift my body so that my left knee is between his thighs, my right foot on the floor. I rock my hips once, barely holding back a groan at how good it feels. "I just—I need—"

My head falls forward, and I watch my lower body roll down against his leg. I do it again, my mouth popping open at that first mounting of pressure. With the full knowledge that I'm not going to stop until I'm in pieces, I look up at Theo, only to find that he's already looking at me. His gaze skates over my face, lingering on my nose and the place where my birthmark should be. Quickly, I hide my face in his shoulder.

"You know what you need," Theo husks, seeming not to notice my sudden self-consciousness—likely because he doesn't share it. This isn't like when he was eighteen and figuring things out alongside me; his words are commanding in my ear, his hands firm on my hips as he guides me into a slow grind against his thigh. "My Nina knows what she wants, and she takes it."

I'm not sure that's true. Twenty-seven years in, and there isn't much evidence to back up his claim. What do I have that's truly mine? Some cheap clothes? Abandonment issues? Estranged family?

"Take it, honey," he murmurs, and his lips ghost over the crown of my head. "Use me. I'm all yours."

Theo.

He didn't even hear my question, but he's still managed to answer it.

I'm all yours.

I press my forehead harder against him, clutching at his shoulders. The seam of my shorts rubs my clit at just the right angle, and I let out a weak, "Oh."

Quicker and quicker, my body moves over his; tighter and tighter, the pressure coils inside of me. Every time I rock forward, his erection bumps my thigh, covered but still evident through his jeans. Sensual memories come storming through my consciousness, and I dig my fingers harder into his shoulders, fighting the temptation to reach for his zipper.

"Yes." Both of Theo's hands are on my ass now, squeezing, encouraging me as I lose all semblance of control. "Yes, Nina."

His permission is enough for me to let go, to let myself unravel right there in his arms. He holds me through it, murmuring in my ear all the while. When my breathing evens out and the world stops spinning, I relax into him, thinking I might stay there for a minute.

But he doesn't let me. He only holds on long enough to gently deposit me back in the passenger seat. I sit there, blinking as the world rights itself. Theo adjusts his pants, takes a deep breath, and sends me a small smile. "You still want Scoop Shack?"

It takes me a beat to catch up. "Yeah," I manage, an odd combination of satisfied and dejected. "Let's go."

Chapter Twenty-Seven

Then

"So you really didn't like my idea of being honest with your parents, huh?"

I crumpled up the wrappers from my burger and fries and tossed them into the grease-stained brown sack between us. Our legs dangled off the tailgate of his truck, swinging over the ground. Two hours ago, we were in the office exchanging admissions of love; now we were parked out on one of the dirt roads near Train Bridge with only the moon and stars to light our way. "I said I'd think about it."

"But you really wanted to say no," he rebutted conversationally, putting his trash in with mine before tossing the bag over his shoulder. It landed in the hole of the spare tire that sat in the bed of his truck. "Which is fine. They're your folks; we'll handle it the way you want to."

"Thanks," I said, even as my stomach twisted uncomfortably. With Mom already suspecting that something was going on and rumors flying around town, keeping it a secret and sneaking around was only going to work for so long. I didn't know what else to do, though. For now, this was the way it would have to be. "I know you think I'm being overdramatic, but—"

"Nah, Sass," he sighed. "I know Kelly. You're right—she would probably make our lives hell."

I leaned my head on his shoulder, and he put his arm around my waist. Silence fell between us, the comfortable kind. For several minutes we were alone with the sound of the crickets. I could have fallen asleep there, his thumb idly stroking my hip, but he pulled me out of my dazed state with, "I'm ready to tell you about UNC."

It took me a moment to catch on to what he was saying. Enough had happened lately that the mysterious reason for his deferred acceptance to UNC hadn't been on my mind. Once my brain caught up, I straightened, peering at his face in the moonlight. "Okay. Sure."

Theo let out a breath. "I told my parents that I wanted to take a year to work in the store and save up money," he said, "but the real reason I deferred was that I was hoping that—I hoped that you would come with me."

I blinked at him. "I don't have the grades to get into UNC."

"It wouldn't have had to be UNC. There are tons of schools around there. Or, you know, if you didn't want to go to school, you could have found a job or—"

"Theo, I don't know what I'm going to do after high school. I haven't decided."

"I know." He clasped his fingers together behind his neck, craned his head back, looked at the sky. I could see the silhouette of his throat bobbing as he swallowed. "I know. Sorry. I was being stupid."

"No," I said quickly, touching his knee, "I didn't mean—"

Theo interrupted me, his voice slightly raised, tone firm: "It was selfish, I guess, but I didn't care. I couldn't be without you."

The words hung in the muggy air between us.

I didn't know what to say, but there was no need to respond; Theo plowed ahead, the words tumbling from his mouth as if they'd been trying to get out for some time: "Every time I thought about going away and leaving you here, my chest would hurt just like it did when we were kids and you were in the hospital. The day came to put down the deposit for the fall semester, and I just filled out the form to defer instead. I hoped that with a year to work with, I could make something happen with you, and by the time you finished high school we'd be ready to make a plan together."

I made a conscious effort to close my gaping mouth, flabbergasted that while Theo and I were going about our normal lives at the store and school, he was making these life-altering decisions based on a *hope* that he and I might become something more, and I was completely oblivious.

"You wouldn't even be two hours away," I said. "You could have come back to see me all the time."

But Theo shook his head emphatically. "I couldn't do it, Nina. I just couldn't."

And even before the words were fully out, I was already thinking about how devastating it would have been for him to leave me behind. Even when I never quite understood why he chose not to go, there was always that undercurrent of relief that he had. That he was still here, with me, where he had always been.

"Okay," I told him. "I get it."

He raised his eyebrows. "Do you?"

"Yeah. I think so." I twisted my fingers together in my lap. "I don't remember my life without you, Theo. I can't even imagine what it would have been like not to have you here."

"Then don't. I'm not going anywhere without you."

I looked out toward the pitch black of the woods and let myself imagine what it would actually be like to leave here together. I might go to college, or I might not. I could find a retail job. Maybe even management—I had all the skills. And at the end of the day, instead of going home to criticism and tension and emotional distance, it would be Theo waiting for me.

I liked this idea. I liked it a lot.

"Maybe I will go with you," I said.

Even in the dark, Theo's grin couldn't be missed. "Really?"

I found myself grinning back. "Yeah."

Just a touch too abruptly, he grabbed my wrists and tugged me toward him. I pitched forward, giggling and catching myself with a hand on the tailgate. Theo didn't seem to notice as he hauled me up and over his lap, his arms tight around me, holding me close.

"Too bad I won't be eighteen until November," I said. "We could have taken off right now."

Theo slid his thumb down the side of my neck. I knew it was sweaty beneath my ponytail, but he kept his hand there, so he must not have noticed or cared. "You'd drop out of high school?"

I rested my chin on his shoulder, my hands splayed over his back, and stared at that spare tire bolted down in the truck bed. "I never really thought about it before now, but if that would get me out of here faster, then yeah. Maybe."

"If we left tonight," he said, "where would we go?"

I knew we weren't really going anywhere. I was still underage, first of all, and we didn't have any supplies or money on us. I knew that in less than two hours, Theo would be dropping me off at my parents' house just before curfew. We'd exchange a few texts before falling asleep in our own beds.

But it was fun to pretend.

"Up north," I said. I'd never had any particular desire to travel, to see new places, but something about the idea of driving off into the night with Theo, being able to choose whatever road we wanted, had my mind churning excitedly. "To a city. New York or Philadelphia or someplace."

Theo barked out a laugh. "Philadelphia?"

"What?" I pushed myself up so that I was sitting back on his thighs. "I've never been anywhere bigger than Charlotte, and Sage said Philadelphia was cool."

"Sage liked Philadelphia? With the Liberty Bell and shit?"

"They weren't doing that kind of stuff. She was there with her mom and sister to see a concert."

His hands grazed my thighs. It was an innocent touch—barely a touch at all—but heat sparked in my belly nonetheless. "Well, what about us? What would we do there?"

"Spend a few days looking around and exploring. Then move on. Go see someplace else."

"Would we ever come back?"

"Of course. It would just be for the summer, and then we'd back in time for you to go ahead and start college this year." I liked the idea that ultimately, we'd come back to our home base—the same one, of course.

"What would you do?"

"Get a job," I said. "Earn money for us."

"And let me live off you like a bum?" he asked. "Hell, you'd be better off staying here."

I shook my head at him. "You could live off me for a while, yeah, but when you finished school, we could switch places," I said. "I could do something for me. Go to school, or—or start a business, maybe."

"Huh," he said, as if he were really considering it. As if this weren't just an elaborate fantasy that would fade like a dream by morning. "That doesn't sound too bad."

"Yeah." Reality set in, and I felt my shoulders sag. "But..."

Theo read my mind. "Yeah. I know." He ducked his head and pressed his lips just above my collarbone. I closed my eyes, savoring it. "We'll get there, Sass."

My legs and butt were going numb from the position that we were in. I went to move away, but Theo slipped his hands past the hem of my shirt to hold my waist. His mouth ghosted up my neck, dropping tiny kisses along the way, and over the shell of my ear. With my hand curled over his head, I let out a hum of satisfaction that turned into a loud gasp when he abruptly sucked my earlobe into his mouth.

"What?" he murmured, his voice giving off warm vibrations against my skin. "You don't like that?"

"No, I do."

He did it again, and I found myself bucking in his lap. The movement put me right over where he was hard. By that point, we'd done plenty of making out and fooling around; I'd felt him there before. Usually I backed off, not ready to explore that yet.

That night, I wasn't in the mood to retreat from Theo. We might not have been able to start a new life together yet, but we did have this little patch of backroad all to ourselves, and I was feeling daring.

"Oh, fuck," Theo muttered. He gripped my hips hard enough to leave fingerprint-shaped bruises, guiding me back and forth over him. "Fuck, that feels good, Nina."

It *did* feel good, and even though I didn't quite understand the mechanics of why, I had figured out how to build the oddly pleasant pressure inside of me.

I pressed closer. Our lips crashed together. Theo didn't bother to go through the motions of being gentle; he gripped me everywhere, mouth open, tongue ravenous, and I gave as good as I got.

It might have been minutes or it might have been hours by the time Theo drew back for a shaky breath and murmured, "You want a blanket?"

Dazed and hot all over, I blinked at him. "What?"

He gestured behind him at the bed of the truck. "To lay down on?"

"Oh." I licked my lips and slid my fingers through my hair, freeing the black scrunchie from my ruined ponytail and tossing it aside. "Yeah. Sure."

Theo disappeared around the side of the truck. I listened as he opened the door and shuffled around in the backseat for a minute. The door slammed shut, and he reemerged with a comforter in his arms.

"It's clean," he told me as he climbed up on the tailgate and spread out the blanket. "I put it in there just in case."

I started to tease him about planning for a night of rolling around with me in the bed of his truck, but the words died in my throat when he tossed something down between us. Even in the dark, I could see what it was.

Are we really doing this? I thought as I stared at the foil packet, and then Theo was laying back on the blanket, taking me with him, sliding his hands down my back and over my butt, and it appeared that the answer was a resounding *yes*.

Our shoes and shirts went first. We laughed in a fit of exhilarated joy when Theo tried to cast my bra aside and instead dropped it on his face, one cup covering his left eye like a pirate.

"Ahoy," I managed through my laughter. Theo plucked the bra off his face and whacked me with it.

Hands slipped lower. Our voices faded out, replaced by sighs and gasps and heavy breathing. The last bits of clothes between us were shed, and Theo reached for the condom he'd retrieved earlier.

I didn't know where to look while he put it on, so I lay on my back and counted the stars in the sky. I got to thirty-six, and then he was moving over me, balancing with his elbows on either side of my head, and suddenly there were no more stars. Only him.

"It's your first time, right?" he asked quietly.

I nodded. Relief flitted across his face.

"Me too." Theo began to rub my shoulders, and I realized that they were bunched up around my neck. He brushed my nose with his and spoke against my mouth: "It's just me, Nina."

I met his gaze, the same one I'd been looking into my entire life, and the tightly coiled tension in my body begin to ebb. *It's just me.* Just Theo, my constant. My rock. The one person in this world who would never, ever hurt me.

I exhaled and nodded. "I know."

"Are you ready?" he asked.

With one more deep breath for good measure, I wrapped my arms around him, pressing my palms to the warm skin of his back and pulling his body ever closer. "Ready."

Chapter Twenty-Eight

Now

When I get to work the next day, there's a police car parked in the fire lane. I'm completely aware that it belongs to Quinton—that's where he always parks when he comes by to see Sage—but I decide to be obnoxious anyway. When I walk through the front door, the bell above my head tinkling to announce my arrival, I call out, "Where's the emergency?"

A woman browsing the produce looks up, startled. From her spot behind the counter, Sage waves her off. "No emergency," she says cheerfully, and the woman goes back to her shopping.

"Maybe we should talk to the police department about not blocking the fire lane," I tell Sage, studiously ignoring Quinton, who leans against the shelves of cigarettes beside her. In my peripheral version, I can see him leveling me with an unimpressed look. "You'd think they would teach them that in cop school."

She motions for me to come closer, patiently waiting as I drag my feet across the floor. I stop in front of the counter, my arms crossed stubbornly over my chest. "Quinton wants to apologize," she says quietly, keeping it between the three of us.

I look directly at Quinton for the first time. His jaw is tight. He gives no indication of intending to speak with me. Turning back to Sage, I ask, "Are you sure?"

Sage nudges him in the side. He casts an annoyed look in her direction, but when their eyes meet, I notice that his soften almost instantly. It reminds me of the way Theo looks at me. "I'm sorry, Nina," he tells me. "I was wrong last night."

"Do you really think that, or are you just saying what Theo and Sage told you to?"

He stutters, taken aback. "Uh—"

"I don't need you to lie to me." I reach over the counter to grab an apron from one of the hooks. "It's a waste of everyone's time."

"No," he says. "That's not it. I've been worried about Theo, and—"

"Theo," I interrupt, crossing the apron strings around my front once before knotting them in the back, "is a grown man."

Take it.

Use me.

I'm all yours.

I repress a shudder and try to extinguish the memory of Theo's deep voice in my ear, egging me on as I writhed on his lap. I've relived the entire scene a million times in the past sixteen hours; meanwhile, Theo seemed completely unaffected as we went back into town, got ice cream, and headed home. He spent most of the time talking about the clients who had been difficult that day, at one point pulling up pictures on his phone and asking my opinion about their yards. The quick brush of our fingers when I took the phone from him was the last time we touched.

No strings attached, he had promised.

I wasn't expecting to feel so disappointed when he stuck to his word.

"I know," Quinton tells me, and I force myself to focus back on the conversation at hand—which has nothing to do with me dry-humping Theo. "But you weren't here. He wasn't okay after you left. I don't want to see that happen to him again."

"I wasn't exactly having the time of my life, either."

"We know that," Sage cuts in, with the tone of an impending *but*, and I realize too late that she isn't here to mediate; this conversation is two against one, with nobody on my side. "We just... I mean, do you have a plan?"

"A plan?" I repeat dumbly.

"Yeah. Like, are you back for good?" asks Quinton. He has softened toward me today, but his tone still isn't friendly. "Or just passing through?"

I look between the two of them and can't deny that they seem to be primarily concerned, not accusatory. All that concern is for Theo, and it's not like they can be faulted for that—he's been in their lives, and I haven't. Even so, there's a little throb of hurt that comes with knowing that Quinton and Theo have both become more important to Sage than I am.

"The plan," I say, "is to work here for a while, get on my feet, and figure out what's next."

"So you're not staying," Sage clarifies.

With a frustrated sigh, I shrug, throwing up my hands and letting them slap my thighs when they fall. "I really don't know. But Theo is aware of all this, okay? I don't know how to convince you guys to trust me. I'm not trying to take advantage of him. There aren't a lot of other places for me to go, but I could have figured something else out if I had to. I told him that. He insisted I stay here."

"Well, yeah," Sage says. "Of course he did. He's still in love with you."

"No." I don't mean to sound so sharp. "No, he's not."

She glances at Quinton, who hitches his thumbs in his belt and regards me coolly. "She's right."

I put my hands up, palms out, warding off their words, even as my brain presents me with a hasty slideshow of everything Theo told me last night. The company. His refusal to bring anyone home to his parents—to date seriously at all. Even things he hasn't addressed with me directly: the house, the star in his logo, the photos in his living room. It all comes together to create a picture that I refuse to look directly at.

"All we're saying," Sage continues as the blood begins to pound in my ears, "is that if you leave again, it's going to destroy him."

I don't know what to say to that. Mercifully, the radio hooked on her apron string crackles, and Judith's voice comes through the static. "Is Nina here yet?"

Sage picks up the radio. "She's right here."

"Send her to me, would you? I need help with this truck."

I've never been so thankful for an interruption. I turn on my heel, not bothering to say anything to either of them as I head to the back.

The truth I don't want to face—that I don't even want to think about—is that leaving might destroy me, too.

***

That evening, I'm already drinking a beer and eating Red Vines on the back patio when Theo gets home. He emerges from the house with two beers in hand, one for each of us, as has become our after-work custom. My heart immediately kickstarts at the sight of him, but he continues to appear alarmingly unaffected by the fact that I recently orgasmed on his thigh. When he sees my bottle already sweating on the table, he raises his eyebrows. "You got started early."

"That's because I'm pissed off."

He winces and comes to sit beside me on the wicker couch, holding out a hand. "Yeah. Quinton called."

"He gave me the most half-assed apology I've ever received in my life." I slap a Red Vine into his palm with a soft *thwack*. "Which is saying something, because you know who was literally incapable of a sincere apology?"

"Daniel?"

"Bingo." I pick up the bag and peer inside. *Damn*—it's almost empty. I'll need to buy more when I'm at work tomorrow. It's amazing how quickly these have become a staple in my diet again. "Anyway, I hope you're not offended that I refuse to take responsibility for you being a bad friend to Quinton."

"Not at all."

"Good."

Theo relaxes into the opposite corner of the couch, letting his knees fall open a little. The position immediately brings me back to last night, and I turn away, afraid of what he might see in my face. We sip on our beer and listen to the birds and cicadas. The alcohol saturates my bloodstream enough that I start to relax a bit—at least, until Theo breaks our somewhat comfortable silence with, "Did they say anything else that bothered you?"

Since it's obvious he already knows what they said, I don't bother responding.

He sighs, sounding frustrated. "You don't need to worry about me, Nina. I think you're doing the right thing by focusing on yourself right now. Whatever you decide, I'll be fine."

"Will you?" I ask, because I'm starting to feel dizzy from the task of trying to square Theo's life with mine. They were so inextricably linked for so long, and I've come to realize that they still are—I just need to figure out how. "The things I've heard from your mom, and now Quinton and Sage... even the stuff you said last night, about why you started the company. You're really going to pretend that you wouldn't care if I left again?"

"Wouldn't *care*?" he repeats, incredulous, and sits up straight, both feet flat on the ground. "Of course I'd fucking care. But if staying here isn't going to make you happy, then that's not what I want for you."

I sit up, too, turning on the couch so one of my legs is curled beneath me. An entire cushion separates us, which is good; otherwise, I might be tempted to do something stupid. Again.

"So what would make *you* happy?" I ask.

His eyes flash with surprise, and then understanding. "I'm happy," he says carefully, "when the people I love are nearby, healthy, and taken care of. Which means that over these past couple weeks, I've been doing pretty damn well."

Of course that would be his answer; of course he would mean it. Theo is the best man—the best *person*—I've ever known. His drive, his selflessness, his constant consideration for the people around him, and his loyalty—few could live up to that character, least of all me. And yet, somehow, I was the one who was lucky enough to grow up by his side. To be loved by him. To have him here, waiting for me, after all this time.

Emotion swells suddenly in my chest, and my vision blurs before I know what's happening. I duck my head, trying to hide, but it's too late.

"Honey." Theo sounds alarmed. "Honey, honey, hey."

"I'm fine."

"You can cry." He scoots close, our knees bumping, and curls his big hands beneath my elbows. I resist when he tugs me toward him; on the second attempt, I give in, falling against his chest as he wraps me up in his strong arms. "Got you. I got you. It's okay to cry, Nina."

I can't remember the last time I let myself.

But out here on Theo's back patio, surrounded only by green fields and him, I let the tears break free, let them roll down my cheeks, and I think it's the most honest I've ever been in front of another person in a long, long time. The logo on his polo is right beside where my head rests; I raise my right hand to trace the star over the *i*.

"I'm sorry," I whisper.

His hand curls around the back of my head. "For what?"

"For not calling after those first few days. For staying away so long."

He lets out a breath that fans over my neck and shoulder, giving me goosebumps. "It's okay, Sass."

"And I'm sorry for spending so much time being angry with you because I convinced myself you didn't care."

At that, Theo tenses up for a second; then he threads his fingers through my hair, keeping my head tucked close against him, and that's how I know I've said the right thing. "Thank you."

I use his shirt to wipe my eyes. The blur around me becomes a little clearer. "And..."

"And?"

"And I'm sorry for being super horny and getting myself off on your leg."

This apology is met with silence. My cheeks are already burning, but I force myself to sit up to look into his face—only to find him grinning.

"What?" I demand, even as I feel the corners of my own mouth rising.

His grin grows, his shoulders beginning to shake. When he bursts out laughing, I join in, wiping away the last of my tears.

"That," he says, "you don't need to apologize for."

Chapter Twenty-Nine

Now

"I want these, too."

I shift our shopping basket, close to overflowing, to my other arm. "Don't you think we have plenty?"

"This is it," Theo says, holding a package of firecrackers in one hand and smoke bombs in the other. He starts to walk toward me but pauses when something else catches his eye. After rearranging the fireworks in his arms, he grabs a cannister labeled 'La Vida Loca Fountain' from the display table. "Okay, last thing."

I watch as he carefully places his newest selections in the basket. "Pyro."

"You're sure not being very patriotic on our country's birthday."

"That's because I usually try to pretend it doesn't exist."

Our eyes meet, understanding rippling in the air between us. It's the Fourth of July, ten years to the day since we were torn apart, and this is the first time either of us have acknowledged it. Every year since I left Amity, I've done everything I could to avoid this day, even sleeping with ear plugs and drawn curtains so I could ignore the fireworks. I'd never forgotten riding away from the Jacksonville police station in my mom's car, head throbbing from hours of crying, and seeing the sky lit up in celebration. I had no desire to relive that.

The tense moment passes, and we move toward the checkout at the front of the tent. The line is long, winding through the makeshift aisles. Theo takes the basket from me and puts his hand on my back, nudging me around a corner as we search for the end of the line. There's a person standing with their back to us, browsing a display. I lose my balance as I squeeze through the crowd and accidentally bump into him, stepping on the back of his shoe.

"Sorry," I say as Theo steadies me.

"It's fine," says the guy, glancing over his shoulder. He does a double take when he sees me before turning around completely, and I balk the second I recognize the cocky smirk of Vince Redding.

"Nina Sullivan," he drawls, crossing his arms over his chest. "I heard you were back in town."

I force a smile. The last time I saw Vince was when he insulted me and wouldn't let me walk away from him. I've run into enough old acquaintances by now that I've mostly gotten past the discomfort, but Vince is one of those people I'd definitely rather avoid. "Hey."

Theo moves in closer, and Vince throws him an unenthusiastic, "Hey, Hoyt," before returning his attention to me. He makes a big show of eyeing me up and down, letting out a low whistle. "Looking good."

"Thanks," I say in a tone meant to convey that I don't mean it.

"So what are you guys doing?" Vince asks. "Having a party?"

"We're going over to my parents' house," Theo cuts in before I can answer, like he wants to remind Vince he's there. "We're headed up to check out."

Vince nods, but doesn't take the hint to end the conversation. "You want to come out with me instead?" he asks me. "I'm meeting my friends up in Raleigh. We're gonna shoot off some shit and then hit the bars."

I think I'd rather relive every miserable Fourth of July of the past decade than accept this invitation. "Sounds fun, but I'm good."

"Come on, now." He nudges my arm. "You can't follow this guy around forever. We're not kids anymore."

"Are you sure?" Theo asks, deadpan. "Because the way you're acting right now reminds me of the time I punched you in the face."

Vince snorts and raises his hands in mock surrender. "Still can't take a joke, Hoyt, huh?" Although he's acting nonchalant, he takes a couple steps backward, putting space between us. "That's okay. You guys probably have a lot to talk about, anyway."

His last sentence is punctuated with a meaningful look in Theo's direction, and then he turns his back to us. We watch as he saunters to the other side of the tent and says something to a woman browsing alone. She giggles, he grins, and he's officially onto a new flirtation.

I look up at Theo, who's staring hard in Vince's direction. "What was that about?"

"Nothing," he says, a little bit quickly. "Let's get in line."

***

When we pull up to the Hoyts' house and see just how many cars are lining the block, I feel a kick of anxiety. Theo told me ahead of time that extended family and neighbors would be at the barbecue. In a moment of bravery, I agreed to go anyway.

"If it gets to be too much," he tells me as we trudge up the drive, weighed down by plastic bags of fireworks, "let me know and we'll leave."

The house is full of the Hoyts' family, friends, and neighbors, and the minute Theo and I step through the front door, we're showered in greetings, pulled into hugs. I stick close to Theo's side; this type of family gathering has always felt foreign to me, since my parents were only children whose own parents died young.

But it's not too much. As we move through the house, everybody we stop to talk to is nothing but warm and welcoming. They don't ask intrusive questions about where I've been or what I'm doing here; they don't stare at my scar or hold the past against me. Over and over, it's *so good to see you* and *how are you doing* and *let us know if you need anything*. When Theo's grandmother sees me for the first time, her eyes grow watery, and she reaches out to grasp my hands in her papery ones.

"Oh, Nina Lynn," she says, "look at you, beautiful girl. Back where you belong."

"Gram," Theo warns, wrapping an arm around her shoulders. "Nina gets to decide where she belongs."

"I didn't mean Amity," his grandmother *tsks*. "I meant standing next to you."

Over her head, Theo sends me an apologetic grimace. "Gram, that's not--"

"Thank you," I interrupt, surprising myself and not even knowing who I'm speaking to—her for calling me beautiful or him for trying to make me comfortable. I squeeze her hand and say, "This is exactly where I want to be," and the way Theo's gaze heats has me looking at the floor.

We go into the backyard, where Cecil is grilling burgers and hot dogs. Randi sits in a lawn chair with a canned margarita in her hand, bare feet propped on a cooler in front of her.

"Kids," she scolds affectionately, and in that moment, I am one. Something that feels suspiciously like joy bubbles up, as if I've somehow traveled back to that time in my life when the world was simple—even though now, it's anything but. "We already have way too many fireworks."

"That's a matter of opinion," Theo tells her, moving some of the fireworks already covering the patio table to make room for his. "Everything was half off, anyway."

"I tried to stop him," I say.

She rolls her eyes, but she's smiling. Behind her, a group of kids chase a soccer ball around the yard. Theo had mentioned that some of his cousins have kids now, and they're standing nearby, talking and drinking. I see them notice us. When they raise their hands to wave, I smile and wave back.

One of the boys, maybe six or seven years old, grabs the ball and holds it over his head. "Uncle Theo!" he hollers. "Come play with us!"

I raise my eyebrows, thinking of the nephews I've never met. "Uncle?"

He shrugs. "It's simpler than Second Cousin Theo."

"They're your first cousins, once removed," Cecil chimes in.

"Know-it-all," Theo says good-naturedly, elbowing his dad in the side. He scoots behind me, resting a hand on my hip. "You okay?"

"Sure," I say, and with a quick kiss to my cheek, he's off. In my peripheral vision, I see Cecil and Randi exchange a pointed glance. But I keep my eyes on Theo, watching as he swiftly scoops the ball from the boy's hands and takes off with it. The kids follow him, squealing, until he throws himself on the ground and lets them pile on top of him.

"Nina, how are things going at the store?" Cecil asks me. "I was there on Tuesday, but I didn't see you."

"That's usually my day off," I say, sinking into the lawn chair beside Randi.

"I saw Judith. She said you've been such a help," Randi tells me, the corners of her eyes crinkling with a warm smile. She reaches into her cooler and grabs me a margarita, popping the tab before she hands it to me. "I told her that I'm absolutely not surprised."

"You always did a good job at Walk a Mile," Cecil agrees. I take a sip of my drink, drawing it out, caught off guard—and a little uncomfortable—with how casually they've started talking about the store. "When we were teaching you and Theo how to make change, you picked it up a lot faster than him."

"Oh, Lord," groans Randi. "Every day for two weeks, if he had rung somebody up, the drawer would be short."

"But Nina was great at it," Cecil says. "And she was a year younger! Eight or nine, I think."

I was nine, and I know because I clearly remember the last time he messed up the drawer. My mom had counted it, found it short, and called me into the backroom. We were missing twelve dollars, and I wasted no time in throwing Theo under the bus in the interest of self-preservation. It didn't work; I was working alongside him, so as far as she was concerned, I was responsible too.

When I told Theo that I'd gotten yelled at for his mistake, he asked me to help him understand how to make change. We took some money from the register and practiced a few times. I watched as he carefully counted bills and coins into the hand of our next customer, giving him a nod when he glanced back for confirmation that he'd done it correctly.

"I won't mess up anymore," he promised me.

That night, and every single night afterward, the drawer was balanced.

I search for him in the yard and find him talking to his cousins, one kid splayed across his back while the youngest one, a toddler, taps his thigh. A warmth blooms in my chest, expanding even more when he catches my eye and shoots me a quick wink.

"You know what else you were good at?" Randi says, and I bring myself back to our conversation. "Upselling."

"That's right." Cecil momentarily stops flipping the burgers to point his spatula at me. "People would get up to the register and by the time you were done with them, they'd be spending twice as much money."

Randi pats my knee. "You were a natural."

"I liked the store," I admit. "Theo and I used to talk about taking over eventually."

It's been so long since this dream was even possible—if it ever was—but since I've returned, I've felt unsettled by it. Like there's something I should be doing, something unfinished. There isn't, of course—the store has been gone for ten years and was on its way out long before that.

But the more time I spend here, the more I want to reach into the past and grasp at those old possibilities.

"So, Nina," Randi says, and now her voice is tinged with hesitation. I take another swig of my drink, bracing myself. "I've been wanting to ask...how is your family?"

"You haven't asked Theo?"

"There are a lot of things I've been wanting to ask both you and Theo," she admits, "but I'm trying to respect your privacy."

It's too early for the stars to be out, so I press the cold aluminum can to the inside of my thigh and focus on the steady numbing of my skin. "My parents are divorced."

"Hmm," Randi hums, sympathetic but unsurprised.

"I know. Big shock. Dad and Brock moved west together afterward, and I stayed with Mom."

"And do you speak to them?"

A peal of laughter rings through the air, and I stare out at the yard, at Theo, as I answer. "Not much. Brock has two kids, but I've never met them. And Mom..." I let out a sardonic laugh. "She's mad at me for ending my engagement, so I guess that's over now, too."

"Oh, Nina." Randi leans forward to put a hand on my arm. Her palm is warm and clammy from the humid evening, and still, it's exactly what I need right now. "I am so sorry. You deserve better."

"It's alright, Ra--"

"No," she interrupts, her normally soft demeanor suddenly replaced with uncharacteristic ferocity. "No, it is *not* alright. I spent so much time watching your mother mistreat you while your father and brother did nothing about it. And--" She closes her eyes briefly. "And neither did I."

I press my drink harder against the flesh of my thigh. "She wouldn't have listened to you."

"You're right. But I still wish I'd said something." Randi moves her hand down to cover mine, curled over the cloth arm of my chair. "And since I'm already making you uncomfortable--"

"You aren't," I lie.

"I'm sorry for keeping Theo away from you."

Involuntarily, I draw back, unprepared for the barrage of emotions *that* dredges up. "What?"

"After the police found you," she says, as if I'm not already having vivid technicolor flashbacks. "We just wanted to protect him. We should have been doing the same for you."

"He's your son," I say stiffly, even as I think of all the opportunities for things to be different, the opportunities that nobody took. Cecil and Randi may have told Theo not to talk to me, but he's the one who listened, and I'm the one who was so hurt from a few days of being ignored that I decided to do the ignoring for the rest of our lives. "Of course you'd put him first."

"But we love you like our daughter."

Cecil's voice cuts into the conversation, startling me. I'd completely forgotten that he was lingering within earshot. He stands with his back to the grill, watching me expectantly, and slowly, I begin to process what he's said.

"We do," Randi reiterates. "Theo grieved immensely when you left, but so did we. We always hoped..." She trails off, her chin quivering a little before she stills it with a shaky smile. "We're just so very glad you're here."

Maybe it's her sincerity, or her squeeze of my hand, or the sound of Theo's raucous laughter moving through the hot air, or the fact that I'd be alone tonight if it weren't for the Hoyts. Whatever the reason, I find the strength to break through the cage of tension holding me back and wrap my arms around the woman who's said all the things I wish I could hear from my own mother.

"Oh," she says, surprised, but hugs me back hard.

A moment later, a pair of arms surrounds both of us, and from somewhere above my head comes Cecil's voice: "It hasn't been the same around here without you, Nina Lynn."

Footsteps run across the patio, growing louder as they approach, and I know without looking that they belong to Theo. He kneels on the ground between Randi's chair and mine, wedging himself into the only opening left. "What's going on?" he asks, slinging his arms over our shoulders. His eyes scan my face, assessing, and I nod to indicate that I'm just fine. "Group hug?"

Randi pulls everybody in further. "Family hug."

***

When the food has been served and night has fallen, everybody migrates to the Hoyts' driveway to watch the fireworks. One of Theo's uncles puts himself in charge of setting them off at the end of the driveway, and the rest of us mingle near the fence, the older adults in chairs while everyone else sits on the ground or stands.

I'm leaning back on the fence, the splintered wood poking my butt through my shorts, when Theo comes to join me. He sidles up to my side; shoulder to shoulder, hip to hip, we stand there together, looking out toward the street.

"You're not setting off you own stuff?"

"Nah," he says as his uncle lights a sparkler and touches it to a cylinder sitting on the asphalt. The air fills with the familiar *sizzle, whine, crack* of a firework streaking upward and exploding in the dark sky. The kids squeal and clap. "I want to watch with you."

I smile at him just as another firework goes off a block away. Another one of ours follows, and it feels like a show.

"You know what this reminds me of?" Theo asks, and from the way his voice has grown quiet, audible only to me, I have a feeling I know where this is going.

I rest the back of my head against the fence and let it loll in his direction. He does the same, and when the next set of fireworks goes off, our faces are only inches apart. "What?"

"That night I was in the holding cell while everything got sorted out," he says, and my chest aches at the way his past pain threads through his words. "I was sitting there thinking my life was over, and all I could hear were fucking fireworks."

"Yeah. I hated them for a long time."

Theo nudges the bill of his cap upward, and another burst of light, another *crack*, lights his face. "Until tonight?"

"Don't give yourself too much credit."

He laughs, then I do; and then he moves a little closer, his fingers brushing the pulse at my wrist. "Nina--"

My phone vibrates in my back pocket, buzzing loudly against the fence and breaking the moment. I wince. "Sorry," I say, pulling it out. "I'm not--"

With my finger poised to reject what I assumed would be spam, I pause.

Because it's Daniel calling me.

"What the *hell*?" I stare down at the screen, stunned. "What does he want?"

Theo lets his hand fall to his side and takes a step back, putting space between us that I have the urge to close. "Pick it up."

"What? I don't want to."

"He's calling you at almost ten o'clock on a holiday," he says stiffly. He adjusts his hat, bringing it down to shield his eyes. Even in the light of the fireworks, they're hidden from me, and a heavy rock forms in my stomach at the idea of him closing himself off. "See what he wants."

I stare at him, because I'm pretty sure that Theo doesn't want me to take this call any more than I do. But then he turns and walks off, toward the rest of his family, and I'm left alone.

I gather my courage and swipe quickly across the screen, catching the call before it goes to voicemail. I lift it to my ear, only managing a weak, "Hello."

"Hello," comes Daniel's voice, impatient as ever.

I wait to feel some sort of wistfulness or regret, but there's nothing. I have no desire to talk to Daniel. No desire to repair anything. I want to get this conversation over with and return to Theo and whatever was happening before we were interrupted.

I step through the gate and into the empty backyard, keeping my voice low. "Why are you calling me?"

Daniel sighs, and I find pleasure in the fact that he's already annoyed. "I've got a company coming to pack and ship your stuff in the morning."

Another round of fireworks; I use my pointer finger to plug my free ear. "Okay? You had to call me this late to tell me that?"

"I just got off work."

"It's a holiday."

"Some of us have jobs, Nina," he snipes, and I barely manage to bite my tongue. "Just give me an address to send it to."

I rattle off Theo's address easily and wait while Daniel writes it down.

"Let me guess," he says. "You're staying with him?"

There's no need to clarify who *him* is. "Why do you care?"

"I don't."

I roll my eyes, thinking *sounds like you do*, but there's no point in starting an argument. We broke up less than a month ago; our wedding was supposed to be four days from now...and yet, the three years I spent with Daniel already feels like distant history.

"Okay," I tell him. "If that's all you needed, I'm gonna go."

He doesn't say anything. I give him one second, two, and then I end the call, deciding that this conversation was the last of my time, my energy, or myself that I'll ever give Daniel Hartley.

A sound behind me has me turning back, and there is Theo, one hand on the fence and the other holding the gate open. In the moonlit shadows, I can see the defined curve of his biceps, the point of his nose.

Silence stretches between us. In the driveway, another firework goes off; Theo waits for it to finish crackling before he asks, "What did he want?"

"Nothing." I slip my phone back in my pocket. "He was asking where to send the stuff I left at his apartment."

"This late?" Theo asks doubtfully. "On the Fourth of July?"

I shrug. "He has a *very important job*," I drawl sarcastically. "Too busy to call at a normal time, I guess."

"Are you sure he wasn't looking for an excuse to talk to you? Feeling you out for another chance?"

"I don't think so, and even if he was, I really wouldn't care. We're done." I make a slashing motion across my throat. "Finished."

Theo removes his hat, curls the brim, and replaces it backwards. I look at him. He looks at me.

"Thank God," he breathes into the silence, his voice thick with relief, and then he's crossing the space between us, and he's right there, his palms are on my cheeks, his mouth is on mine.

His kiss is so intensely familiar, yet still like nothing I've felt before. This is not the euphoric make-out of our last summer together. Tonight, we have years of pain and separation and grief behind us, between us, and I feel every ounce of that heavy history in the press of his fingers, the caress of his lips, the stroke of his tongue.

"Theo."

He pulls back, and even in the dim light I can see his face shuttering, prepared for disappointment. "Yeah, Sass."

Feeling his grip on me loosen, I wind my arms around his neck to keep him close. I prop my chin on his shoulder, letting my lips brush his ear when I speak against it. "Let's go home."

Chapter Thirty

Then

"Nina Lynn."

The annoyed voice cut through my thoughts. I paused, price gun in one hand and a pair of seasonally inappropriate shamrock slippers in the other, and looked up. From my spot on the floor of the stock room, Mom towered over me. "What?"

She let out a huff and crossed her arms over her chest. "You aren't listening to music, are you? You need to be able to hear the customers."

"No, I'm not." I finished tagging the slippers, covering the price on the original tag with a bright red $4.99. After tossing them into the box beside me, I pulled my hair back to show Mom that my ears were empty. "Sorry. I was just thinking."

I had wished many times for my mother to take an interest in my life beyond what she believed needed to be fixed, but at this moment, I was glad to be safe from further questions. Because where my mind had been—in the back of Theo's truck with his body moving over me, sweet words spoken against my skin—wasn't anything she needed to know about. We had snuck off a few times since, but it was that first time that I was hung up on—that moment when Theo and I handed over the only pieces of each other that we didn't already have.

For a week, I'd been reliving that night, and for a week, I'd been terrified that she'd somehow know. But as she skirted past me to move into the office, it was clear that she was oblivious.

I ducked my head so she couldn't see me smiling.

"Well, I was *trying* to tell you that when you're done tagging that clearance, you need to go cover the register so Theo can take his break," she called out to me. I heard the office chair creak as she sat down. "And then make sure the clearance gets put out before you leave for the night."

"Yes, ma'am."

All noise from the office ceased, and I grimaced to myself, realizing how deferential my tone had been. I had been raised to speak to adults that way, but when I pulled out the pleasantries with my own parents, they often assumed that I was up to something.

Generally, they were right.

I held my breath as I waited for my mom's response. It finally came as a pointed, "Thank you."

I rushed through marking the rest of the clearance and breathed out a sigh of relief when I plowed through the one swinging door, box of slippers propped on my hip, putting distance between myself and my mom. There didn't seem to be any customers around. When I got up to the register, Theo was leaning on the counter and working a page in the sudoku book he kept behind the counter for slow nights like this.

"Hey," he said, flipping his book shut as I approached. His eyes sparked with mischief as he looked at me. I wasn't the only one who'd been on cloud nine lately. "What's all that?"

"Those ugly shamrock slippers." I dropped them on the ground. "You can have your very own for only $4.99."

"What about my employee discount?"

I clucked my tongue. "You know I can't do math in my head."

"Sure you can. Round it up to five dollars and think of it as five hundred cents, and then—"

"Theo," I whined. "I don't care."

"Fine." He leaned toward me, smirking. "I'll take pity on you 'cause you're hot. Fifteen percent off would make them $4.25."

"Great. Sign me up." I jerked my head toward the front door. "My mom said you could go on break."

Theo stretched his arms over his head. His t-shirt rode up over the waistband of his jeans, exposing his belly button and a dark smattering of hair. I tried not to stare. "I don't need one. I'll hang out with you."

The bell at the door jangled to announce someone's arrival, and I stopped ogling Theo long enough to cast a quick, "Welcome to Walk a Mile," over my shoulder. Then I leaned in toward him, lowering my voice so only we could hear. "Go on break. It'll make my mom suspicious if we're just hanging out up here by ourselves."

"Why?" he asked. "We've done it a million times."

"Do I really have to explain to you *again*—"

I cut myself off when Theo's eyes darted to the right. I turned abruptly, expecting my mother to have come up beside us, but instead saw the customer who had just entered.

Except he didn't really look like a customer. He didn't look like he belonged here at all. He was wearing a tailored suit, hair perfectly swooped above his forehead, and towered over both of us. He reminded me of the main character in a law drama I liked to watch sometimes.

"Can we help you?" asked Theo.

The man responded with an easy grin. "Hey, y'all," he said cheerfully. "You sure can. Nina and Theo, right?"

I furrowed my brow, trying to remember if I'd met him somewhere before.

"That's right." Theo answered for both of us, the slightest edge in his voice.

"Rick Redding," he said, pointing to himself with a thumb, and I felt my eyes go wide. "I'm not sure we've met. Y'all know my son Vince, I think."

He was still being conversational, but when he mentioned Vince, his voice lilted up into something that sounded like a warning.

I turned to look at Theo, only to see that he had come out from behind the counter and was standing at my side, tension radiating off his body. "Yes, sir," he said. "He was in my class. Nina's a year behind us."

"Right, right. I remember seeing you at graduation now. Exciting stuff, going out into the world," Mr. Redding said, and then clapped his hands together. "Listen, is it just you two in the store today? I was hoping to chat with one of y'all's folks."

"My mom is in the back," I said. "If you wait here, I can go get—"

"Actually, it might be better if I talk to her in private," he interrupted. "Mind walking me back there?"

Theo cleared his throat. "Sure. It's just this way."

His hand grazed mine as he turned away. I wanted to grasp it, to let his touch quell the anxiety bubbling up in my chest, but I knew I couldn't do that right now. Instead, I watched as Theo led the way down the center aisle. Mr. Redding followed a pace behind, striding forward in that same deceptively casual manner.

By the time Theo returned, I was practically vibrating with anxiety. He joined me behind the counter, and I could see the worry marring his features.

"What did he want?" I whispered.

Theo pressed his lips into a thin line for several seconds. "I don't know," he said finally. "But when I went into the office and told Kelly he was here, she looked like she'd seen a ghost."

"Do you think they might be raising the rent again?"

He let out a breath. "It's July second," he said. "It was due two days ago. Hell, Sass—I'm wondering if maybe they didn't *make* the rent."

My stomach bottomed out, and I opened my mouth to argue, stopping short when I realized that he could be right. There was a reason we hadn't recognized Mr. Redding when he came in—he and his wife may have owned half the town, but they had reached the level of success where they could delegate their business, pocket the profit, and spend most of their time at their vacation home.

Whatever he had come here to talk about, it couldn't be anything good.

The bell at the front door jangled again, this time to announce the arrival of actual customers. Theo showed the family to the kids' section while I arranged the shamrock slippers on the clearance rack. As I was finishing up, Mr. Redding came around the corner, and I practically jumped out of my skin at his reappearance. He breezed on past without so much as a glance at me, strides long and back straight, with the air of a man who knew he had won.

Chapter Thirty-One
Now

As soon as we climb out of Theo's truck, he's pressing me against the wall of the garage, kissing me thoroughly. We eventually stumble into the house only to get sidetracked again in the kitchen, where he puts me on the counter and wedges his hips between my thighs. He tastes of salt and sweat, and I'm sticky myself. But he kisses hungrily across my neck and my collarbone, taking me as I am.

"Sass," he sighs against my skin. "I've got bad news for you."

"What?"

Theo raises his head as his mouth curls into that cocky smirk. "This is romantic."

With a scoff, I knock his hat onto the floor so I can twist my fingers through his thick hair. Less than a week has passed since the night when we hastily agreed to that no-strings-attached, non-romantic, one-sided orgasm—what a shitty deal for him—and I'm already willing to renege on it. "Good."

He grins and then grabs at my thighs, pressing into me. His mouth returns to my skin, gently sucking my earlobe, and I let out a gasp.

"You like that?" he murmurs. "You used to."

I let my head fall back as desire shoots up my spine. "Yes."

"What about this?"

He palms my breast over my clothes. I glance down at my chest—not flat, but nothing to brag about. Theo's hand completely engulfs me; he pushes up to create swelling cleavage over the neckline of my tank, then leans down to kiss me there. "That good?"

"Yes, Theo." I tug at his hair, urging him to look at me. "It's *all* good. Can we go upstairs now?"

He laughs. "Taking me back to your room?"

"Actually," I hedge, "I was thinking we'd go to yours."

For a second, Theo freezes. I immediately start doubting myself. I haven't seen Theo's room; it's at the very end of the upstairs hall, and the only occasion I would have to go down that way would be to snoop—which I'm certainly not above, but even for me, that seemed a step too far.

But in the next moment, Theo's expression clears, and his easy smile returns. He steps back, offering me his hand. I grab it as I hop off the counter. He yanks me into him, and we're right back to it: stumbling across the kitchen, up the stairs, and down the hall, kisses growing deeper and hands taking more liberties as we go. When we fall through his bedroom door, I force myself away so I can look around.

If his room at his parents' house is a showcase of Theo as a kid, this is the adult version. A lamp on the nightstand gives the room a muted, soft glow. His king-sized bed is backed by a dark oak headboard and covered in a gray comforter with matching sham. A dresser against the wall has a large TV on it, and on the wall across from us, floor-to-ceiling curtains are drawn. Like the rest of the house, the room is neat and devoid of clutter.

"Cute," I tell him.

He reels me in again, looking amused. "Cute?"

"I mean, it's very gray." I run my hands over his chest. "Very manly."

"Hmm."

"And very clean."

"Well, that is my brand."

With a laugh, I kiss him again, pressing our smiles together. Somewhere beneath the pure joy of this moment, I know that I'm being reckless. I know that every second I spend in Theo's arms puts both of us at greater risk for another heartbreak.

And I just can't bring myself to care.

We fall onto the bed, me pulling Theo's shirt over his head, him removing mine. He drapes half his body over me, his knee wedged between my thighs. My breath catches when he traces a line up my abdomen and curls his hand gently around the side of my neck. "When was the last time you had an orgasm?"

His thumb is resting in the hollow of my throat, and I swallow very deliberately, letting him feel the movement there. I watch as his gaze darkens, just as I intended. I want him to be just as affected by me as I am by him. "The other night."

"I meant before the truck."

"Yeah, I'm not talking about the truck." I stretch a little, arching my back and pressing my palms into the cool sheets beneath me. Theo's eyes rove over my body. "I've had, like, four since then."

Briefly, he looks confused. Then understanding floods his features, and I don't miss his quiet—but unmistakably sharp—intake of breath. "Yeah?" he asks, voice strangled. A jolt of satisfaction zips through me. Even after all this time, I can still knock confident, unshakeable Theo off-balance. "What've you been doing here at night, Sass?"

"Touching myself." I let my hand trail along the cups of my bra, the button of my shorts, and he watches, entranced. "Using my vibrator."

His eyes snap up from the show I'm putting on. "You have a vibrator here?"

"Yes."

"What have you been thinking about while you get yourself off in my house?"

My hand dips just an inch into the front of my shorts, and I cock a brow at him. "What do you think?"

He makes a noise in the back of his throat, something between a groan and a growl that I can feel in the tremor of his body. He presses himself along my thigh, letting me feel what my words are doing to him. "Can I ask you a question?"

"You already did."

Theo fixes me with an unamused look. He smooths my hair back from my face, his voice soft when he asks, "Did Daniel take care of you?"

I understand what he means. "Sometimes. A lot of times, I'd take care of myself afterward."

I thought Theo would be thrilled to learn that Daniel wasn't the greatest lover. Instead, his face morphs into disbelief, and then unadulterated fury. "I hate the idea of you with him," he says, "but I think I hate the idea of you being unsatisfied even more."

"Then don't leave me unsatisfied."

I go to kiss him again, but he maneuvers his mouth just out of my reach. He settles his weight more fully over me, pinning me to the mattress. With his hair mussed and his lips swollen, he looks completely undone—and I haven't even gotten to see him *undone* yet. I wiggle beneath him, impatient. "What is it?"

"I want you to go over to the curtains," he says, "and see what's on the other side."

I glance at them, confused. "Isn't it just a window?"

Theo rolls off me. "Go look."

I'd really rather stay right here and explore his bare torso, laid out so enticingly in front of me, but his eyes dart between me and the curtains expectantly. I haul myself off the bed, feeling him watch me as I walk away in my bra and denim shorts. Across the room, I pull the curtains apart. I'm still expecting to see some kind of window, just because I can't think of what else would be there; instead, it's a pair of French doors, leading out to a balcony.

"Oh," I say, surprised. "Can I walk on it?"

"'Course."

I open the door and slip out, back into the hot summer air. The balcony is whitewashed concrete with a metal railing, just big enough for two or three people. I lean on it as I look out over Theo's land, trying to figure out how I've never noticed this was up here.

"We're on the west side of the house," he says from behind me. "You can't see it from the road or the driveway."

I look out at the dark outline of the trees. "Do you come out here a lot?"

"Sometimes." His front presses lightly against my back, his hands rubbing the bare skin around my waist, thumbs snaring in my belt loops. "Look up."

I drop the back of my head against his shoulder, turning my face to the sky. The gasp that escapes is purely involuntary.

"Oh, wow," I whisper. You can always see the stars in Amity, but from this spot, they shine especially bright. There are too many to count, and the biggest ones seem a little too close. If I didn't know better, I'd think that I could pluck one from the sky to keep for myself. "This is beautiful."

Theo nudges my cheek with his nose. "You remember what I told you about the business?"

It was just about you.

Since that night, I've had my suspicions about the house. I whirl around to face him, only to find him leveling me with the most unaffected, infuriating look. "I *knew* it."

"Knew what?" he asks, playing dumb.

"That this house was part of your..." I flap my hands around, searching for words. "Your plan to make yourself suitable."

The corner of his mouth ticks upward. "That's not *exactly* it."

"Then explain," I say, a little impatient.

"The business thing... I was twenty-two and still holding onto a lot of that shit from what happened with us. By the time I was in a position to build this house, I'd matured a bit. It wasn't, 'oh, let's build a house for Nina.' It was more, 'I'm going to build a house for *me*, and if I ever got lucky enough for Nina to find her way back, I think she'd really like a place where she can look at the stars." Theo pauses, watching me carefully. "Do you like it?"

A beat, and then I admit: "Yes."

"Good." He moves toward me, backing me against the rail. His fingers deftly undo the button of my shorts; they fall to the ground, and I kick them away, not shy in the least as I stand before him.

He drops kisses down my sternum, my stomach, and my breath hitches when his teeth close over the waistband of my panties. He tugs, and those, too, fall to the concrete I'm standing on. I watch as he pushes my legs apart, rests his nose in the hair I haven't had the opportunity to wax in much longer than I would prefer. "Nina."

"Hmm?" I ask, at a loss for words.

His mouth moves down to my thigh, nipping at the outside, and then inward.

"Look up, Nina," he says against my skin. "Look at the stars."

And I do. Arms spread out on the railing behind me, I let my head fall back so I can stare up at the clear night sky. Theo's hands grip my hips, holding me in place, and a second later a rush of sensation has me gasping as his mouth closes over my center.

One of the mysteries of my adult sex life has been that, even as I tried new things with Daniel and a handful of other men, it always seemed to pale in comparison to the fumbling missionary sex I used to have with Theo. I eventually decided that I was viewing the past through rose-colored glasses, that I was romanticizing my first time, my first love, and building it up to be something it really wasn't.

In this moment, I know that I've been lying to myself. Because this isn't the first time a man has gone down on me, but it's the first time *Theo* has, and the sensation is unlike anything I've experienced with others. That elusive feeling I've been chasing since I was seventeen is back, and it's stronger than ever.

His fingertips dig into my skin, holding me firmly over his mouth as his tongue works me over. My hands cling to the railing on either side of me; the metal bar digs into my back. My upper body arcs backwards, and the sensation of floating above the ground only heightens the thrill in my chest, the tightening in my core. I surrender to it, knowing that Theo would never let me fall.

Theo's mouth leaves me, and for a moment, I'm bereft. Then his lips are back on my inner thigh, leaving little suckling kisses on the sensitive skin there as he pushes two fingers inside of me.

"Fuck," he mutters. He crooks those fingers toward himself, pressing them against my inner wall. I gasp.

"Nina. Tell me the truth. When you're using your vibrator and thinking about me, do you get wet like this?"

"Yes." No hesitation. No shame. No point trying to lie.

With his free hand, he hoists my leg over his shoulder. I let him maneuver me, gripping the handrail tighter as I shift my balance to one foot. "Next time," he says, his warm breath washing over me, "I want to watch."

I open my mouth, intending to voice my agreement—honestly, I think I would be willing to jump off this balcony right now if Theo asked me to—but he applies new pressure to that place inside of me at the same moment he begins to suck on my clit, and what comes out instead is a desperate, keening rendition of his name.

One of my hands leaves the railing to thread through his hair. All my inhibitions fly out the window, and I use my grip to push his face further into me. He has the same idea; he winds his arms beneath my thighs, encouraging me to move my hips. I do. I ride his face, and with that added friction, the symphony of sensation is seconds away from overtaking me.

"Open your eyes," he says, quiet but commanding, and it's only then that I realize they were closed at all. "Look up at the stars when you come for me."

And I do. I stare at the sky, and I grip the railing so hard my hands hurt, and in the distance, a firework sounds at the exact moment those stars explode right in front of my eyes.

Chapter Thirty-Two

Then

The day after Mr. Redding came to speak with Mom, I woke up to a gentle rapping at my bedroom window. With a groan, I rolled over and saw Theo on the other side, peering in at me.

"What?" I hissed. He cupped one hand behind his ear, indicating that he couldn't hear me, and used the other to wave me over.

I hauled myself out of bed, adjusting my tank top and shorts as I went. It was bright outside, and with Theo's face pressed right up against the glass, I didn't miss his gaze lingering on my bare legs.

"Back up," I called, flicking the window where his nose was. He blinked as if coming out of a daze, and I pushed the window up. "What are you doing here?"

"You weren't answering your phone."

"Because I was sleeping," I said. "We don't all get up at the crack of dawn."

"Or before ten, either." Theo propped his elbows on the windowsill and leaned in to give me a kiss. I accepted it, annoyance over my disturbed sleep evaporating.

It seemed like he was holding back, though, not melting into me like he usually did. I pulled away. "What's wrong? Wait, what time is it?"

"Almost eleven."

"Why aren't you at the store? I thought you were opening today."

Wincing, Theo pulled his phone from the pocket of his shorts. He clicked the screen a couple of times, then showed me a text from his dad. *Don't come to the store today*, it said. *We've got it covered.*

"Did they tell you not to come in?" he asked.

I doubled back to my bed to retrieve my own phone from under the covers. Behind me, I heard a grunt, and then the *thud* of feet on the floor as Theo came into my bedroom.

"Shh!" I spun around, phone in hand. "My mom is home."

"Neither of their cars are out front," he said.

I frowned. "Really? She wasn't working today. I wonder where--" I cut myself off as I read the text waiting for me. "Okay, my dad sent me the same thing. That's so weird."

Theo came up behind me. We were quiet for a moment as he peered at the text.

"You wanna go up there?" he asked. "Make sure everything's okay?"

"Yeah." I nodded, even though my gut already knew that it wasn't. "We should check."

***

"What the hell," muttered Theo when we drove by the front of the store and saw the 'closed' sign still hanging in the window.

"Maybe they decided to close early for the holiday?" I posited without much conviction. We were closed for the Fourth of July every year, but the days before and after were always business as usual.

"If they did, it was pretty last minute," Theo said, "considering we were both planning on working today."

We drove around the side of the strip mall and entered the back parking lot, where I immediately spotted both of my parents' cars. Cecil and Randi's SUV was there, too.

"Nobody was home when I left," said Theo. He pulled the truck into an empty space. I unbuckled my seatbelt and flung the door open. "Wait, Sass, maybe we should--"

Ignoring him, I hopped down and slammed the door shut.

Theo's footsteps sounded behind me, scurrying to catch up as I marched up to the back entrance of the store. As I drew closer, I could hear noise coming from inside. "They're in there talking," I told Theo.

He came to a stop at my side, keys out, reaching for the door. It clicked open, and he motioned for me to go in ahead of him.

The entrance deposited us in the back hall, right by the single swinging door. Raised voices in the office made me stop abruptly, and Theo bumped into me from behind.

"Whoa," he muttered, hands falling to my shoulders.

I held a finger to my lips. "Be quiet!"

"You be quiet."

The roar of my father's voice startled us, and we both fell deadly silent as he shouted, "God fucking damn it, would somebody in this room tell the fucking truth?"

"I don't know what to tell you, Frank," said Randi. "Last I looked, the money was there."

"And when they tried to withdraw the rent twelve hours later, it wasn't. How's that happen?"

I looked at Theo, wide-eyed. "You were right," I whispered. "They didn't pay the rent."

With his mouth set in a grim line, he wrapped his arms around my shoulders and tugged me against him. I set my hands on his forearms where they crossed my chest. He was the only thing holding me up.

"Frank," came Cecil's voice, sounding uncharacteristically heated. "You're right on the edge of accusing my wife of something. I suggest you back off."

"I'm not on the edge of it. I *am* accusing her. She handles that account. What else am I supposed to think?"

"Everyone in this room has access to it, you dick!" shouted Cecil, voice booming in a way I had never heard before. Judging by Theo's sharp inhale behind me, neither had he. "Hell, the kids could probably figure out how to get into it if they wanted! Have you spoken to your son lately? I heard he was back here snooping around a few weeks ago."

"Brock did not do anything." My mother entered the conversation. Of the four of them, she seemed to be the calmest, which was decidedly outside the norm. "He has a good job. He doesn't need to steal."

Someone snorted in response. My mind was spinning. The rent hadn't been paid because somebody emptied the store's account. There were only a handful of people who could have done it, and most of them were standing in the building right now.

I glanced at Theo over my shoulder, remembering the day we caught Brock in the office. He had been cranky, refusing to tell us why he was there. "Do you think...?"

"I don't know," Theo said.

"Theo told me that Brock was in the office, by himself, looking at things he had no business looking at," Cecil continued. "Nina was there, too. She didn't say anything to you?"

"No, because she doesn't tell us anything," snapped Mom, voice rising to a more familiar pitch and volume, "especially not concerning *Theo*."

For a second, I swore my heart stopping beating. Theo drew me closer, nestling his chin in the crook of my shoulder.

"I'm not sure what that is supposed to mean," said Randi stiffly.

"You know exactly what I mean. All of you do. Your son, an *adult*, has been sneaking around with our underage daughter--"

Cecil cut my mother off with a disbelieving laugh. "You're shitting me, right?"

"No, I am not. I've heard from people all over town that they--"

"Obviously something's going on between them," Cecil said, and Theo exhaled hard into my ear. "I'm not talking about that; I'm talking about you trying to make Theo out to be some kind of predator. That's pretty fucking low, Kelly."

My eyes found a black smudge on the wall, and I put my focus on it. I counted the number of sides, the number of angles, noted the way it shifted from gray on the left to jet black on the right. I refused to look away from that smudge. I felt like the world might collapse around me if I did.

"That doesn't matter," my mother shot back, "when she is *seventeen*."

"Kelly, *stop*." It was my father, his tone commanding. "Not that you asked my opinion, but I really don't give a shit if Nina and Theo are dating. We can talk about it later. We can figure out who emptied the account later. Right now, we all need to calm down enough to figure out how we're going to pay the rent."

An uneasy silence fell. I could hear Theo's breathing, feel his chest rising and falling against my back. I, on the other hand, felt like I wasn't breathing at all.

"Hell," said Cecil. His anger seemed to have evaporated; now, he just sounded defeated. "Maybe we shouldn't."

"Shouldn't what?" asked my dad.

"Pay the rent. Even if we came up with the money, what's the point? We can all see the writing on the wall. Let's just close. Let Redding kick us out. Be done with this."

There was no reply, not that I cared to hear it. I pushed against Theo's arm. As soon as he released me from his grip, I turned on my heel and walked out the door.

Neither of us spoke as we climbed back into the truck. Theo started the engine, and then we just sat there in the blast of air conditioning, staring at each other.

"Let's leave," I said finally.

And because it was Theo, he didn't have to ask for clarification. He knew exactly what I meant. "You want to swing by your house and grab some stuff?"

"No." I couldn't bear the thought that someone might come home and stop me. I had to get out of here, to put distance between myself and whatever was happening to life as I'd always known it. "I just want to go."

Chapter Thirty-Three

Now

When I open my eyes, it's to a square of bright sunlight in the ceiling above my head. I blink as I come to, fragments of last night entering my mind: the Fourth of July. Hanging out with the Hoyts. The balcony, and of course, Theo—his hands, his mouth, the rumble of his voice between my thighs...

Look up at the stars when you come for me.

I look over at him now, passed out on top of the covers wearing only his boxers. He doesn't have a gym body; he has the body of a man who works with his hands every day, and in the daylight, I can make out every ridge of his subtly defined muscles. As I watch, he makes an unintelligible noise and curls further into his pillow.

When we came in from the balcony last night, I had no intention of sleeping anytime soon. But Theo intercepted my hands as they reached for his zipper, kissed each palm, and directed me to sit on the bed.

"One more thing," he said, grabbing a remote off the table. I frowned, a little put out that he stopped me to turn on the TV. But the remote didn't go to the TV; instead, he pointed it at the ceiling above the bed. I watched as the set of wood slats I'd assumed was a large vent rolled away to reveal a skylight showcasing the same stars we'd just been looking at.

If the story behind the balcony had surprised me, this had me absolutely floored.

"You want to sleep under the stars?"

"Yes," I said, a little breathless. We huddled together in the bed, still half-dressed, and for the first time, I counted *real* stars until I drifted off to sleep.

Now, instead of the endless stars, all I see is the harsh light of day. The return of reality. The truth is, I'm a disaster. Theo has his shit together. It's become increasingly clear that our feelings for each other are nowhere near resolved, and I'm beginning to feel guilty about the fact that while I was engaged to Daniel, Theo was busy carving out a place for me in his new life. Everywhere we've gone together, I've seen women making eyes at him, women who would have no qualms about moving in here and sitting on that balcony and letting him take care of them. Women who don't have anywhere near the baggage that I do.

I roll onto my side, wanting to look at him. His mouth has fallen slightly open; I reach over and gently press beneath his chin. I don't mean to wake him, but he stirs at my touch. "Nina?"

"Hey." I scoot to his side of the bed as he opens his eyes, blinking rapidly as they adjust to the sun. "Morning."

Theo yawns and grabs for his phone, checking the time. "Damn it. I should have already left."

But he makes no move to get out of bed. He types out a quick text, and then he's turning back toward me, propping himself up on an elbow to mirror me. We study each other for a long moment before he squeezes his eyes shut with a frustrated sigh. "Fuck."

"What?"

"You know what. I can see the regret all over your face."

He flops onto his back, letting his forearm fall over his forehead, and stares at the ceiling. His expression is hard, his jaw tight. I can see the pulse beating at his throat. Disquieted, I sit up, adjusting my bra strap just to have something to do with my hands.

Nobody says anything for what feels like forever. I wish I could evaporate into the floor, through the balcony doors—anywhere to escape this tension. Briefly, I consider getting up and walking out of his bedroom; then I decide that would be a little too on-the-nose for my history, and I force myself to stay put.

Just as I open my mouth—to say what, I don't have any fucking clue—Theo intones, "This is my fault."

I glance over my shoulder at him. "Huh?"

He glares at the ceiling for another moment, then sits up abruptly, swinging his legs over the side of the bed. Perched on the edge of the mattress with his back to me, he speaks to the floor. "You kept telling me you didn't want this, and I convinced myself you were starting to change your mind."

"It isn't that I don't *want*--"

"Nina." Theo's fingers lace together behind his neck. "It's fine."

But it's *not* fine, and the taut muscles across the expanse of his back make that clear. Crawling on my knees,

I move over to kneel beside him. He doesn't move away, but he doesn't look at me, either.

"You know I'm trying to figure out what's next for me," I say finally. "I don't want to drag you into it."

That makes him lift his head, and he's incredulous. He gestures broadly: at me, at the balcony, at himself. "What part of *any* of this makes you think I don't want to be dragged into it?"

"You have so many options other than me," I tell him. I can immediately tell that he doesn't like that, but I press forward, desperate to make him see where I'm coming from. "You've built this amazing life--"

"I built it for *us*."

"Except that I don't even know how I fit into it."

He must hear my doubt, my insecurity, because his expression softens. With that, he looks much more like my Theo.

I adjust so that I'm sitting on my butt, my legs dangling beside his. "I like working at the Wilsons' for now, but I don't have any idea what I want to do long-term. And I need to do *something*. I meant what I said, before. I've got to prove to myself that I can stand on my own two feet."

He listens carefully, nodding along. "Alright," he concedes. "I can understand that."

"And, I mean..." I blow out a breath. "What do *you* want?"

"You."

The word comes out quickly, a reflex. Even as my belly flutters, I roll my eyes, because I should have seen that coming. "Okay, but what else?" I think back to last night, when he was running around the yard with his cousins' children, grinning and laughing alongside them. "Do you want kids?"

He shrugs. "Yeah, I think so. Someday. But I'm not in a rush."

"Well," I say, both relieved and upset to discover this sticking point, "I'm not sure I do."

"You're not sure?" he asks, furrowing his brow at me. "Didn't you and Daniel talk about it? Shouldn't that have come up with someone you were about to marry?"

I really don't want to discuss Daniel again; talking to him on the phone last night was more than enough. But it's a fair question, so I answer. "He wanted them, and I told him I was okay with it."

"And let me guess. He was going to keep working insane hours, and you were going to do everything by yourself."

"We would have had a nanny to help."

Theo snorts. "I don't think Fran Fine is looking for a new job at this point."

"Shut up," I say, but I'm unable to completely hold back a laugh. I bump his shoulder with mine. "I'm just saying...now that I'm not marrying him, I can really think it through and decide if it's what I want eventually, or if I was just going along with what *he* wanted."

"So think it through. Take your time," he says, still infuriatingly casual. "It's not a dealbreaker."

"Theo!" Exasperated, I jump to my feet and stand in front of him. He leans back on his hands, letting his eyes do a slow scan down my body. His shirt from last night is on the floor next to us; I crouch down and grab it, then pull it over my head. "You're being insane."

"How?"

I prop my hands on my hips. "Because you've built your entire life around this *hope* that we'd see each other again. And now you're willing to give up on the other things you want, just to be with me?" I shake my head. "You know what? *You're* codependent, too. Not financially, but emotionally."

His eyes flash, and for a moment, I think I've gone too far. He stands, putting us back on the same level. "Yeah, I guess I am," he snaps—not angry, exactly, but fierce. "I love you. I'm not ashamed or embarrassed and I don't need to get over it. You can take it or leave it, but you're going to have to deal with the fact that I *have* loved you for my entire life and I *will* love you for the rest of it."

The room stills around us. My breath stalls in my throat. I gather the hem of his shirt in my hands, scrunch, release. All the while, he stands there and stares at me expectantly, not a trace of regret or apology in his expression.

"Theo," I say, soft. "You don't know that."

"I *do* know that," he argues. "Every day, people get married to someone they only met a couple of years earlier, and nobody questions it. I've had my entire life to think about how I feel about you, and I know. This is it."

"But you haven't *known* me your entire life," I remind him. "We didn't talk for ten years."

Theo lifts his chin. "On that first day, at the country club," he says, "did you feel like you were talking to a stranger?"

I look down at my feet, sunk into his plush carpet, and think back to that day. I was shocked, stunned, even a little scared to be confronted with the past so unexpectedly—but we were far from strangers.

He reaches toward me, hesitant. I don't move, and he takes that as permission to grasp my arms. I wait for him to say something. Anything. When he doesn't, I lift my eyes, and he squeezes. "You do what you need to do," he tells me. "I'll be here when you're ready."

"Why?" I demand. "*Why* do you want to spend your life waiting around for me?"

Theo's thumbs brush the base of my neck, and he gives me a small smile, tinged with something melancholy. "Because you're worth the wait."

Before I can argue, he pulls me into his arms. I hug him back, letting myself relax fully into him, and I think, *I love you*. The words float into my mind, a gentle acknowledgement.

I love you, I think again, purposefully this time, and it still feels like the most fundamental truth I've ever known.

I love you, I want so badly to tell him. But that would be cruel when I'm not even sure I can stay, when I'm not sure I *should* be letting him love me to his own detriment—so what comes out instead is, "I don't deserve you."

"That isn't true." His fingers slide through my hair, gently pulling at the tangles that formed as we slept. I close my eyes against his shoulder and let the sensation soothe me. "I know you weren't brought up to believe this, but you deserve everything the world has to offer, Sass. Including a short guy with a big nose who's gone for you."

Even though he's just proved my point—why is *he* reassuring *me*, when I'm the one making everything complicated? --I laugh. "I like your nose. And you're not that short."

"An even six feet, according to my driver's license."

"You're still lying about that?"

"Not actively," he says, "but that's what I put down when I was sixteen, and you can't really go into the DMV and say 'hey, I need to change my height because I shrunk.'"

I pull back, letting my hands linger as they fall away from his body. "Good point."

For a long moment, we hold eye contact; then Theo turns away, letting out a sigh. "I've got to shower and get to work. I'll see you for dinner?"

"Sure."

He smiles at me, his eyes sparking. He chucks my chin, and then, as he moves around me and heads for the master bath, throws out, "Love you so much."

My response comes as a reflex—not the loaded, adult *I love you*, but the refrain of our childhood that eventually grew with us. I wonder if it could ever grow big enough to encompass who we are now. "Love you so much."

Chapter Thirty-Four

Now

When I arrive at work later that day, I'm relieved to see that Quinton's car is nowhere to be seen. Inside, Sage is ringing up Mrs. Bryant, who used to frequent the shoe store and who, frankly, I was surprised to learn is still alive.

"Good morning, Mrs. Bryant." The groceries are bagged; while Sage counts out her change, I grab the bags off the counter, looping two over each wrist to get them all in one trip. "I'll bring these out to your car for you."

"What a doll," Mrs. Bryant drawls, leaning heavily on her cane. "Aren't you sweet, Nina Lynn."

I'm not sure I've ever been called 'sweet' in my life, but I return her gummy smile with one of my own. It takes a while to get out to the parking lot at Mrs. Bryant's pace. She gives me a hard butterscotch candy as a thank you, and I pop it into my mouth as I trudge back into the store, tossing the wrapper in an outdoor trash can as I go.

When I come back in, Sage is waiting for me. "I'm sorry about the other day," she says in a rush as I grab an apron. "We feel bad. Quinton, too. Theo read him the riot act and I think it actually got through this t--"

She stops abruptly, staring, and I pause in the midst of tying my apron. "What?"

"You have a hickey!" she scream-whispers. I slap a hand over my neck, the apron strings falling limp at my sides. "No, the other side!"

"Oh god," I groan. "I swear I checked before I left!"

"It's kind of under your ear lobe," she says, poking the spot with her index finger. "Right there. I saw it when you turned your head."

I tug at the scrunchie holding my ponytail in place. "I'll just put my hair down."

"No, don't do that. It's so freaking hot in here today." Sage crouches down and shuffles through her purse where it's stowed beneath the counter. When she stands, she holds up a tube of concealer and a compact, triumphant. "Did you forget that I'm the master?"

The answer is that yes, I did forget, but as soon as she says it, I can't believe that I did. In high school, Sage took care of everyone's hickeys—her own, mine, Lori Ann's, even random girls who happened to enter the bathroom while we hogged the mirrors. The summer that Theo and I were together, I needed her help so frequently that she ended up teaching me her tricks. It's another memory that fell victim to my desperation to suppress the past.

"Judith's in the back," she says. "Turn that way and I'll take care of it real quick."

I tilt my head to the side, exposing the area. She dabs concealer onto my skin. "Thanks."

One second passes. Two. I can feel the question coming; it's just a matter of when--

"So he's not still in love with you, huh?"

"How do you know it's from him?"

Sage pauses what she's doing and moves her unimpressed face into my line of sight. "Please. Give me some credit."

I let out a little laugh in spite of myself. "We made out."

"And...?"

"That's all."

She tilts her head. "Come on."

I laugh again, and it feels like we could be back in high school, comparing notes about boys and giggling. It's been so long since I had that kind of connection with another woman; I haven't had it at all, really, since I left Amity. Suddenly, I'm tempted to tell Sage everything.

"I'm not really sure what we're doing," I admit. "It's not smart, whatever it is."

Moving back to my side, she taps beneath my ear to blend the concealer with her finger. "Maybe," she says, "if you know you'll be leaving."

I don't know that. Not at all. The urge to stay has grown every day since I've been back in Amity, every hour since Randi and Cecil pulled me into their family hug, every minute since Theo held me in his arms and said *you're worth the wait*.

I still want to find a place for myself that isn't carved from someone else's. Can I do that in Amity, in Theo's house? In his bed?

Desperately—*desperately*—I want the answer to be yes.

"How did you know you were going to stay here?" I ask Sage.

She takes a minute to set aside the concealer and grab the compact. "I don't know if we'll be here forever," she says, powdering up her sponge. "Quinton could make more money being a cop in a bigger city."

"Is he looking for something else?" I ask, surprised to feel a pang of sadness at the thought of them moving away.

"No, not really." Sage gently nudges my jaw, and I tilt my head again. "We're good for now. Our families are here. His grandpa isn't doing too well, you know."

"No," I say softly. "I didn't realize that."

"Yeah, so. It doesn't seem like the time to leave." She pats her sponge along my skin, blows on it, and declares, "Done."

"How does it look?"

"Perfect," she says, kissing her fingers with a flourish. "Nobody will ever know."

With a sigh, I finally finish tying my apron. "Thank you. I hope Mrs. Bryant didn't notice it."

"Mrs. Bryant needed me to remind her that quarters are different from nickels. I think you're fine." She looks down for a second as she flips her makeup back into her bag. "Anyway," she says, "you know what I think? About you and Theo?"

"What," I ask, wary enough not to inflect for a question.

"I don't think you need to worry about where you're at," she says, "as much as who's there with you."

Chapter Thirty-Five

Then

We drove for hours.

The first entrance ramp we came across was heading southbound, so that was the direction we went. It was late in the afternoon by the time we decided to pull over in Savannah, just over the Georgia state line. We got burgers and shakes from a drive-thru and then sat in the parking lot, eating on the tailgate like we would back home.

"Did they call?" I asked Theo when I saw him looking at his phone. He shook his head, and my shoulders slumped in relief. I hadn't heard from my family, either. I figured they were still preoccupied with things at the store, which was fine by me.

"So what's the plan, Sass?" He took a slurp of his milkshake. "We ever going back?"

I turned my face up to the sun, letting it beat down on me. The sky was clear and bright blue—odd, since it felt like a giant gray cloud had followed us all the way from Amity. "What if I said no?"

I was so busy basking in the sun that it took me several seconds to realize that he hadn't responded. When

I looked over, he was staring out at the road, and my stomach dropped like a lead ball.

"What?" I asked. "You want to go back?"

Theo exhaled. He flicked his dark eyes over to me. "I don't know. I have enough in my bank account to last us maybe a month—if we lived in the car."

"We can find work."

"Without our birth certificates or social security cards?"

I knew he was right and shoved my burger in my mouth so that I didn't have to admit it. We'd have to go back eventually—to what, I didn't know, but our parents would be looking for us, and Theo needed to take his place at UNC. We couldn't drive around aimlessly for the rest of our lives.

"I have no idea what the hell is going to happen with our parents and the store," he said, "but we'll have each other, Nina."

"But what if we don't?" I burst out. Anger surged through me at the memory of what we had overheard earlier. "You heard my mom. The things she said about you. I've been telling you this entire time that she couldn't find out about us because I wouldn't be allowed to see you. It's obvious she knows and is willing to stoop real low to stop it."

Theo's jaw ticked, and a bead of sweat slid down the side of his neck. He stirred the straw around in his milkshake. "You don't think she might have been right?"

I stared at him. "Right about what?"

"Maybe I shouldn't be with you right now."

If I'd thought my world was knocked off its axis this morning when we stood in the hallway and listened to our families' business implode in real time, it was nothing compared to this. I was absolutely blindsided and completely taken aback that Theo, of all people, would be rejecting me.

I set my food to the side, no longer hungry. My fingers curled over the edge of the tailgate, anchoring me, and I stared at him in disbelief. "You want to break up?"

He shook his head sharply. "No. No, of course not. But maybe we should just...wait. Until you're out of high school and out of the house, and we can do what we want without worrying about Kelly."

"And what do you think it would be like in the meantime? We'd go back to normal?" I challenged. "If we go back, Theo, I'm not going to be allowed to see you. Ever. And if the store does close and my family moves, or yours does, there won't be any sneaking around or knocking on my bedroom window in the middle of the night."

Theo watched me, looking torn. I needed something to do, so I gathered my hair up and off my neck, securing it with the band on my wrist. "I can't be without you, Theo."

I almost got it out smoothly, but my voice broke on his name, and then he was in my space, hauling me close with one arm while the other gripped my cheek. He angled my head so that he could look right into my eyes. "You think I want to be without you, Sass?" he asked in a tone that managed to be both soft and fierce. "After an entire lifetime that's revolved around you, you think I want to just let that go?"

I took a shaky breath. "I don't—"

"You know that year we were together in Mrs. Everett's class?" he interrupted, moving his mouth over mine—not kissing, just letting his words wash over my lips. "All I ever heard was 'Theo, stop staring at Nina. Theo, Nina is fine. Theo, let Nina worry about herself.' I know you don't remember any of that, but my parents will tell you. It was the main topic of the parent-teacher conference." He stroked his thumb across my birthmark. "I've never known how to leave you alone. But I also love you more than I've ever loved anyone else, and I don't want to be the one who takes you from your family or sets you up for a shitty future. Someday we'll have our life together, honey, but it's not time yet."

As if on cue, my phone began to buzz in my pocket. I disentangled myself from Theo and pulled it out with the tips of my thumb and forefinger, as if it were a bomb ready to go off. The word *Mom* jumped out at me.

Theo made no move to intervene. He watched me as I watched the screen, both of us absolutely frozen until the call went to voicemail. A few seconds later, my phone vibrated with a text: *Where are you?*

I turned the phone out to show Theo. He grimaced as he read the message. "Guess they noticed," he said dryly.

"Yeah." Keeping the phone turned in his direction, I pointedly held the power button down until the screen went black. "Too bad I'm not telling her anything."

"Sass—"

"What?" I threw my hands in the air, forgetting that I still held my phone. I barely managed to tighten my grip before it went flying. "What, Theo? You know my family. Why the hell would I be in a rush to get back there so I can get yelled at and locked in my room until the end of time?"

He let out a loud sigh, as if dealing with me was more than he could take. As we'd grown older, we had developed this dynamic where I was the risktaker and he was the voice of reason. It worked for us. We balanced each other out.

Right then, though, I wasn't in the mood for practicality. I couldn't stomach the idea of facing my parents and learning which of them had drained the store's account. I would have to deal with what was going on back home eventually, but not yet. Not when I was two states away with miles of open road ahead of me.

I hopped off the tailgate and snatched up my black crossbody bag. Inside was everything I had with me—wallet, lip gloss, claw clip, earbuds. It sure wouldn't get me very far. "I'm not going back," I announced. "But you have a safe drive."

I turned on my heel and stomped off across the parking lot, my bag thumping against my thigh. I was determined not to look back at Theo. I wanted him to chase me. To reassure me that he'd never leave me alone. I wanted to be more important to him than the sensible, responsible option.

I was a few feet away from the sidewalk and starting to lose hope when I heard my name. The knot in my chest loosened, unraveling completely when I heard Theo jogging up behind me.

"Okay, okay." He put himself in my path, hands on my shoulders. "Come on. We don't have to go back."

"Really?"

"Yes. Just let me tell my parents that we're together and safe," he said, and swiftly cut me off when I opened my mouth to protest. "I won't tell them where we're going. But I don't want people out searching, thinking we're dead or something."

"Alright," I conceded reluctantly. "Okay. But after we text them, you turn your phone off, too."

"Deal."

We walked back to the truck, where we took a selfie. Theo sent it to both of his parents, as well as a message that we carefully crafted together: *Nina is with me. We're taking a road trip. Just stopped in Savannah. All good.*

As soon as the text cleared, he powered off his phone and dropped it in the cup holder. I looked over at him, slouched in the driver's seat with both hands on the wheel. He looked tired, and guilt began to creep in.

Maybe he was right before. Maybe we shouldn't be doing this. Maybe we should just go back now, find out what had happened to the store. Face the consequences of running off. Get it over with.

I was about to voice my thoughts but stopped when Theo turned to me. He let out a breath, like he was releasing his stress, and gave me a genuine grin. I couldn't help beaming back. All thoughts of turning around evaporated from my mind.

"Alright, Sass," he said, turning the key in the ignition. "Vacation time."

Chapter Thirty-Six

Now

Theo makes dinner for us, and when the kitchen is clean and the dishwasher is humming along, we head out to the patio. I lay in the hammock; he sits in the chair with his feet on the table. We drink our cheap beer and talk about our days and watch the sunset. I ask if Theo knew about Quinton's grandfather; he says that he did. He tells me that Randi wants us to come over for dinner next week, and even though it feels very couple-ish, I agree after only the slightest hesitation.

Despite the fact that he had me gasping up at the stars last night, that I fell asleep in his arms, that I basically rejected him this morning—it's all so overwhelmingly normal. The new normal we've created over the past few weeks, anyway.

I'm starting to think that when Theo said he'd wait forever, he meant it.

"You want to go to the beach this weekend?" he asks.

I wedge my cold bottle into the top of my cleavage, trying to cool off. "What?"

"The beach." His eyes snag on my chest. "We could go for the weekend."

"Excuse me," I tell him. "Stop looking at my tits."

A smirk lifts the corner of his mouth. "That's not what you were saying last night."

"Theo!"

He laughs, amused with himself, and I try to hide my own smile behind another sip. "Okay, sorry. When was the last time you went to the beach, though?"

I think for a second. "Labor Day. We went to Cape Cod with Daniel's family."

"Were the Kennedys there, too?"

There's a small throw pillow sitting next to me in the hammock; I sling it at his head, and he cracks up as he bats it away. "When was the last time *you* went to the beach?"

Theo's laughter fades, his wide grin following close behind. "The last time I tried to go," he says, and I can sense how hard he's fighting to keep his voice light, "I got arrested and threatened with kidnapping charges instead. So I thought a redo might be nice."

"Minus the cops?"

"Ideally, yeah."

With this tenuous place we're in, going away together is probably the stupidest thing we could do. I know it, and I'm sure he does too. "I have to work Saturday morning."

"Let's leave after that."

"For *Jacksonville*? We wouldn't get there until dinner time."

"Nah. We'll go to Wilmington."

I cast him a wary glance. "And stay the night?"

"What? Are you afraid you won't be able to keep your hands off me?"

He waggles his brows, a clear sign that he's messing around. But the memories of his skin beneath my hands and his mouth between my legs and his soft bites at my neck are just too potent for me to say anything but, "Yes."

"Well," he says, dropping his voice an octave that slides straight down my spine, "maybe that's the point."

***

Against all better judgment, I agree to go.

Back in my bedroom, I sift through the clutter that has begun to accumulate on the floor, deciding what I'll need for a night away. The amount of shit I brought from New York seems asinine as I pick out a change of shorts and crop top, underwear, and only the most basic toiletries. Daniel will supposedly be shipping the rest of my things soon. Nothing still at his apartment has any value besides monetary; it'll be mostly clothes that I probably won't even want. I should have told him not to bother.

While I'm packing, I realize that I didn't bring a swimsuit and make a mental note to grab one on the road. I zip up my duffel bag, preparing to flick it into the corner, when a flash of pink catches my eye.

It's my vibrator, peeking out from its hiding spot beneath my pillow. My cheeks immediately heat when I think of how many nights I've laid in this bed and gotten myself off, thinking about Theo while he slept, oblivious, down the hall. How many times, if we're being completely honest, I did the same thing in my mom's house. In Daniel's apartment.

I stare at it, wondering if I should slip it into my bag. I've internally sworn that I won't sleep with Theo in Wilmington, but I don't even believe myself. And he did say that he wanted to watch...

"Sass?"

Theo's voice tears me from my wandering thoughts, preventing them from derailing completely. My head snaps up, my spine straightens, and I whirl to face him. He's leaning on the doorframe, hair damp from the shower, wearing black joggers and a Tar Heels t-shirt speckled with water.

In an instant, I know that I'm going to fold. Maybe now. Maybe in Wilmington. Maybe further down the road, if I can hold out that long. But it's time to face facts: no matter where I am, no matter what I do, I will always be on the brink of running back to Theo Hoyt.

"You okay?" he asks, walking into the room. "You were just staring into space."

"Yeah." I move to the side, trying to block his view of the bed. "Fine. Just thinking."

Theo looks at me with a frown, his eyes searching mine, and then looks past my shoulder. I hold my breath as he scans the bed. When his catches on a sharp inhale, I know I've been caught.

"Shit," he tells me, mischievous smirk firmly in place. I could be kissing it in half a second. I know he wouldn't push me away. "Right before I came in here, I told myself that I was going to be a gentleman tonight."

We're standing so close now. I can smell the remnants of his soap and shampoo. I toss my head in what I hope is a confident, unruffled manner, even though inside, I'm shaking. "Only tonight?"

His tongue darts out to wet his bottom lip. I'm not sure I've ever seen him do that before. Based on the way my thighs immediately clench, I think I would remember if I had. "I booked separate hotel rooms for Wilmington," he says, a strain in his voice. "I'm trying, Nina."

I know that he is. Theo is trying so hard to be there for me without pushing too much, to let me know I'm cared for without creating expectations. If I allowed it, he would give me whatever I want, whatever I need, and never ask for anything in return.

I won't allow it. Not anymore.

"I was thinking about bringing it to Wilmington," I say, crowding into his space. His eyes widen momentarily before his hands find my hips. "What do you think?"

"You know what I think."

"Yeah?" I lean up to kiss him. His mouth is warm and responsive, instantly opening against mine. For a few seconds, it's a fierce back-and-forth. He presses his body against me; I press back harder. All I taste is him; in the next instant, I make sure that all he tastes is me. We both give. We both take.

Until I pull back, trailing my palms slowly down his front, and sink onto my knees. My fingers linger on his abs, and when I glance up, I see Theo watching me with an expression that somehow manages to contain both arousal and concern.

"Nina, are you sure you want--"

"Yes," I interrupt. "Unless you don't."

The bark of laughter that escapes him is a little strangled, as if he's short on air. "Does it seem like I don't want it?"

In response, I curl my fingers over his waistband. Our heavy breathing is the only sound in the room as I pull at his joggers, letting them slip over his hips and thighs until they're pooled around his ankles. My hands are shaking a little when they return for his boxers; his hands close over mine, gently guiding, and we take care of them together.

Then he is *there*, heavy and hard in front of me. I bat my hair out of my eyes, letting out a shaky exhale that washes over him; he shudders, thighs clenching, as his hands fold over my shoulders.

"Nina," he murmurs, "look in my pocket."

I tilt my head back, studying his striking jaw from this new angle. "Why?"

"For your hair."

I'm still confused, but I feel around for his pants and wedge my fingers inside the pocket. They close around something soft. I pull it out, and it's the black scrunchie that I was wearing the night of our first time, the one I last saw in Theo's childhood bedroom.

"You're just walking around with this?" I ask him.

Shrugging, he combs his fingers through my hair, holding it in a ponytail at the nape of my neck. I take it from him and secure it with the scrunchie. "Came in handy, didn't it?"

I don't respond; instead, I slide my hand over him, giving him a couple of experimental pumps. Right in front of me, his stomach ripples with the sensation. I lean in until my lips meet his crown, and as I slowly take him into my mouth, I look up through my lashes to see his head thrown back, the tendons in his neck protruding sharply.

"Fucking hell," Theo groans. His hands are back on my head, just resting there. I love that he doesn't push. I love that he just takes what I give him. "You're so good."

Pleased, I press as close as I can, holding onto his legs for balance. The tip of my nose bumps his abdomen at the same moment he hits the back of my throat. I like being filled by him, but I don't have time to get used to the sensation before he's pulling out, grasping my arms, dragging me to my feet.

"What?" I ask, breathless. "Why did you stop me?"

He hauls me close and presses his nose into my cheek. For a long moment, we breathe together, wrapped in each other's arms.

"Will you lay on the bed?" he whispers against me. He runs his hands up beneath my shirt, tracing the ridges of my spine. "Please."

Yes. Yes. Yes.

Whatever self-control I thought I possessed is officially lost. There's salt on my tongue and a mattress bumping the back of my knees, and I think about that first time: the blanket, the truck, the cicadas.

The sky.

I pull back and put a hand to his face. "Your bed," I say. "Under the stars."

Theo grins at me, absolutely blinding, and we take off. He seems to forget that his pants are around his ankles;

he trips after two steps, barely managing to regain his balance before he faceplants. I howl with laughter and run down the hall, grinning as soon as I hear his footsteps thundering behind me.

In his bedroom, the skylight is already open. We only have the moon and stars to see by as we finish undressing—just like that first time. I lay back on a soft blanket, just like that first time. I listen as he tears open a condom, and I count the stars until he moves over me.

Just like that first time.

Theo balances on one elbow, and with the stars behind him, I'm hit with an overwhelming sense of déjà vu. One hand smooths my hair off my forehead; the other trails across my collarbone and over my breasts, teasing my nipples into tight peaks. "How many stars did you count?"

"I only got to sixteen." I lean up to kiss him briefly. "You were quick."

"Hopefully that doesn't continue," he says, and my quiet laugh turns into a sigh when his fingers dip between my legs. "Are you ready?"

I arc into his hand. "I don't know. Check."

He presses a finger inside of me for just a second; he's there and gone so quick that I barely have time to gasp before he's spreading his hand, dragging my arousal around my inner thighs. "Feels that way to me."

"Then I'm ready."

Theo doesn't need another word. He settles himself on top of me, grasping me behind the knee to hitch my leg up and over his hip, and enters me in one smooth thrust.

"Oh!" I cry out, because this is not the slow, hesitant, little-by-little sex of our last summer together. This is sex between two people who have history and experience, and as much as I hate thinking of him getting that experience after me, I have to admit that I'm enjoying the benefits.

"It's alright," Theo says, squeezing the flesh of my thigh. He draws halfway out of me and then slams in again. I whimper—not from pain, but from the total overwhelm of having him around and inside of me after so long. "You can take it, honey. You always did before."

"Not like this," I argue, winding my arms around his neck and pulling him down to me. Our kiss is messy, a little sloppy, in accordance with his quick thrusts. "Theo--"

"I got you, Sass." He traces a thumb down the side of my face. "I got you."

Our gazes hold. I'm just about to lose myself in his eyes completely before they dart to the side, to my scar. For what feels like an interminable second, he stares at it; then he's back to looking in my eyes, driving into me again and again, as if he never looked away.

But even as I'm physically pushed toward release, that short moment has snagged in my mind, cooling the embers in my belly. I put my hands on either side of Theo's face and hold him there until he realizes that I'm wanting to say something.

"What?" he asks, slowing.

A bead of sweat rolls down his nose; I brush it away with my thumb. "Do you hate the way I look now?" My voice is quiet—it's a question I don't want to ask, but have to.

For his part, Theo looks startled. "What?"

"You were looking here, just now," I say, touching my scar.

His face softens in realization, and he shakes his head, resolute. "No. No, Nina, what I was thinking was—I don't think I've ever seen you look as beautiful as you do right now."

"Oh," I say, a little subdued. I think back to every comment my mother ever made lamenting my birthmark, steadily chipping away at my confidence. I don't want to hear that I looked better as a teenager, but I don't want to hear this, either. I should have kept my mouth shut. "I thought you didn't like that I'd had work done."

"It's not about that." Theo gives a little pump of his hips, reminding me that he's still buried inside of me. A moan rises in the back of my throat, and I swallow it down. "To me, this is the most beautiful you've ever been. Not because you weren't beautiful before, but because this is the way you came back to me."

"Oh," I say again, and I feel like I can breathe. I run my hands up the smooth skin of his biceps, taking his stubbled face in my palms. My heart swells with affection as I hold him there. He's every version of himself in that moment: the boy I grew up with, the teenager who made me feel things I'd never felt before, the only man to ever own my heart completely. "Theo."

"Hmm."

"I love you."

It's the first time I've said it without *so much*—for us, the shorter version is the more meaningful. He doesn't seem surprised, though; his lips drift upward into a lazy, soft smile, and he pecks me on the mouth. "I love you too."

"Love you so much," I throw in for good measure.

"So much," he echoes. He sits up, pulling out of me and rolling away; I have only a second to whine before we're spooning, my back to his front, and he's pulling my top leg back over his hip, and then he's pushing back inside. The new angle is different, deeper; from the first stroke, I'm grinding my hips back into his. We come together again and again until Theo warningly says, "Nina..."

"Don't stop," I beg. One of his arms is banding over my stomach.; I grab onto it and hold. "Please, Theo, oh my--"

"Take it," he growls, just like that day in his truck. I want to record Theo saying *take it* in this demanding, rumbly tone so I can play it back whenever I want for the rest of my life. His hand falls down between my legs and he circles my clit, drawing a moan from me. "You're gonna come for me, aren't you?"

"Yes."

"Yes," he repeats, and as if on command, the tension in my body coils tight and then unravels. I gasp and buck; he holds me still and fucks me through it, coaxing aftershocks with his fingers. My world is just beginning to right itself when Theo shouts into my ear, curls himself over my back, and empties himself inside of me.

We lay tangled together for a minute or two, catching our breath, until he asks, "Are you okay?"

"I'm amazing," I say truthfully, looking back at him over my shoulder. "You?"

"Same."

He withdraws from me carefully, gripping the bottom of the condom so it doesn't spill. I stare unabashedly at his bare ass as he walks into the bathroom to dispose of it; when he emerges, he stands next to the bed, and I enjoy the full-frontal view.

"When we go to Wilmington on Saturday," he tells me, "bring that vibrator."

"Done," I say, draping myself comfortably over a pillow. "You're in charge of the condoms."

Theo grins. "Deal."

Chapter Thirty-Seven

Then

We called it a night when we got to Jacksonville. Not wanting to turn our phones on and subject ourselves to the barrage of messages that were surely waiting, we drove around until we came across a cluster of chain hotels. We picked the one we thought would be cheapest, and I waited at a side entrance while Theo got us a room.

By the time he came to let me in, I was hot and sweaty. "What took you so long?" I demanded as I stepped into the blessed air conditioning.

"The guy at the front desk was convinced my ID was fake."

"Probably because you put your height down as six feet."

"Hey." Theo flicked my ear. "It's not like he was standing there with a measuring tape. Good thing you didn't come in, though. We'd be in the back of a police car by now."

There was a vending machine by the elevator. I dug out every coin in the bottom of my bag, and we bought as many snacks and sodas as we could carry. My arms were so full that I had to use my elbow to hit the up button. When the elevator arrived and we stepped inside with our loot, I lost my grip on one of the soda bottles I was carrying.

"No!" I cried, watching it roll out of the elevator and across the tiled floor outside. I started forward, but the doors closed in my face.

Theo doubled over with laughter.

In our room, we piled everything in the middle of the giant bed and splayed out, eating our fill of junk food and shuffling through the TV channels. We were in our bubble, the same one we'd occupied together for our entire lives. Whenever my mind started to drift back home, all I had to do was look at Theo. I didn't need to count stars. He was there to ground me.

When our stomachs were full and our eyes were starting to droop, we huddled together in the middle of the bed. I was cold in my t-shirt and shorts, but instead of getting up to turn down the air conditioning, I tugged the comforter over us and curled into Theo's side.

"Your breath stinks," I said when I got a whiff of sour cream and onion.

"Yours isn't too great, either."

I lifted a hand to my mouth and breathed into it. The scent came back to me, and I found that he was right. "We probably should have stopped for toothbrushes."

"We'll have to go to the store in the morning." Theo wrapped both arms around my shoulders, pulling me more fully into his chest. I smiled when I felt his lips press into my hair. "I'm so fucking tired. I'd never be able to fall asleep in these clothes otherwise."

I glanced at the local news channel we had left the TV on. It was muted, but I watched the weather woman move her hands over the coast of Florida, showing balmy temperatures for the next several days.

The map zoomed out to show the entire southeast region, and my stomach clenched, again, as I was reminded of home and everything that was waiting there. A thought that had been gnawing at me for hours rose up again, and I found myself shifting so I could see Theo's face.

"Theo?"

He looked down at me, eyes half-open. "Yeah."

"I don't think Randi and Cecil would take that money."

Theo grew very still beneath me. He paused before admitting, "I don't, either."

The implication was clear: the culprit was someone in my family. I knew it had to be. Theo's family was the perfect one. His parents were still in love with each other. They supported Theo in everything he did and let him live his life. They were hard-working, honest people, and there was no way they would have tanked our business.

Not that my parents didn't work hard. They certainly did. But honesty and integrity weren't always there, and even though Dad and Cecil were best friends, I wouldn't put it past Dad to do something like this if he thought it was for the good of himself and his own family.

"I don't know anything about it," I told him. "You believe me, right?"

Theo's face softened. He brought a hand to my cheek, and I leaned into his palm. "I know, Sass. You love the store. You'd never do that."

Even though it was true, his reasoning didn't sit quite right with me. "I also wouldn't do that to *you*, or your parents. If I knew what was going on, or who did it, I would have told you already."

"I know."

With a sigh, I let my eyes fall closed. I fixated on his warm touch, the callus on his thumb as it stroked my birthmark. "There's just no way any of this is going to end well, is there?"

A few beats passed with no answer, and I opened my eyes just in time to see Theo rolling on top of me. His hands found mine. Our fingers interlaced together, and he pressed them into the pillow above me. His hips pinned mine to the bed, and the intimate position set off a few sultry flashbacks in my mind, but when Theo put his face close to mine, stopping just short of my lips, it was clear that wasn't what he had in mind.

"I'm gonna be honest with you, honey," he said, his nose brushing mine. "No, things with the store probably aren't going to end well. Things with our families are probably not going to end well. Things for us aren't going to be easy for a while."

With every word he said, anxiety constricted my chest further. I had no idea what things would be like when we returned to Amity, but I did know that they would be unrecognizable. Our days at the store were over. Our days lived side-by-side were over. Our lives, as we'd known them, were over.

"But here's what I do know," Theo continued, squeezing my fingers with his. "We, you and me—*we* will end well. I don't know how we'll get there, but we will. When you're ready, we'll go back and deal with everything. Together. No matter what our parents say."

"I'm scared," I whispered.

It took a lot for me to admit something like that, and he knew it. Keeping our hands joined, he brought them to rest between us, right over my steady heartbeat. "So am I. But you know what?"

"What?"

"We're not going back tonight." Keeping his eyes up and trained on mine, Theo ducked his head to press a chaste kiss to the back of my hand. "We're not going back tomorrow. All I'm really worried about right now is getting to fall asleep with you next to me. We've never done that before."

I wrinkled my forehead in confusion. "Yes, we have. We used to take naps in the back room and—"

He cut me off with a laugh. "I don't mean when we were little kids, Sass. I mean since we got together. It never feels very romantic to have sex with you in the back of my truck and then drop you off a block from your parents' house so they don't know you were with me."

"Oh."

Theo kissed me gently. I extracted one hand from his hold and slipped it under his shirt. I pressed closer, jutting my hips up and letting my mouth fall open against his, but he retreated.

"Not tonight," he murmured, forehead rolling against mine. "Just let me hold you."

I let out a breath. "Okay."

We shifted around so that we were on our sides, my back to his chest, one of his arms locked securely around my waist. I could feel his hot breath on the back of my neck when he leaned in and said the words that had been lighting me up inside for my entire life.

"Love you so much, Sass."

I cuddled closer. "Love you so much."

And despite everything, I thought that this might be our best night yet.

Chapter Thirty-Eight

Now

Saturdays are always the busiest day for the Wilsons, and I'm glad for it. If it were slow, time would be crawling while I wait for my shift to end; instead, my mind is (mostly) too occupied to relive the past two nights in Theo's bed, and every time I get a second to look at the clock, a nice chunk of time has passed.

Today was also supposed to be the day I married Daniel—something I had completely forgotten until I woke up this morning and saw a text from Brock that said, "Congrats from me and Dad." I stared at the message for a while, trying to decide how to respond, but I didn't even know where to start. I gave up. Neither of them had bothered to RSVP either way when I sent them invitations; if they wanted me to expend my emotional energy on them, there were opportunities prior to my would-be wedding day.

So, with all of that going on, I'm happy to be distracted at work today, and I'm glad to be going to Wilmington later. Theo dropped me off this morning before heading to his office for a while; when I finally hopped out of the truck after about ten minutes of making out in his front seat, Sage was standing on the sidewalk. Her smug expression let me know that she'd seen everything.

"Do you need my services before we open?" she asked, and cracked up when I responded by hip-checking her.

I'm on the register with four people in line—I've been meaning to ask Judith about the possibility of adding a second register, because this backup is frequent on the weekends—when the bell announces the arrival of a new customer.

"Your total is fifty-six ninety-two," I tell the woman in front of me, then holler toward the front door, "Good afternoon!"

As I glance up, I realize who has entered the store: Quinton and Theo. Quinton is in uniform; Theo is in the shorts and non-work polo he was wearing when he dropped me off earlier. They're standing just inside the door, speaking quietly and looking troubled.

My customer finishes paying and leaves. "You can start unloading," I tell the next person. "I'll be right back."

Quinton walks off without acknowledging me as I approach. I come to a stop in front of Theo, feeling my heartrate kick up at his expression. "Hey. My shift isn't over for another hour."

"Quinton went to find Sage so she can get on the register," he tells me, his voice tight. This morning, he fucked me in the shower; when he dropped me off, he was still riding the high. Now all of that is gone, and tension radiates from him. "I don't know if...I think he should come with us. Just in case."

"What?" I prop my hands on my hips, confused and started to feel a little panicked. "Come with us where? What the fuck is going on?"

"It's Kelly," Theo says quietly, and my stomach drops like a boulder. "She's at my parents' house looking for you."

***

We drive in silence to the Hoyts' house, all of our earlier buoyancy and excitement gone. Our overnight bags sit in the back, where we put them this morning. I'm not sure what's about to happen, but I have the sinking feeling that we won't be going to Wilmington after all.

"Theo," I say, low and scratchy, as we approach the turn for our old neighborhood.

"Yeah."

"Today was supposed to be my wedding."

He inhales deeply, reaching up with one hand to adjust his cap. "Well," he says flatly, "that might explain it."

My mother's car is parked in front of the Hoyts' house, which ends the remote hope I'd been clinging to that this is just a misunderstanding. We climb out of the truck as Quinton's police cruiser turns the corner, stopping a couple houses down. The sight of a police car still makes my heart kick, even though I know who it is and why he's there.

"I'll text him if we need him," Theo says under his breath as we walk up to the front door. Our hands brush, and

I expect his fingers to twine through mine. They don't. "Hopefully she'll just go away."

I stop on the porch, short of the door. Something is off between us, and I want it fixed before we go inside. "Wait."

He turns back, his hand on the doorknob. The living room curtains are open, but the sunlight reflecting off the windows prevent me from seeing inside. Our parents could be watching us right now. "What?"

I'm not sure if his tension is coming from the situation—if so, join the club—or if he's upset with me for some reason. I don't like the silence we sat in on the way over here; I don't like how, after weeks of him taking every opportunity to touch me, he pulled his hand away from mine just a minute ago. "I haven't talked to her," I say desperately, unwilling to let him believe that I've double-crossed him somehow. "I have no idea why she's here."

To my relief, Theo's face softens. He reaches a hand toward me, and I grab on, relaxing a little when I feel his warm touch again.

"I know," he says. "I'm sorry. I'm pissed off because she's ruining our trip, and this whole thing...it's a little too familiar."

"I know," I echo, and squeeze his hand. "We'll see what she wants, and then we can go."

He glances pointedly at our hands. "You want to go in like this?"

"Yes."

That gets me a small smile, and a bit of the cloud surrounding us lifts. I drift closer to his side as he pushes the door open, leading me into the house. The living room is empty, but hushed voices in the kitchen come to an abrupt halt when the door swings shut behind us.

My mom appears in the doorway a second later. Randi and Cecil flank her, their eyes wide in apology. Mom takes one look at our joined hands and throws hers in the air. "Oh, of *course*."

"Something to say, Kelly?" Theo asks lightly.

She comes out of the kitchen, his parents following right behind. I instinctively step closer to Theo; she rolls her eyes. "I knew this was why you left Daniel. I should have come up here earlier. *You* should have intervened," she snaps at Randi and Cecil. "Do you understand what she gave up?"

"I dumped Daniel because he very creepily stalked me with your help, and then put his hands on me," I tell her.

She lets out an annoyed sigh, like this is such an inconvenience for *her*. "He said he touched your arm."

"He left a bruise!" I yell, and Randi puts a hand over her heart. "I know now that I should have ended things with him for a lot of other reasons, but I definitely wasn't going to stay with someone who hurts me."

"As you shouldn't," Cecil tells me pointedly, and when my mom glares at him, he openly glares back.

"I'm not going back to him," I tell my mother. "I'm just not. And he doesn't want me back, either. He's already shipped my stuff."

"Shipped it where?"

I don't say anything, but my eyes involuntarily dart in Theo's direction, and her face clouds over with understanding. "Oh," she says. "To your kidnapper's house."

"Alright, Kelly," Cecil cuts in, exasperated. "You told us you wanted to have a serious conversation--"

"I am having a serious conversation!" Her voice goes high with fake concern. "If my daughter doesn't want to be with someone who hurts her, *Theo* certainly isn't a better option."

Cecil waves a dismissive hand, laughing without humor. "You're fuckin' nuts."

"Hey," Randi chides him. "How about everybody--"

"I don't care that he got away with it. She was only seventeen."

"When you were seventeen, you got pregnant with Brock!" Cecil yells at her, and even Theo looks shocked that he went there. "You know what? Get out. We shouldn't have even let you inside. You're not going to stand in my house and disparage my son, who cares about Nina more than anyone on this planet." He takes a step toward my mom and sticks his finger in her face. "And for the record, nobody cares about *your* daughter less than *you* do."

"Dad." Theo gets between Cecil, whose face is a shade of red I wouldn't have thought possible, and my mother, whose face is quickly turning a similar color. "Back off, alright? Let Nina and Kelly talk."

Cecil lets Theo push him into the living room. Randi stays rooted where she is, looking uncertain. My mother props her hands on her hips. Her face is tightly drawn as she looks me up and down. I imagine what she must be seeing: cheap clothes, chipped nails, the roots of my hair coming in dark.

"Well," she says finally. "You seem to have made your choice."

I envision myself on Theo's balcony, counting the stars. "I want to be here, Mom. At least for now. Is there no part of you that can understand that?"

She studies me for a long moment, her face unreadable. "You know why Walk a Mile closed, don't you?"

"What?" I ask, taken aback at the abrupt shift in conversation. I glance into the living room, where Theo and Cecil are watching us carefully. Randi is standing near them now, and her palm covers her mouth. I look back at my mom. "Yeah, everyone knows. You drained the store's account after the Reddings raised the rent. You guys couldn't pay it."

"I drained the account?" My mother presses her palm against her sternum, all wide-eyed innocence. "No, Nina Lynn, I most certainly did not."

I stare at her, disbelieving, and then look over at the Hoyts. Their expressions have taken on varying degrees of guilt—including Theo's. Slowly, the pieces come together, and I'm looking directly at him when I say, "It was *you*?"

"It was me," Cecil volunteers with a grimace, like he knows how this is hurting me. "I didn't come clean to Randi until afterward, and we only told Theo a few years ago."

"But why?" I ask. It doesn't make sense. "Why would you do that?"

Cecil and Randi exchange a look, and she nods her encouragement. Theo, I notice, is still looking at his feet. I think of Vince at the fireworks tent just a few days ago: *you guys probably have a lot to talk about*. The loaded looks directed toward Theo. This is what he meant.

"Nina," Cecil says, his voice soft with apology, "I'm sorry you believed it was Kelly. Theo told me about what you overheard before you ran away, and that you thought it was her. It wasn't. The business was tanking, and I wanted out. Frank wouldn't let me. The rent raise was the final straw." And then, as if my mind wasn't spinning enough already, he looks back at my mom. "But your mom *does* know something about the rent."

Her eyes dilate. "Excuse me?"

"We know you got Rick to raise it," Randi tells her, and I nearly give myself whiplash snapping my head back around. "Everyone thought it was because of the fight Theo and Vince got into, but it wasn't."

"How do you *know* that?" Mom demands.

"Rick talked after y'all had been gone a few years," Cecil says simply. "We aren't mad about it. We got out, you got out. Everybody got what they wanted, except Frank."

"And the kids," Randi adds, the regret evident in her voice. "We really hurt the kids."

Theo is trying to catch my eye. I refuse to let him, turning away from all of them as I pace to the front door and back, just to release some of the excess energy building within me. All this time, I've blamed *my* parents for the end of Walk a Mile, and myself by extension. Very recently, I've stood in this house and felt guilty about it. I've wondered how Randi and Cecil could even stand to be around me.

It makes perfect sense now.

"So, to be clear," I say, finding my voice, and everyone goes deadly still. "To be clear, everyone in this room has been lying to me."

Nobody responds.

"Right." I nod to myself as I pace back to the door that I last entered with Theo—the person I've always trusted more than anybody. Now I just feel betrayed and alone. "Alright."

"Sass--"

I grab the door, yanking it open so hard it slams against the foyer wall. Randi winces; I don't apologize. "Don't," I tell him, and then the rest of them. "Don't talk to me. Don't follow me."

And then, under my breath as I walk outside, "I don't need you, anyway."

Chapter Thirty-Nine

Then

"There it is!" I shrieked. "Over there!"

"Okay, okay. I see it." Theo flipped on his turn signal and checked over his shoulder before switching lanes. "Calm down. You've been to the beach before."

"Only in Wilmington," I said. My family used to make that trip every other year or so. Usually, we could only afford a vacation when the store was doing well. That hadn't been the case for a while. "And not since, like, eighth grade."

Plus, there was the added thrill of flying down the coast of Florida in Theo's truck, windows rolled down, wind whipping my hair around my face. We had decided before we left Jacksonville that we would head to the beach, so we stopped at a supermarket to buy new clothes and swimsuits. The sun was out, the sky was bright and blue, and I could see the water glittering in the distance. It was easy to leave reality behind with this escape laid out before us.

"I see a gas station up there by the exit," Theo said. "Let's pull over there to change and—"

He stopped abruptly. I tore my gaze away from the ocean and glanced over at him. Immediately, I knew that something wasn't right: his eyes were trained on the rearview mirror, and his hands had the wheel in a death grip. "What?" I demanded. "What is it?"

"Nina," he said, his tone measured and even, "listen to me. You need to stay calm."

I twisted around in my seat, trying to figure out what he was talking about. Just as I caught sight of the flashing red and blue lights, the sound of a siren reached my ears, and for a second, it felt like the world stopped. "Oh no. No, no, no." I glanced wildly at the dash. "Were you speeding?"

"No," Theo said grimly. We were still in a middle lane. He glanced over his shoulder at the stream of cars blocking us from moving to the right. "I need to get over."

"You can't stop!"

He looked at me, incredulous. "You want me to take a cop on a high-speed chase?"

"Maybe we can lose them," I said desperately. It was amazing how, in just a matter of seconds, I had fallen from a giddy high into a pit of black dread. "It's so crowded out here. Try to get in front of this van and—"

"Nina, shut up." Theo put one hand on top of his head, clutching at hair he didn't have. His face was positively pale. "Fuck."

The police car was right on our tail. Whatever small shred of hope I had that they were coming after someone else was gone. Theo turned on his hazards and took advantage of a break in traffic to get to the right lane.

"Theo!" I clutched my bag to my chest, as if it would protect me from what was about to happen. "You know they're gonna take me back home. You know my parents—"

"You're seventeen," he said, raising his voice to drown mine out, "and I've taken you across three state lines. You understand I'm about to get arrested, right? Trying to outrun the police is just going to make this worse."

My heart was pounding so hard, I swore I could feel it beating in my toes. He had to be mistaken, didn't he? He wasn't going to be arrested. He'd done nothing wrong.

The seat rumbled beneath me as we pulled onto the shoulder. We slowed, and I looked ahead to the exit we were supposed to take, envious of the cars getting off the highway and turning toward the beach. I looked around for something to count, but there was nothing. No stars, no clouds.

In the rearview mirror, I saw two uniformed men climbing out of their car and made a strangled sound. Theo leaned over and put his hand on my knee. "Sass, it's okay," he said, speaking quickly, urgently. "You're not in trouble. They're just going to take you home."

"Are you really going to get arrested?" My voice came out high-pitched and panicky, the opposite of his calm reassurance.

Theo winced. "I think so. But I'll come home as soon as I can, okay? I'll come for you."

"They'll never let you see me." I looked back and saw the cops ambling around the car. They were almost to us. "Oh my god, oh my—"

"Nina." Theo put his face directly in my line of sight and continued rambling, words falling out one right after another, trying to get out as many as possible in the time we had left. "Do what they say. I love you. I love you so much, and I promise I will find you. Okay? I promise, as soon as—"

One cop appeared by his window just as there was a sharp rap on mine. I whirled around to find the other cop standing there with a phone. I watched as his gaze immediately zeroed in on my birthmark. The window between us came down. Theo must have done it, because I was frozen in place.

"Nina Sullivan," said the cop. It wasn't a question. He turned his phone toward me, and I stared at my own junior yearbook photo. "Your parents are looking for you."

Chapter Forty

Now

Nobody follows me.

It's what I asked for, and it's something I should be used to by now, but as I walk away from the Hoyts', I find myself listening for footsteps.

I stop by Quinton's car and rap lightly on the tinted window until he rolls it down.

"All good?" he asks.

"All good," I lie. "You can go. Thanks."

He gives me a two-finger salute, taking my word for it. I turn the corner, headed toward my family's old house. Up until now, I haven't seen it; purposefully or not, Theo has driven around the other way whenever we've come to see his parents.

Now I trudge up the cracked sidewalk toward the spot where my world first began to fall apart. I'm not filled with dread and anxiety, like the day I returned to Amity; I'm oddly detached. It's not like seeing the house again is going to be any worse than the situation I just walked out of.

Our front yard, with its tall oak tree, comes into view at the end of the street. As I draw closer, I start to make out more details: the yard is littered with toys, there's a service truck parked out front, the white paint that was peeling ten years ago now appears to have fallen off in sheets.

When I get to the sidewalk in front of our neighbors' house—and it is the same people; I recognize their Oldsmobile—I stop, cross my arms, and stare. I think about my memories from that house, and most of what comes to mind are arguments, slammed doors, tense silence.

We never were a very happy family.

It's not our house anymore, and the longer I stand there and stare at it, the more that truth settles deep in my bones. The closing of the store devastated me for years because it ended both the life I knew and the life I imagined. Now, looking at the house I grew up in, I have a realization: that life was fleeting to begin with. My parents' divorce was inevitable. Brock was always going to distance himself from the rest of us. Walk a Mile may have been successful decades ago, but the fact is that most stores like it don't survive these days.

Ultimately, it doesn't really matter who raised the rent or took the money. It doesn't matter that Theo and I left when we did or that my parents took me to Raleigh. Things changed because they were always going to, and even if that summer had gone entirely differently, my life would have become unrecognizable anyway.

I take one more long look at the house. The front door opens. A woman with a toddler on her hip steps out, laughing, closely followed by a man in coveralls. That's my cue to turn my back, and I walk away, leaving the house to the people who belong there.

***

The next place I go is the pond. It's a good half hour away on foot, and by the time I collapse on the dock, I'm dripping in sweat.

I reach for my phone, groaning when I find my pockets empty. I don't remember having it at the Hoyts' house; it must be in Theo's truck. Fantastic. Based on the sun, I figure it must be getting close to three. We should be getting close to Wilmington by now.

I take my shoes off and dip my feet into the pond, then lay back and close my eyes against the hot sun. My shoulders and ears are already feeling tender. As a kid, I hated the smell of sunscreen and often came home sunburned. Then the doctor who did my surgeries introduced me to an expensive dermatological skincare line that I followed religiously for years—after all, I'd taken the time to fix my nose and birthmark; I might as well keep my skin looking good. Being out here at the pond, unprotected, feels like its own kind of rebellion.

I only realize that I've drifted off when movement on the dock vibrates beneath my back, jerking me awake. Startled, I jolt upright; by the time I twist around to see who it is, my sixth sense for Theo's presence has kicked in, and I already know.

He stands a few paces behind me with his thumbs hooked in the pockets of his shorts. His hat hangs off his belt, but his hair is flat from wearing it, stuck to his forehead with sweat.

"I found you," he tells me.

"It's about time."

Theo laughs quietly, taking a hesitant step forward. I scoot over, silently granting permission for him to sit beside me. He slips off his shoes and carefully tucks the socks inside; then he sinks down next to me, his feet dangling off the end of the dock with mine.

"I'm mad at you," I tell him, just to get it out there.

"I know. I'm sorry. So are Mom and Dad."

He sounds sincere, but I don't let him off the hook that easily. "Why didn't you tell me?"

"This is going to sound like a cop out," he says, and I fix him with a preemptive glare, "but I honestly didn't think much about it. And then when I did, it didn't seem that important."

"Why wouldn't it be important?"

"I don't know, Nina," he says with a shrug. "It's not like it would have fixed your relationship with your mom."

I look down into the water. Our feet look distorted, side-by-side. "No."

"Plus, the fact that she was the reason for the rent increase almost seemed worse than her taking the money." Theo runs a hand through his damp hair, moving it back off his forehead. It sticks out in twelve different directions. "I didn't think it was worth dredging up, with all the other stuff you've been going through, but I was obviously wrong."

I snort. "You think?"

"I'm sorry," he says again.

There's no reason for him to keep apologizing. He's already said it twice, and I can tell he feels bad. I focus on what's really bothering me about this. "I just can't believe Cecil would do that."

"I was mad at him for a long time after I found out," Theo tells me. Our elbows brush, and neither of us moves away. "I started to blame him for you being taken to Raleigh. But eventually I realized that the store wasn't going to survive anyway, and Kelly was never going to let you be with me. If it hadn't happened the way it did, I think the same things would have happened some other way."

It's essentially the same conclusion I came to earlier. I hum in agreement.

"Everybody was just fucking desperate," Theo adds. "You and I were too wrapped up in each other to notice how bad it was."

"I've never been wrapped up in you in my life."

"So who was the girl in my bed yelling 'don't stop' at the top of her lungs last night?"

I kick my foot into the pond. He laughs, shifting away as the water splashes his bare legs, and then clears his throat. "Anyway, I hope you can forgive me. I asked Quinton, and he said that if you want to stay somewhere else, he and Sage have a guest room and--"

"What?" I interrupt. "What are you talking about?"

"If you don't want to stay with me anymore," he clarifies. "I wouldn't blame you."

"Do *you* want me to move out?" I ask, my voice small.

"No." Theo immediately shakes his head. "No. Of course not. I want you there as long as you want to be there."

I look out over the pond, at the trees towering over us on the other side. The last time I was here, Theo and I held hands and jumped off this dock. Together. And although I'm not sure of all the things I want, I know that I do want *that*.

"I love you," I tell him. Now that I've gotten in the habit of saying it again, it comes out so easily, as if those words were created solely to fall from my lips to his ears. "I want to be with you."

He watches me carefully. "But?"

"But I don't know what else I want," I admit. "I know we had this conversation before, and I know you said that was okay. But Theo, I really don't know if I want to be in Amity forever, or just for right now. I don't know if I'll ever want kids. I don't know if my life will end up fitting into yours."

Theo touches the back of my hand; instinctively, I turn it over so we're palm-to-palm, threading my fingers through his. "Can I make a suggestion?" he asks.

I nod.

"What if we stopped worrying about your life and my life," he says, "and figure out *our* life?"

"Explain," I say, my throat thick.

With his free hand, Theo reaches up to trace my cheekbone, and I feel the electricity in each notch of my spine. "There's never going to be anything that I want more than I want you, Nina. I love you so much—so *much*—and I missed you every single day we were apart. I never want to miss you again. Anything I might have to sacrifice to make that happen is worth it to me."

I attempt to smile at him, but it's weakened by the fact that my chin is quivering embarrassingly. "Are you sure?"

"I'm *sure*."

I lean in and kiss him. His lips are salty with sweat. We both desperately need a shower. Even so, I feel the same as I did on this same dock all that time ago: like I'm flying.

When Theo draws back, he murmurs against my mouth: "Wilmington? Or home?"

"How about both?"

"Wilmington now," he confirms, "then you come home with me."

Come home with me. I didn't even realize until this very moment how long I've waited to hear those words.

"We'll build something together." Theo frames my face in his palms, his forehead hot against mine. "You want to?"

And although I don't know anything, I do know the answer to that.

"Yes."

Epilogue

One Year Later

It's July in North Carolina again, which is another way of saying it's hot as hell. Even so, the parking lot of the Wilsons' store is full of cars and people, all of them gathered near the wooden, open-front enclosure with plants spilling out and a purple awning that reads *Nina Lynn's*.

Early this spring, I approached Theo with the idea of creating a retail nursery under the umbrella of Hoyt Landscaping. My vision was to put it on the same lot as his office, but we ultimately decided that would be too out of the way. We scouted out a few more locations in the area, and although I would have liked an excuse to work near him, the right fit wasn't there.

Then, while setting up the first spring flowers on the crammed sidewalk outside the Wilsons' front door, I had an idea. I took it home to Theo to talk over; the next day, we came in together with a proposal for Judith. She took it to her family, and now we're about to officially open for business.

A pair of strong arms encircle me from behind, and I crane my head back to look at Theo, grinning. "Are they almost ready?"

"Almost," he says. "You need to get up there."

"We need to get up there," I tell him. "This is ours. I still think it should have your name on it instead of mine—you're funding it."

Squeezing me tighter, he presses a kiss to the back of my head. "Nah, Sass. This was all you."

I relax my body into his and give myself permission to be proud. It's something I'm still working on, but getting better at all the time.

Sage and Quinton walk up, hand-in-hand. "Hey," Sage tells me. "Judith is ready."

Reluctantly, I disentangle myself from Theo, glancing toward the crowd we're about to wade into. "Guess it's time."

The four of us move across the lot toward the nursery. We're stopped several times by people wanting to chat and congratulate us. Cecil and Randi are in the crowd; they take turns hugging Theo and me hard, as if we weren't just at their house for dinner three nights ago.

"Did you hear from your mom?" Randi asks quietly in my ear.

I swallow, my good mood deflating the slightest bit. I've been in occasional contact with my family over the past year, and I invited all three of them to the opening today. Dad and Brock sent their congratulations, but couldn't (or didn't want to) travel. Mom never responded to the text I sent two weeks ago. Part of me thinks that this—me opening my own business in Amity, securing my roots here and, in her eyes, repeating all of her mistakes—might be the final straw for our relationship.

We'll see.

"No," I tell Randi, trying not to sound too despondent.

She draws back and chucks my chin, the same way Theo has since we were kids. "Well, *I'm* proud of you," she says fiercely. "For this, and for getting your GED, and for so many other things, Nina Lynn."

I nod, ducking my head to hide any emotions that might be betrayed in my expression. One thing I'm crystal-clear on these days is who has been there for me, and who hasn't. Who's worth my energy, and who isn't.

When we get to the front, we find Judith and Mrs. Wilson standing to the left of the entrance, which is blocked off by a giant red ribbon. Mrs. Wilson beams as she hands me a huge pair of scissors.

"Sorry," I tell her. "I'm ready now."

Mrs. Wilson makes a motion to Theo. He winks at me, then puts two fingers in his mouth and whistles loudly. The conversations around us fade out, and the crowd begins to turn toward us. "Hey, y'all," Theo yells once he has everyone's attention. "We're ready to get started here."

Mrs. Wilson takes over. Her voice doesn't carry as well as his, but everyone is quiet, reverent, as she talks about her late husband's great-great-grandfather starting the general store at the turn of the twentieth century. It's the oldest business still open in Amity, and she receives a round of applause when she thanks everybody for making that happen.

"And now," she says, switching gears, "we're proud to partner with Nina Lynn Sullivan--"

She is cut off by loud applause. Sage, Quinton, Randi, and Cecil are in the front row, hooting and clapping their hands over their heads. Theo touches the small of my back, and I move closer to him—a little embarrassed by the attention, but trying not to be.

When everyone is quiet once again, Mrs. Wilson continues: "We're proud to partner with Nina, and Hoyt Landscaping, to bring you beautiful, seasonal plants year-round." She moves aside and smiles at me, gesturing toward the entrance. "Let's get in there."

I look over at Theo and hold up the scissors. "Come on."

"Honey," he says quietly, so only I can hear. "This is yours."

I grab his hand with my free hand. Someone near us makes an *aww* sound. I move us toward the center of the entrance, scissors poised over the ribbon. "This life," I remind him, "is ours."

Theo grins. Gently, he holds onto my scissors-wielding hand, keeping it in place as he leans in and kisses me. Cheers rise up around us, and I internally roll my eyes. We've lived together for a year. We go to The Hutch with Sage and Quinton every Thursday night. Last weekend, we went to a jeweler in Goldsboro to look at rings; while there, we ran into our high school classmate Amy Baird, who still lives in town. It's not like the two of us being an item is news to anybody here.

But I also don't take it for granted that we have people who are pulling for us, so I take my time kissing him, and then I turn back to the entrance of our—my—nursery.

With one hand, I hold onto Theo's.
With the other, I cut the ribbon.
And right now, everything feels absolutely perfect.

Thank You

After I released my first book last year, I assumed that every subsequent novel would be so much easier. I'm not sure what led me to that conclusion, because that did *not* turn out to be the case. At all. Getting Walk a Mile written, edited, and ready to publish was a task that I fumbled multiple times. This is a one-woman operation (cover art aside—thank you, Lorissa!) and I felt the brunt of that while trying to get Theo and Nina out into the world.

But here they are, and I'm so thankful to everyone who decided to read their love story. I hope you will stick around for the next one I have to tell.

Thank you, as always, to my family—in particular, my parents who have always believed that I would be a writer, and my husband who doesn't really understand the romance novel thing but claims to enjoy mine anyway. I'm a lucky girl.

About the Author

Eliza Lane lives near Kansas City, Missouri with her husband and many pets. She became attached to her first fictional couple at the age of nine, and the rest is history. This is her second novel.

Follow her at:
instagram.com/elizalanebooks
elizalane.substack.com

www.ingramcontent.com/pod-product-compliance
Lightning Source LLC
La Vergne TN
LVHW041742060526
838201LV00046B/881